TABLE OF CONTENTS

INTRODUCTION

by T Cooper & Adam Mansbach

Introduction

Dear Reader, Browser, or Shoplifter:

Those who forget history are doomed to repeat it. We can't remember who said that, so here we are repeating it.

We're Americans, and as such, we can't remember shit. Perhaps that's why, as we write this, the massive, orchestrated effort by the current administration to revise history even as it occurs is experiencing almost total success. Events are being reduced to sound bites; sound bites are becoming mantras. The truth—if you edit carefully enough, omit artfully enough, distort brazenly enough—becomes lies. And lies, if repeated relentlessly, become truth. Especially if they are wedged immovably between the covers of the kind of history text that bored you to tears in high school.

You ever wonder how it's possible that history—the story of everything that's ever happened—got so damn sterile and uninteresting that you and your friends spent most of tenth-grade American History ditching to smoke cigarettes in the parking lot?

Well, to haul out another old saw, it's because *history is written by the winners*. Those stale-ass textbooks, just like our received cultural memories, are packed with names, dates, places, and single-sentence summaries of events that, in reality, resonated differently for hundreds of millions of people.

The goal of this collection is to move beyond the obvious and the canonical: to challenge, tease, and expand upon the hegemonic single-narrative of mainstream American history. Here are some of the moments and people left out of the textbooks. Here is what *else* happened on some of the dates and during many of the eras we were forced to memorize in school, or incorporate into the stride of our daily lives.

So why use fiction as the way to get at the truth? Two reasons. The first is that's what the best fiction is: a lie that reveals the truth. (That's somebody else's line too, by the way. We're most likely totally mangling it, but since we can't remember who said that one either, let's just apologize to his estate and move on.)

The second reason is that history *is* fiction. How can it not be? History becomes fiction the minute someone attempts to write it down, to retell it in any way, shape, or form. So many factors intervene between the moment history unfolds and any attempt to relay it: power, pain, bias, sadness, tragedy, elation, time, fear, desire—to name just a few. Plus, there's the problem of who gets to tell the story. Howard Zinn addresses this issue beautifully in his important, comprehensive book, *A People's*

History of the United States. In fact, that was a title we considered borrowing for this book—you know, doing the cutesy thing where you insert an extra word with a little arrow:

Fictional
A PEOPLE'S /\ HISTORY OF THE UNITED STATES

Because in some ways, this collection is meant to capture the spirit of Zinn's book. These are stories that take up the same challenge of speaking for the voiceless— who all too often are voiceless because somebody who will later be made into a statue is standing on their necks.

As you can see, the name of the book ended up being *A Fictional History of the United States with Huge Chunks Missing.* This is simply an accurate description, not an attempt to preempt readers who might ask questions like, "What about the Watts Riots?" or "What about Eleanor Roosevelt's purported lesbian relationships?"

To such questions, we say: Right! Good point, boss. What *about* those things, and so much more? How about the entire eighteenth century, for instance? We totally left that out. By all means, send a letter to your favorite author, asking exactly why he or she did not take up a particular historical event and write a story about it for this anthology.

But even if every author in America had returned our e-mails and letters (and in one case, text messages), this would still be a patchwork history, an anecdotal history, one with huge chunks missing. The stories in this book reflect the moments that moved this particular, eclectic batch of gifted and courageous writers and cartoonists. Of course, there are millions more stories, and we hope this collection provides some impetus for them to be told. We think the seventeen pieces that did make it between these covers are riveting, inventive, timely, funny, and— most pressingly for us—politically vital.

A Fictional History of the United States with Huge Chunks Missing picks up—and yanks on—the thread of America's supposed commitment to seeking the truth . . . even if that truth happens to be revealed in fiction.

T Cooper & Adam Mansbach
New York City
May 2006

ca. 2000 B.C.E.–present

THE DISCOVERY OF AMERICA

by Paul La Farge

The Discovery of America

1

There is a story that America was discovered by the Icelanders, who came across the North Atlantic in boats centuries ago, when the ocean was warmer and perhaps not quite as wide. They got to Greenland, and by some accounts went south as far as Virginia, where they left Icelandic artifacts: spearheads and mead jugs and the skulls of their enemies, the Danes. It is a certain fact that the skulls of Danes have been discovered in Virginia, although the purpose for which the Icelanders carried the skulls across the ocean and buried them there can only be guessed at.

2

According to another story, America was discovered by the Basques, who sailed the Atlantic in fishing boats, in search of cod. The Basques may have been blown across the ocean by a storm, because in those days storms were more frequent than they are now. Indeed, in the earliest times, when Europe and America were so close that you could practically jump from one to the other, the air between them was a perpetual storm, vast and greenish-black, which shot lightning into the narrow body of water that would one day become the Atlantic. Imagine how each continent must have looked to someone standing on the other shore in those days: a black land, lit only in flashes, where it seemed always to be raining. Nonetheless, the Basques took to their boats and crossed the ocean to America, where they left artifacts: wool caps, leather wineskins, and sturdy Basque shoes. None of these artifacts have survived, but when the French arrived in Louisiana, hundreds of years later, they found a tribe of Indians there whose language was unlike any they had ever heard, with the possible exception of Basque.

3

An old story has it that America was discovered by the Phoenicians. They discovered it on a clay tablet, where a scribe unfamiliar with the Phoenician alphabet had written *west* for *east*. They rowed across the ocean and there it was, America, big and green and full of animals! They landed in what is now New Hampshire, sacrificed some children, and rowed home. The holds of their galleys groaned with fur and copper. Their discovery would be widely known, but the Phoenicians, jealous as always of their trade secrets, erased America from their tablets, and claimed to have discovered England instead.

4

Long before anyone reached the eastern shores of America, this story goes, the continent was visited from the other side, by Japanese fishermen who were blown across the Pacific by a storm. They reached the Aleutian Islands, which were just like the country they had left, but rockier and more desolate, and infested with a small black biting fly unknown in Japan. Driven almost mad by these insects, the Japanese fishermen sailed down the coast as far as California, which looked just like China, only it was more arid and there were no temples. For reasons that this story does not supply, the fishermen wandered inland as far as New Mexico, where they lived for many years. They taught the natives to make pots, and to paint them with decorative patterns; they taught them the Japanese words for *blue* and *yellow*, and showed them how to burn their dead. There was so much they wanted to teach the natives! But most of their knowledge was useless in this desert country: no point in showing the natives how to fish, or how to build boats. As for the rest—the construction of huts, or the weaving of *tatami* mats—the natives already had their own way of doing things. Discouraged, the Japanese fishermen traveled overland back to California, where they found their boats half buried in sea grass. They cut themselves free and set out to sea; almost at once they were carried back to Japan by a storm blowing in the opposite direction. To this day, in parts of New Mexico, you can find fragments of pottery with designs on them that could be Japanese; also, Japanese and Zuni share the words *ha* and *mo*, which mean *leaf* and *spherical object*, respectively.

5

And this is not to mention the Hindus, who visited America some 3,000 years ago. We don't know how or why they came, but we know they were here. The absence of Hindu monuments in the New World proves it: The Hindus were a Turanian people, and the Turanians did not construct monuments, not back then.

6

Dywed y chwedl fod gan Owain, frenin Gwynedd, nifer o feibion, ac mai enw ohonynt oedd Madog . . . Don't you speak American? This story, which is almost certainly true, maintains that Owain, king of Gwynedd, had a number of sons, one of whom was named Madoc. Owain was the last independent Lord of North Wales, and when he died in 1170, his sons fell out among themselves. One of them, Madoc, took his retinue and crossed the high and far seas to a land which seemed to resemble Wales in character and climate, although, as they soon discovered, its extent was much greater than anything Welshmen had previously known—it was so big, in fact, that they had to invent new units of measurement to talk about the distances they traveled. Enchanted by all this open space, Madoc and his men went westward, leaving behind a trail of Welsh bibles, blue-eyed children, and legends. For centuries, explorers looked for Madoc's colony. It was thought to lie beyond the Tuscaroras, beyond the Paducahs, beyond the Mandans, but apart from a few blue-eyed, fair-haired Indians, the explorers found no trace of Owain's son. He must have kept going. Imagine Madoc coming to the shore of the Pacific and crossing that ocean, too; imagine Madoc and his men in Hawaii, in Japan. Imagine Madoc in China. He is very old now, and his blue eyes are dim with cataracts. But his children will keep walking west across the steppe when he is dead, and his grandchildren, and his great-grandchildren.

One day they will come back to Wales. Then, perhaps, they will discover America again.

7

There is also a story that America was discovered by the Danes, who crossed the North Atlantic in their sturdy Danish boats, vastly superior in craftsmanship and sea-worthiness to the boats of the Icelanders, and trod in their sturdy Danish boots, which were lighter and warmer than the boots of the Icelanders, on the shores of Nova Scotia. They traveled south as far as Virginia, which they found to their liking, and settled there, and the Danes would be there still if the Icelandic latecomers hadn't descended from the north in their leaky, cramped vessels and killed them all—out of disappointment, probably, that they hadn't discovered Virginia first.

8

Muammar Abu Minyar al-Qaddafi, the Libyan head of state, tells the story of a certain Arabian Emir who, long before the Danes had lashed together their rough craft and crossed the inconsiderable gap between Iceland and Greenland, navigated the length of the Mediterranean, through the teeth of Gibraltar, and across the whole width of the Atlantic Ocean, before making landfall on the Florida coast. *So damp!* the Emir sighed, overseeing the swamps which could all have been his, if only he chose to disembark his fierce Arab warriors on the shore. *So smelly! And so unclean!* The Emir, a wise leader, prized the health and happiness of his men more than the dubious fruit of a greenish tangle more than half underwater. He turned his ships around and sailed due east; favorable winds conveyed him so quickly in this holy direction that he was back in Arabia before the sun had set three times. He made a map of his voyage, and named the land he had seen for himself—but then, in a fit of modesty, he ordered his name struck from the map and replaced by his initial, *K*. The barbarous Frenchmen who pillaged his culture some centuries later found the map, and wondered about the mysterious land named *Emir K.*, which they, being French, pronounced *kah*.

9

As for the fact that the Chinese were the first to visit America, we can infer it from the fact that they did *everything* first.

10

Though another story has it that America was discovered by Americans, who had been living in Europe for many years and made up their minds at last to come home. The proof: In parts of Germany and what is now the Czech Republic, if you dig, you can find spear points and axes of a distinctly American design.

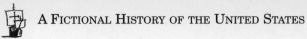

11

And there is even another story, which has it that America remains to be discovered. Who will discover it, by what means, and what artifacts they will leave behind to prove that they were here—all of these things are unknown. The only certain thing is that the discoverers, when they come, will ride on the wings of a storm.

1426–1524

WAMPESHAU

by Alexander Chee

Wampeshau

The most plausible explanation is that the [North Salem] rocks were erected by the Chinese and the women Verrazzano met were the descendants of Chinese concubines. I suggest that the first settlers of North America came not with Columbus nor any other European Fleet, but in the Junks of Admiral Zhen Wen's fleet, landing around Christmas 1421. Perhaps New England should now be named New China.

—From Gavin Menzies, *1421: The Year China Discovered America*

1426, NARRAGANSETT

The boy stands on the prow of the ship in the early night, watching the forest's edge along the coast. The red sails are tied to the masts. In the dark they look like trees again.

The boy calls it his father's ship and he thinks of it this way. He's the son of a concubine and the fleet's astronomer, the chief navigator, born after their long passage up the coast of this country and raised during the mapping of its inner reaches. He is five. A warrior braid stripes the wind behind him as he hops up and down in place.

He wants to fly.

The fleet is all boats of teak, dragon-shaped junks with red sails like wings raised for flight that never descend. Fifteen ships fill the harbor, and each of them is like a mother and a litter, with barges towed behind for the horses, the deer and cattle, and the concubines.

The concubines are not allowed to sleep aboard the ships except during storms at sea, which has the sailors, on this journey, oddly anxious for bad weather.

In the astronomer's cabin, the concubine brushes her hair. She can hear the *tap tap* of her son's feet landing on the deck.

The captain of the fleet's guard is the boy's idol, and has filled his head with stories of China and its heroes and monsters.

I want to be a dragon, he told her a few nights before, as she put him to bed.

And why is this? she asked.

A dragon can fly in the air, swim in the sea, and run on land, he said.

In the candlelight there in the blue stone walls of her room, she smiled at her son.

Perhaps I'll be a dragon too, she said.

He had looked at her to see if she was mocking him.

She remembers China differently than the guard's captain.

She pulls the hair from the brush and drops it over the side of the boat. She is as afraid that the fleet will never return as she is that it will. Here, on the other side of the world, her son enjoys freedom from a disgrace that will present itself the moment he realizes he is not his father's legitimate heir. She has received no sign from the astronomer as to whether he will make her one of his wives on their return or not. But she knows he loves his son, even if she does not know how he feels for her and her future.

She thinks of this as she approaches him in the dark, walking the wooden sides of the boat again after years in the comfort of the village.

I should have named you Bird instead of Wing, she says.

He turns at her voice, his face wet from his efforts.

Yes, he says. You should have. Then I could fly.

Come to bed, she says. Even birds sleep.

Every now and then in the life of a child, he adds up what he has from his parents and something is missing, she considers, as she leads him back. She can feel China through the wall of night. She knows she will be lucky if this is his grudge.

After she has seen her son to bed, she stops to bid goodnight to the astronomer in his quarters, but he pulls her back inside the door.

Is there a storm tonight? she asks.

He undoes the catch of her gown.

They were to leave at dawn, but the last patrol has not returned. Thirty men, including the guard's captain, were due back the day before, and made no appearance during the night, not even a messenger. The admiral has thus postponed their departure.

The astronomer sits in his cabin with his son, at work on his morning calligraphy—even on this morning, even on the open sea. He knows his son is besotted with warcraft and so he keeps him strictly mixing his ink, the first of the tasks to master in the art.

When he originally began this practice at his father's own side, he did not understand how it would support him later in life. How this practice, of writing out the lines of Chinese classical poetry, with its descriptions of the land, could keep his country in sight when nothing else would.

To be an explorer is to practice the art of getting lost, he considers, as he thinks of the missing guard. Each one, he has discovered, learns how he will keep his home known to him.

The brush curls wetly as he inspects it. It shines, the viscosity is perfect, there is no precipitous drip. The hairs instead are plump.

Have you written a poem for our departure, as I asked? he says to his son.

I have just a line so far, he answers.

And what is it? he asks.

I do not know our land but it knows me, he says.

He meets his son's eyes. That's very good, he replies.

Further south, three ships were trapped in a bog and were declared lost. A fort was created from the timbers and the ballast stones, a guide tower raised to warn the ships coming from behind the bog. A copper mine was discovered, rich and of fine quality, though all were reluctant to add to what must return when the number of boats had been reduced. Objects were made to trade with the tribes found along the coast. Saddle ornaments for the horses given as gifts or in exchange for food, jewelry as presents for their women.

We sell a bit of their own land back to them, the admiral noted to the astronomer.

Trade was a Ming way. Each people met along the way were left with a gift of the emperor's favorite chickens, and horses and ponies were typically traded for grains and vegetables.

Some had never met a horse.

The brush moved down and then back and forth, like the movements of a mare.

Eventually there had been some in the fleet who would not return. Who chose to remain. Colonies, it was thought optimistically.

The fleet's creation had deforested much of their country. China is the land of the young tree and the old woman, his mother had said sadly, visiting him at his offices down at the harbor before he left.

Come home quick as you can, she said.

The expedition fleets filled the horizon as they left for as far as he could see, making it seem in the distance as if they were continents peopled by masts covered in red sails, and the glittering teak junks were the shiny new lands the fleets themselves sought. The rush of the boats down the waves in the open sea made it seem at times as if they could, on the next wave's crest, fly.

But they could not. And the southwestern fleet of Admiral Zhen Wen had shrunk first to twenty, then to seven, then to, now, just three boats. Colonies were now strewn along the coasts and islands of these farflung countries, and they were built of the ballast stones and timber wood of the lost boats, inhabited by their survivors. The first to be left were confident of further expeditions, of how their new towns could become cities known to China. The next, less so, but, to keep in spirit with the first, made themselves brave with their new mines, the distilleries outfitted for rice whiskey but using new grains found there, and the fine weather. Still, he shuddered as they passed near the skeletons of the boats, what had to be left, unable to be harvested.

In discussing the decision to delay their departure, the admiral had said, I am in no rush to leave behind those who would not be left.

The astronomer shrugged, bowed, and took his leave.

Now he pushes his brush across the page. He copies out his son's first line.

His strokes are what he will remember of that morning. The mixing of the ink determines the character as much as the paper, the brush, and the man. Wing had not mastered the ink previously, and so for months his pages have frustrated him. The streaky characters make it seem as if the sight of his own country is dimmed, and it feels portentous as they wait. But then, he is not the astrologer. He is the astronomer. The one who knows from the stars, whenever he walks outside, how far they are from home.

By evening the night patrol has not returned.

With the next morning, the fleet divides. Another colony is born from those who will not leave off their waiting. The admiral departs, taking with him the astronomer's best student. For the astronomer, the constellations are like the lines of poems. For his student, stars are new poets. The astronomer has heard what they have to say, while his student has only just now made out their voices.

In just two nights, he thinks, China has grown to include the land he will live on now.

His son, Wing, still hops. Angry when his mother calls him from what he calls his *practicing*.

Each missed practice for him is just another day he cannot fly.

The Guard's Captain

The dark is littered with our footprints.

My patrol runs along the edges of the wind. It is a tricky art, not easily mastered nor used lightly.

The wind can be run like a dune. I leap at the top of one current, sail briefly through several others until I hit another rising one, and run on that as well, feeling it change shape beneath me.

We were attacked at night, our horses stolen, and in order to return to the fleet in time for the departure, we had no choice. Our nearest pursuers, a tribe who'd always condescended to trade with us, chased us on our own horses. They shouted with astonishment as we fled through the air.

They're out of sight, on the far side of the horizon. But we run still, knowing the ships were to have left the night before. And while we are important to the mission, they cannot stay too long for us without putting the entire mission at risk.

At the edge of the forest we move to the treetops and leap along the forest roof. After the wind, it's like running across hard land. While at first we shouted as we tossed ourselves from the peaks of the wind, now we do not speak, we do not look at each other. There is nothing to say, until we return. We are the dark wind above the trees.

The harbor and the signal fire come into view. A single boat waits. We arrive to find our concubines, our friends, who waited for us. Our admiral on the sea again.

I envy him. For him to go home, all he has to do is put to sea.

The chief astronomer moves toward me in greeting. He is a compliment to me, from the admiral. But then his son Wing runs out from behind him, shouting. And I can tell in his remaining, there is a father's forbearance.

His son loves me enough to have hated him forever if they left me behind.

1436, NARRAGANSETT
The Guard's Captain

Wing is in the yard practicing again at fighting the wind. He's said he wants to call it Sword Wind School.

I don't laugh.

It should be like the way the wind moves around you, he says. You go here, it goes here. It should teach the sword to be like that.

Yes, I say.

He stands with the sword out to his side, eyes closed, listening to the wind with just the surface of his skin. His form, as the sword takes on the wind, is perfect. If he were not so dear to me, I would blindfold him in battle, just to see a man die that way from him.

Sword Wind School means the wind is his teacher. He must get it to speak to him and tell him how it fights.

Wing is anxious to go back, wants to see the emperor, wants more teachers than just us or the wind. He is seventeen. His warrior braid shines as it winds out behind him. He wears just a strap; his body is dark from the sun and gleams.

He is among the first of our new generation and he

was born in the year of the Water Dragon, in a dragon hour, six-metal star.

Sword Wind School it will be—that's what this means. It means even the emperor will know of his name.

When do you teach me how to fly? he asked me several months ago.

Go ask a duck if you want to fly, I said, and pulled at my arms. Do you see wings here?

He smiled. He was an easy, friendly boy. But so is any dragon when he wants something from you.

Wing is there, I said, and pointed at him. Teach me to fly.

There is always a point in the training when it is right to teach this, and it is always difficult to teach the young because it requires an acute level of awareness, something that is like listening and like seeing and like scenting, but not precisely like any of them. And it often either comes or does not come in the student. There are many, many bitter proficient warriors who throw themselves the wrong way too many times.

It is a movement of all the senses together, like when the arms swing and the legs thrust and you run. Up the wind.

It is very dangerous, of course. If the years of training and conditioning leave you able to shatter a stone with your knife-hand punch, then yes, if you fall off the top of the forest here you can survive. But if not, and you find yourself upwind and there is no next step to take, no next current in the air, then there is nothing for you except the ground.

I am not convinced the Eight Immortals know to find us here. There are other gods in this forest here, closer to the ground, but they have never made friends with us and I do not trust them to catch the future founder of Sword Wind School if he falls.

I walked him to the edge of the field where the grass grew blue and sweet and waist-high. I drew out a piece of it and poked his smooth forearm.

Grass, he said.

Grass, I said. And then hopped onto the next few blades, and ran across the surface of the field. Butterflies came up like a bright orange smoke around me. I leapt to the ground in front of him. Start with grass, I said.

He jumped up and sank down into the grass.

Don't rely on the grass only, I said. To run is a conversation with what is underneath you. To run hard is to shout. Don't shout. Ask.

He raised an eyebrow.

Ask, I said. And move on before the grass gives way.

We spent that day—me running the tops of the field, him hopping in place at the edges of it—breaking it down.

Yesterday, he ran across the top of the field.

I worry that we are lost. We are the mapmakers of the

emperor, and it is, in a sense, our function to be lost and then find ourselves, again and again. We are made to find the edge of what is known and pursue a path into the heart of it.

There is no safety to it, though. And it is a long time to be in danger. We've stayed too long here; what we are doing here at the settlement could be either a part of our mission or a part of a slow rebellion. Another ship from the fleet, from another mission, could come at any time to find us, to see if there is word of us.

What will they think of our smooth walls and towers? Our pipes and water? Will they stay or arrest us?

The harder decision, of course, is that we must divide, if it is a true settlement. Some will remain and others return. For now we have been content to put such planning ahead, in the future.

Sometimes I fear it will be our children's children returning home to China. I had wanted to bring my grandmother the new flowers, found for her all over the world, unlike flowers anyone has ever seen. I want to sit with her and show her each one, and tell her the country it is from.

I do not want to lay them on her grave.

Wing

To learn wind-walking, I undertook a fast.

I still don't understand how the fast works. I only know that first there is the terrible hunger, when even the smallest piece of fruit is in danger. At that time, even the smallest piece of food can be bigger than whatever you're looking for on the other side.

But this was the point, I understood later, about being able to walk on the grass.

I woke in the middle of the night on the fifth night of it. The fierce hunger had receded. It was like the moment when the tide is low and a way can be made to the island. There was in its place an amazement that seemed a kind of echo of the moon and the glow of the night. And in those moments, it's as if your hunger has stripped the world clean again. The wind outside begins to tell you how far it traveled to get here. The air has a weight and shape and color to it, like water.

I woke to see that the night was an ocean. Also the day. That we rode our horses as if along the bottom of the sea. The breezes broke and crashed against the walls.

I batted at it, feeling it move around my hand.

I stepped outside and went down to the edge of the field, where I listened to the grass explain to me the way to ask its help correctly. When the morning came, the captain found me there, asleep.

The secret to it is being a good guest. The secret to it, the grass explained, is that even the wind will help you if you agree not to linger.

My mother brushes her thick white hair out and then turns to my own, which she oils and braids.

The junk is the most beautiful thing I've ever seen or hope to see. The scarlet sails like the spread wings of dragons set to launch into the sky and lit by the sun. Out the window of our house, down the hill to the glittering sea, is the view of the world I have known all my life.

For my first flight, I wait until the sun sets. I wait for stars.

For me, they're like night fires of the tribes I see from my patrols. I have watched but never approached.

I have become a soldier. I study war. When a man walks toward me, I can see how I would take him apart, where he would not know to keep back a fist, or how the sword, in his hand, would swing only to here, or out to here. The fight is over before he has swung at me, and I know how I will bring him down.

If I had no ability like this, my father might have been more tempted to make me his unwilling student.

It is your father's gift, my mother says of it. Dipped in my own.

My mother reads men also, but differently. My mother has brought down many men, in her way. My father does not understand why she stopped with him. He knows he loves her, but he does not, it seems, see how she loves him.

She is still a beauty. She has to her an elemental quality. I know my mother is beautiful because of the expressions on the faces of the men and women around her, like wind on the field, known by the shape it makes against the grass.

Sometimes I think it will never happen. That we will

never return and I will never meet the emperor. I become certain that I will die out in the woods of this country we are trying to know. At those times I ache for a home, one that I have never met and know only in my blood; one that pulls at me like the wind and leaves me knowing always how even though this world is the only one I know, that world, that is the one that knows me. And it is tempting to see, in the stars, a path through the night sky that leads to Beijing. But I will not try this yet. I will, for now, remain here with the only family I have known.

I stand on the top of the tower of blue stone the color of the moon's features, that has stood overlooking the harbor most of my life. It has been home to my father's work. It is also the repository of the lighthouse not one boat has used in the years since the admiral's departure. The colonies left behind do not know we are here; we have never sent expeditions south, and they have never sent expeditions north. A well-supplied return fleet, as we all know, would take only months to make the trip from China through all the colonies that were left—if they were known to the fleet. My mother tells me my father has confided what we all fear, that the admiral failed to return to China.

When I was young I thought the stars spoke to him, before I understood what it was he did. Later I laughed at myself for being foolish enough to believe this. Now I laugh at myself again for being foolish enough to miss how it is the stars speak to my father. He has taught me enough of what it is he does so that I can look up anywhere at night and learn where it is I am, even how to know the skies of China if I were to run my way along the sky.

No one has ever studied enough to replace him, and for this reason it will be soon that we return. None of our generation wants his job, and he has said again and again to the captain that he cannot teach an unwilling student. And if we do not leave while he can see us home, we will never return.

Yes, a ship took us. A wind, the sea. But these alone will not get you home. To get you home, you need a star. And someone to listen.

The dark around me in the night is like the deep of the sea. I step into it like a drowned sailor determined to return to the surface, the hard edge of the coastal wind, and run until the fires below are almost gone. The wind has been my teacher now for years. It knows me.

1445, NARRAGANSETT
The Concubine

He said he knew his way home in the dark.

The night Wing left, he did so because he thought he could feel his way along the landmasses in the dark. There's a way the wind feels over land that is not the same as over the sea, he said. And there is a scent to it.

I do remember knowing land was near, the scent of the pine in the wind, on the long voyage here.

I remember when the concubines decided not to take the teas that would have kept our wombs clean. I remember because I think of it as the night my son was born. We were on the open sea between a large island and the vast continent we live on now. It would be a new world for us, we decided. And so we went from being gifts to the men of the countries we visited, to giving, of these men, the gift to the expedition of the new generation.

When I tell you my son was the finest of them, I do not exaggerate out of maternal love. He was the finest of them.

We are on the sea again, my husband and I. And our son runs the night sky with the guard's captain. It was decided they should try. Their chances there and ours in a boat alone are one and the same. He has a map his father made him, a trail of stars through the sky that should lead him directly along the coast we traveled. And the teacher he has loved since he was a child.

Confucius said of this love, when two people are at one in their inmost hearts, that it shatters even the strength of iron or of bronze. And when two people understand each other in their inmost hearts, their words are sweet and strong, like the fragrance of orchids.

We are going to our deaths, perhaps, but we are not waiting for them. There is no shame in what we try.

For myself, if this ship is to be our last rest, I am happy. There is no longer any question of me returning to the concubine's ship. I may not return home in triumph as a wife, but I leave this land that way. Wife, mother, lover. In the dark deep-sea nights of the crossing, my husband and I lose the years between us. In the dark we are young again, and it is my premonition that perhaps eternity could be like this with him.

I do not pray to my own ancestors, but to my husband's. My father sold me. I want nothing from his ghost but that he should leave me alone, and not trip my son and his teacher on their voyage home.

1524, NARRAGANSETT
Governor of the Chinese Settlement of Narragansett

They have the skin of ghosts but none of their powers. It's a little terrifying to look at them, until you realize they cannot reach out and race through the walls to where you sleep, or pull a storm out of their pockets. They have the one shape, not many. Their language is a little difficult to understand, all of the sounds different and they seem to slip over the ear. There is no joy in their discovery I can see. It may be they are under the rule of a bitter king who has forced them out.

They seem ill-equipped, and you do not equip an exile. You give them a horse that will die near the border, a ship that can sail out of sight but not much farther. They arrived in a single ship—that suggested a lack of planning.

I was not prepared to be so interested in them.

They appear to have almost no sense of anything like our sciences. It is interesting that they resemble ghosts as much as they do, given they have not the slightest awareness of either our *chi* or even their own. In this, they are like the opposite of ghosts, so alive it has made them numb.

We watch them unobserved. Our patrols unnoticed, our settlement unknown to them.

The Narragansett have named them already, call them the *Wampeshau*. I cannot help thinking there is a sign in it. All the years our people have waited, all the expeditions that have left, nothing has returned to us except them.

The country of the Wampeshau is not unknown to us, my father tells me before our meeting with them. And when we do go to their settlement, and are made welcome there, we are shown their map.

It is not even close to our map in showing our lands. I try not to laugh at their indication of a deep inland sea where I know the people of the plains to live, where we have traded horses and copper. I do not even attempt to make it clear I am a member of something besides the Narragansett tribe, who have begun to marry with our children.

My grandmother was a concubine in the fleet of Admiral Zhen Wen, and my grandfather a king in a distant land who she served as a matter of her service, honorably. I have from her a necklace of ivory he gave to her, said to come from the enormous beasts that ran his country, made of their white tusks. My skin is darker than some of my generation, but it matters less. I have the appearance of a Wampanoag, taller and darker, my hair as straight as theirs.

For a hundred years, our settlement has waited for a sign from China without fail. This morning we saw this ship, and thinking it was the return of the fleet, loaded our boats with flowers and wine. When we drew close and saw that it was not a red-sailed junk, we still greeted them with cheering and hope in our hearts, but our shouting nearly stilled when their white, white faces peered from inside the odd ship.

They did not speak any of our languages.

There will be no fleet's return. I can feel it in my dead heart at the table. My father and I both admire the map greatly, for the appreciation of our guests, but I know he, as I, hides laughter and grief. In it is a story of our lives, reaching past my birth and death at once. I will never greet emissaries from my father's country. The traditions we keep here, the sciences we have kept alive, our new discoveries, all at once seem to me shuttered and mute.

The Wampeshau admire my town. They marvel at the roads. Their leader is a man named Verrazzano. How? I want to ask him as he walks the road. How is it possible? But it isn't for me to know. It isn't for me to think of, in this hour. I want to know if there was news in his country of our fleet, even though it is clear from his face that we surprised him. I want to know if the rumor could be true, that Wing and his teacher have never touched down, and can be seen sometimes in the sky above us, never to return to the earth below. I want to know this and more, but for now there is the road,

made of the belly of our old ships, and the sea, admit-
ting, after all this time, just this man and his one boat.
They do not even have supply ships alongside.

He eyes our women curiously as they wait in line,
greeting him. In another time they would have gone to
his boat for the use of he and his crew. But this is no
longer our way. This is not how we honor the memory of
our settlement's first mothers.

He and his men look like scarabs in their metal suits,
and there is a sound like swords clattering as they move.
We turn from the women's salute in the fierce light of the
midday, and make our way back to the shore.

1846

WEST

by Benjamin Weissman

West

I n late spring three covered wagons crept sluggishly up to a semi-thawed Convict Lake, and a party of five, three men and two women—or was it two and two-thirds women and two and one-third men, since one of these people, Twyla, switched back and forth several times through each day—stepped out of their wagons and settled in for the night. They were a happy bunch in their rust-colored garments, a result of communal washing in iron water. The wagon covers were old and droopy, with the hoops protruding in sets of threes like ribs on a dying giant.

As the sun sank and the sky lit up in an explosion of guava pulp and whipped cream, their bone-dry horses, Moon, Ten Bananas, and Cantankerous Bastard, slurped the icy lake water like it was equine happy hour. Alpenglow cast the landscape into a pink fizz. Pointy, snow-covered Mt. Morrison, a 14,000-foot peak, towered above them, and parts of it could be seen reflected in the clouded, half-iced lake.

I'm going to make spaghetti for dinner, unless someone objects, said Raymond, a perpetually stooping, seven-foot-tall, forty-year-old man with a giraffe neck, a big honking nose, and a protruding Adam's apple.

Lily, his wife, a short, muscular, garlic-colored, garlic-tempered woman of thirty, wanted meat but she wasn't going to say anything. The last time they'd eaten crow cobbler or squirrel succotash was weeks ago in Nevada. Lily took a swig of whiskey and rubbed her belly. This non-meat diet, she said, and then screamed, wasn't good for ladies who were preparing their wombs to make strong healthy babies. She raised the back of her hand to her head, closed her eyes, inspected for a fever, and then whispered under her breath, I just can't stand this anymore.

It was urgent that iron be in her blood now, and she turned in the direction of Gore, maybe because his name rhymed with ore. Also because Gore was a tall, blond, castrated, semi-reformed sex-offender gentleman traveling with them, a sensitive, literate fellow, a Melville scholar who was writing a personal essay entitled "Bearded Duo," who suddenly took on the appearance of a butcher shop dinner to her. Why is swine the coveted meat we dream about, Lily sang to herself, la-la-la, mood swerving toward delirium, when you got Gore standing there looking quite steak-ish, like the hot link man, who will be perfectly adaptable as hash and tripe chopped up with potatoes, and then there's smoked jerky to last for who knows how long.

Their journey west was long. Weeks of protein, she said directly to her axe—a small maneuverable tool with a sweet lily flower burned into the pine handle—which she grabbed, and then ran toward Gore, lifted the heavy blade up into the air, and swung it down across his neck. Gore saw the whole thing coming but didn't seem to mind.

A head never came off so easily, like a fish bowl nudged off the end of a table, and it thumped to the ground, spun a half-circle, and came to a stop with the aid of his nose, something her husband Raymond thought comic, which caused him to laugh for one nervous second, and then say, What the hell.

Lily stood silent, breathing hard, staring at the bloody end of her axe. There was a profound stillness in the air. No one moved, including Gore, who teetered erect and headless. For a moment it seemed very possible that he would bend down and pick up his own head. But he did not. A crow flew by and squawked.

That settles it, Raymond said, I guess I'm grilling Gore. The reign of vegetarian cuisine had ended, even though Gore continued to stand, a geyser of blood hissing up from his torso like a juicy Roman candle. A few heartbeats later a swaying Gore took a step forward, crumpled at the knees, and fell shoulder first onto the dirt, a cloud of dust poofing up around him. Battle, a small hairy man with tiny ears and a thick beard growing right up to his eyes, walked up to the dead man, untied his boots, and yanked them off, measured one sole to sole with his own: same size, sweet, Vibram soles with steel shanks, and cheerfully switched them.

Lily dropped her axe, pulled off her blood-soaked garments, asked Battle to burn them once he got a fire started, and walked naked in the direction of the lake. Damn, Battle said to himself though everyone heard him, trembling, eyes cueball-sized, that's a lot of woman. Raymond stripped Gore of his clothes, carried him over his shoulder and rested him on a log, rubbed lard all over his body, and couldn't help a protracted stare at his genitals, the castration marks, penis intact. Raymond thought, for some reason, ignorant bastard, that Gore's package would be missing, but it wasn't, because every man including all the earth's sex offenders need something to pee out of. And there it was, pale, at rest. Equally present were his deflated testicles, sewn up cruder than stitching on a catcher's mitt.

Smaller thread next time is my advice, Raymond said to himself, a long day, a rough journey, self-talk more available than the two-way variety. Deballed, he said, gritting his teeth, deballed, and shook the confusion, horror, and sympathy out of his head. Raymond pulled out his ultra-sharp knife and poked Gore in the calves several times. Around both thighs he made a dozen incisions, and into Gore's arms and shoulders he stuffed garlic cloves. He rubbed sage and a random assortment of green needles and leaves all over him so he was good and herby; for aromatic purposes he crammed a few old black-tipped carrots and mushy pears into his trunk. Battle gathered an armload of pine logs and small sticks for kindling, and after much effort a fire was blazing in a round pit.

You know, I never knew Gore very well, but I can taste fragments of his life in every bite. Is that weird? Twyla said, dabbing her lips with the hem of her dress, like right now I feel him tapping the keys on a miniature piano.

I know what you mean, Battle said, I see him burning up insects with a magnifying glass.

Sex offenders, Lily said, spend their whole lives looking for ways to turn their evils around and contribute to society. But Raymond, who ate quickly with both hands, his protruding teeth chomping, his lips smacking and splashing, couldn't hear her. Raymond, Lily said, it's deafening, your eating.

It's probably best, Twyla said, if we can't hear ourselves.

I hear you, and I apologize for this method, but the extra added air flow in the mouth improves flavor expo-nentially, Raymond said, grinning at his unortho-dox pronunciation.

Really, Battle said, nodding, fascinated. Twyla's jowls puffed out and her eyebrows thickened. At first it appeared she was vomiting, but she was just manning up ·for the evening. She burped, threw bones over her shoulder, grabbed more meat. Battle shifted gears, prepared himself for homosexual sex later in the evening with his wife.

This is a unique situation, Raymond said to Lily, picking up Gore's head and taking note of the blond stubble that glinted ever so faintly on his cheeks and chin, because it's usually men who impulsively commit violent crimes and it's men who succumb to cannibalism.

Succumb? Where did you come up with *succumb?* Lily said, disgusted.

Well, we could have had noodles for dinner. You chose murder and meat. You're a succumber. I'm making that word up for a new crime of murder and people-eating over chickpea stew and bark mushroom dumplings, and if anyone needs me I'll be lying under the wagon masturbating. And with that, Raymond pulled out his special flannel rag, touched it to his cheek as his other hand snuck down the open side of his overalls toward his testicular area. In Lily, Raymond's odd behavior had found support, his proclivities protected. He faked heart attacks regularly for attention.

Okay, dear, Lily said, but make sure you get all the chowder in the jar, don't spill, remember we . . . are . . . trying . . . to . . . make . . . a . . . bay . . . bee.

The horses, who were all listening, whose vocabularies were extensive and growing daily, sometimes by the minute, took notice because whenever Raymond moved a muscle his odor tripled in strength and their nostrils flared; no living, breathing thing, no microbe or amoeba, could resist such a smell. Raymond seemed to be developing a religion centering around urine. For instance, he believed in something called *smelly footprints,* whereby he pissed inside his shoes and if he happened to disappear on a walkabout he could be found by Lily or their horse Ten Bananas just from his smell alone.

But I think it's interesting, Twyla said, resuming the cannibal conversation, that Lily was the one who took a hatchet to Gore's neck—Lily, not Battle or Raymond, but Lily, sweetheart, she who wanted to eat a fellow man, she who had the wherewithal to proceed.

I didn't hear much objection, Lily said. All I'm hearing are burps and sighs now and a lot of happy bellies.

True, but guilt is forthcoming, Battle said, there's no way you can do this without your conscience experiencing some type of primal revolt, there's nothing worse we could do to each other.

Women can be just as violent and human-eating as men, Lily said. Don't think the fellas got some sort of monopoly on cannibalism.

Well, no women in the Donner party ate people, Twyla said, smiling, leaning affectionately toward Lily, only men.

Times change, sister, Lily said, and the two women bumped shoulders, raised their hands, and high-fived. At that instant a set of dark fir trees swayed wildly in the wind like finger-wagging judges.

After dinner they stared into the fire. A pack of coyotes yipped in the distant beyond. We are surrounded by darkness, Battle said, as if a sermon were forthcoming. Out there, pointing over his shoulder, is the void.

I'd rephrase that, Raymond said from underneath the wagon. We are inhabited by darkness, heart and soul. To return to one of the great philosophical questions man faces, we ate our friend Gore.

Well, he wanted to be eaten, Twyla said, her voice rising in pitch, softening back to her womanly self a bit, beard waning, lips thickening, shoulders narrowing. Why else would he yell *eat me* to those roughnecks who were hassling us back on the trail?

Good point, wife, Battle said, and why did Gore taste so good? Answer that. It's not like we lowered ourselves to cannibalism. I think we chose a seldom-traveled high road. And from somewhere very far off someone handed each of them a slice of apple pie.

Raymond remained under the wagon listening to the debate. The idea that he was married to such a violent woman stimulated the crap out of him. He banged his forehead against the rear axle. I'm succumbing, and with that, two white jets roped into a spotty mason jar, followed soon after with snoring.

Even though Battle had all the polysexual wonders of the world with Twyla, which needless to say included amphibious genitalia that did everything but fold clothes, he had a secret crush on Lily, or at least he was mesmerized by her monolithic ass. She stood on top of her wagon wearing a brassiere, period, sans lower garments, legs planted wide, arms akimbo, airing out the flesh before bed. Lily was thought to be a tumor in her mother's uterus; when a doctor discovered that the mass was actually a little girl, he said she'd be an ugly little thing. Lily—born at home, pushed out onto the living room floor on newspapers—rotated half a circle, climbed down off the wagon, meaty buttocks flexing and churning like a steel machine, Lily's monster ass, the cheeks like two round hostile comedians, taunting the world, with a deep dark ravine down the center.

Ladies and gentlemen, Battle said to himself, drunk off his own brain fumes, this murderess most definitely has the ass of God, yes folks, it is a gleaming white layer cake, but it is only a display item. She climbed down from her wagon, picked up her axe, walked over to the fire, and sat on a tree stump. She leaned forward and rested her elbows on her knees.

You don't mind if I just sit here with my rump in your face for a second, do you, Battle?

Nah, Battle mumbled, barely audible, and the horses raised and lowered their heads. Folded this way Lily now looked like she was composed primarily of ass. Battle sat behind her staring directly at it. Rump, he whispered, rump, rump, rump. Yes, Lily's rump was XL and round, but from this perspective much larger than his already perfect understanding of it, of them, the two, the massive cheeks, since it took up his entire field of vision, as if her rump were a quarter-mile wide with a tiny bulge of fat extruding from either side. Battle thought he was going to die if he didn't stick his head into Lily's rump. He didn't want to just smell, touch, kiss, gnaw, or grip it, he wanted to inhabit it with his mind, he wanted to go through the knotted flower into the big dark cave that he pictured as a high-ceilinged church that echoed with dark red walls.

Lily had a curious look on her face. She turned to

face Battle and the fire. She cradled her axe, kissed the blade, and then began to sing:

Beautiful how sweet the flesh cracks
When playing with my sharp beloved axe
O she's an intelligent girl
As precious to me as a gleaming pearl

Lily dropped her axe, grabbed her hair with both hands, and pulled. This isn't hair, she said to Battle, these are nerve endings!

Okay, Battle said. Then she clomped back to her wagon, flopped face down onto her mattress, rolled over onto her back, and stared at the top of the canvas ceiling. Then she looked at a picture Raymond had just hung up on the sidewall. What is that absurd picture doing here? A painting of cows skiing down a mountain.

From underneath the wagon Raymond said, Perhaps an attempt at interior design.

A hollow gulping sound could be heard. Battle knew Twyla was engaged with Moon, their horse, his huge soupspoon tongue incessantly kissing her, five solid minutes. Battle stuck his own tongue out, a weak pale thing coated white and smelling like an onion, that couldn't be counted on to turn a screw. His eyes were dark, desperate dots that seemed to operate independently of each other. Battle brooding, uneasy: You can see why women prefer horses. Look at their rear ends. They are tremendous. He reached back inside his pants and gripped his own sorry behind. Who knew? Why didn't someone tell me that my rear end needs maintenance? A horse stands five feet high and seven-eighths of it is buttocks with a giant lock of hair running down the middle. How do you compete with that?

Twyla stood in front of Moon. When he finished licking she said, before you came along I only felt loved by my dolls. They never looked away.

That night Lily dreamt with gritted teeth of a giant dreaming pig named Jealousy Song whose adorable ears wiggled and eyelids fluttered as she slept; a small stinky pen with buckets of mash and slop, a big scalding sun high in the sky, more mud than could ever be known, squishy everything, water and more mud and a fresh young child underhoof, stomped and rammed and bitten to death and eaten completely within minutes, bones tossed up in the air, played with, buried.

Raymond's disruptive digestive problems forced him to sleep outside by the fire. An enormous ten-foot snake slithered up to him and decided to show his affection by dropping the bottom half of his mouth like a fork lift and scooping up Raymond's feet. After that the knees, thighs, and torso were easy; soon came the head. The effect of the enveloping snake around his body was warm and comforting, and Raymond's snoring sleep grew deeper, but air was scarce, and soon nonexistent, and he opened his eyes in this dark wet place. He pushed and kicked and tried to stand up, but nothing worked so he began to scream for help.

A groggy Lily, waking after a restful ten hours, heard her husband's faint call but didn't know where to go. All she saw was this long silver sack like a swollen elephant trunk moving in little jerks, wiggling, murmuring by itself. In her sleepy state her first thought was baby and pregnancy and she sighed a little chipmunk orgasm sound, coo, the miracle of life, hopefully me someday, but then she saw a little black eye at the far end taking her in and she knew at that instant that it was a snake and she lunged at it, carefully sliced open its center as if she were unzipping an old sleeping bag, and out rolled her long, lanky, drippy husband, gasping for air.

In the morning Raymond had a bowel movement that frightened him, something along the lines of a beet-red opossum, a true growler, and it stared back at him in grave seriousness. The fuck, he screamed, leaping backwards, falling, scrambling to his feet, zigzagging hysterically back to Lily, and without hesitation she asked if he had returned. He, she said so calmly. At first Raymond was perplexed by her question, but then realized she was right on target. How did she know? How utterly perfect; suddenly the matter of what to do with Gore's wagon had ended. Reincarnated, Gore would remain with them on the slow crawl west. It didn't seem right to travel with a man you had murdered, eaten, and shat out, but there were worse things. And really, when a crowd of new-ish acquaintances go on and on about how wonderful you tasted, it hardly seems right to hold a grudge. Flattery will keep a wagon train together.

We're all just passing through, Battle said, handing Gore his boots back. Gore forced out a smile and nodded.

Thank God you weren't the type of man or creature that dispels his entrails as a defense mechanism when plucked from life, Twyla said to Gore in full earnestness.

Gore, eyes downcast, pinched his face like he was contemplating double-time or about to sneeze, and said, You're welcome.

It was a cloudy day, more milk in the sky than actual blue, plus a small breeze. Within an hour the wagons were loaded up, the horses watered, grinning discretely at each other, ready to hit the road.

1865

Dixie Belle: The Further Adventures of Huckleberry Finn

by Kate Bornstein

Dixie Belle: The Further Adventures of Huckleberry Finn

Letter of May 26, 1865

My Dear Friend Tom,

It has been nearly two months since General Robert E. Lee hanged up his fiddle, and it's only today that the very last of the organized Confederate troops are turning their weapons over to Union soldiers. I am writing to you after so many years and on this particular day because for the first time since the war begun, there's a good chance there ain't no rebels in the hills to ambush the United States Postal Express, and so this letter may ackshully get all the way to your door.

I have addressed this to Tom Sawyer, and I hope with all my heart it is Tom Sawyer who is reading this letter and that he ain't dead and buried out on some battlefield. But whether it's him reading or maybe some surviving relative, have you got any idea yet who's writing to you with such fancy, fine, and dainty handwriting? It's me, Huckleberry Finn hisself! Not that anyone in the city of Nawlins has ever knowed me by that name. No sir. I go by Miss Sarah Grangerford, of the Jackson, Mississippi Grangerfords, honey, such a pleasure to make your acquaintance. There are a few folks know me as Elexander Blodgett, but the crawfish aristocracy and not a few soldiers and officers around town know me better as Sassy Sarah from Madame Violet's Parlor of Elysian Delights, and I sure would appreciate if you don't tell anyone that Huck Finn ever was my name.

Speakin of names, the illustrious Mister Twain and I have crossed paths again, right here at Madame Violet's! I am sure you will see him soon yourself. He asks after you constantly. I am trying my best to persuade him to write stories about this new life of mine the way he done before, but he seems to have some misgivings, which doesn't make sense because I heard that *The Adventures of Huckleberry Finn* made him some good money, more even than *Tom Sawyer.* How about that! I never read either of em all the way through. Have you? *You* tell Mister Twain to write us into another book of his. You was always the one who could sell arrowheads to injins and chains to niggers. Have you seen the old man since we knew him, Tom? He has the same tobacco smell and the same crow's feet about his eyes, only much deeper now, and his hair is gone all snow. He always tells me to send you his warmest regards and hopes for your well-being should I ever see you again alive. I certainly hope

I am being successful in delivering his message through this letter.

Well, I am bustin with all sorts of good stories to tell *someone,* and they are the truth mainly with only some stretchers. So, if it ain't Tom Sawyer readin this letter, then whoever you are, I hope you enjoy the tellin. I'll start back when I took my leave of Miss Watson and the Widow Douglas. Much as I appreciate those two god-fearin good women and all the charitable work they did on me, I reckon I was never cut out to be the well-behaved boy they expected me to be in return. So I let em kiss me goodbye and I set out down to the courthouse to collect the $6,000 that you told me Judge Douglas was holding for me. You remember? My pap never did get his hands on it, you said, and the judge still had it? No hard feelings, Tom, but it might've been better for all concerned if you hadn't stretched the truth quite so far. The day I showed up to collect my heritance, the good judge instead made me the gift of bein a two years all-expenses-paid guest of the great state of Mississippi for what did he call it? Vagrancy and Public Noosance. He did it to self-improve me, he said, and if there ever were any $6,000 I never did see a nickel of it. Sure enough though, I learned a great deal about life, liberty, and the pursuit of happiness as a guest of hizzoner's sheriffs. Soon as I was fully rehabilitated from being a public noosance and released back, I hightailed it as far as I could from respectable society, and headed down to the river, which is the only place I ever felt free. I spent a year and some workin engine room on all sorts of steamboats, ferry-boats, and fish-boats. Tom, I was happy as any river snipe ever had a right to be. Did you know I love to tinker with engines? But when your time is up, your time is up, or so they say, and I landed down here in Nawlins just three days before we heard that war had broke out between the states. From that time on, any sort of river travel got a whole lot harder to do without the Union interferin in your business, and it was clear to me that I was stuck to death in the largest city of the newly con-stitutionalized Confederate States of America. What lit-tle money I had saved ran out. I was a fine mess with not even two bits to pay a barber to cut my hair, which by this time had growed down to my shoulders, as long as my pap's but nowhere near as greasy. I had the choice of stayin in the city or livin out in bayou territory, shootin possums and Union soldiers. Well, I was never very fond of eatin possum, nor have I ever shot a human bein in my life, though if I was to do, it would be a Union soldier rather than a rebel. So I stayed in the city and took myself whatever slop jobs I could find on the waterfront, where everyone worked long hours for not one penny but for two tasteless meals and a sweltering bunk-room filled with too many hard-working newly mancipated niggers, Creoles, and no-account tars like me. I was beginning to reconsider my thoughts about possum.

Then came April 1862, a dark month for the Confederacy but a darker month for Nawlins. The Union Admiral Fraidy-Guts invaded the port like it was no more than a mud castle made by children. He fit an almighty battle, sinking eleven of our ships and clearing the way for the soldiers to march in and take the city, which they wasted no time in doing. The Occupation dried up most of the river trade and most of us dock rats found ourselves out of work. Both armies were lookin for fresh meat for their cannons so they sent recruiters down to the waterfront every day. The Rebel recruiters were sly. They had to be. If they was catched, it was prison and certain death as traitors. Still, some niggers and bums sided with the Rebs and resisted by all means the Occupation. The Union recruiters on the other hand were full of themselves and with good reason: They was holding all the cards in this game, and they offered us positions in their army like they was offering us a place in heaven, which place I have never been very anxious to visit anyways.

Well, I reckon you are about all out of patience wondering what a boy like me is doing calling hisself Sarah and writing you with handwriting so like a girl's. Well, wait jest a minute more because I'm getting to that part.

I suppose I owe it all to the papists. There sure are a whole mess of em here in Nawlins, and most of em residing in the frenchy quarter. A couple years back they built themselves three entire new churches in that part of town. Well, I heard tell Our Lady of Perpetural Sorrows would feed the poor, and none bein so poor as me and since I hadn't had a bite to eat for nearly two days, I saunters my way down to the frenchy quarter. It were a summer-time sabbath morning. I never been inside a catholick church and I didn't figger on spending so much time on my knees. I was beginning to wonder when that perpeturally sorry lady would make an appearance and start feeding us poor folk, when all of a sudden this priest feller in skirts commenced ringing a bell and everybody in the place gets up off their knees quick enough and marches up to a little fence they got inside the church, right up front. Then this fancy-dressed priest pours his-self about the biggest cup of wine I ever seen and I'm wonderin is he going to share it or drink it all hisself. Well, one by one each of them catholicks dropped to they knees, turned up they faces, and opened up they mouths like baby birds waitin fer worms. My turn at the little fence came soon enough and I dropped to my knees like I been a catholick all my life. The frenchy priest looked down at me and muttered something or other and it was-n't even in the French language, but I closed my eyes and opened my mouth. Durned if he didn't drop a insignifi-cant crust of bread on my tongue which I chewed and swallowed even though it was dry and dint particularly taste much. Naturally, I opened my mouth for more.

"Move along, my child," says this priest to me.

"Well, sir," I say perlite as I can, "I'm still hungry."

"Well I ain't a'feeding you," he says. "I'm a'blessing you."

"Priest," says I, "ef this is a blessing, then I'd ruther have a curse as it would likely leave a better taste in my mouth."

He made to push me away and I think I took a swing at him. I'm not all that sure what happened next because I fainted dead away from hunger right there at the little fence. I know I didn't get any more bread. The next thing I do know is I'm flat on my back out in the middle of some dusty road in the frenchy quarter at high noon, and I'm lookin up at the prettiest angel I ever did see. She was lookin down at me and the sun was behind her head, all halo-like.

"Ma'am," I inquired perlite as I could, because the catholicks had jest showed me how ornery they could be if a feller wasn't perlite enough, "are you Our Lady come to feed me?"

She jest tosses her head back and laughs. "I may feed you, boy," she says, "but first you come with me out of that awful hot sun."

I was surprised to see that Our Lady was a quadroon beauty, tall, long of limb, with skin the color of creamed-up coffee. I let her lead me across the road and through a pretty little wooden gate set into a row of nicely trimmed hedges and we come into a well-kept garden. A nice breeze springs up, so cool and fresh and sweet to smell on account of all the flowers. Of a sudden, I remembered my manners and tip my hat and out spills all my scruffy long hair down over my face and shoulders, which I think is gonna put her off, me being such a bum.

She laughs about the loveliest, deepest, richest laugh I ever did hear and says, "Better and better," and smiles a smile like to break my heart she is so lovely. "Young man, you want to earn yourself a dixie?"

Well, that settled it for me: She was not Our Lady, for I had never met a catholick willing to part with a nickel, let alone one of the famous ten-dollar notes writ on the back of them in French with the word *dix*.

"Ma'am," I said to this beautiful woman, "I will do whatever it is you want for jest a little bit of supper, being as how I haven't et a bite for nearly a week now."

She jest clucks her tongue and marches me into the house attached to the garden, and I find myself inside a cozy kitchen presided over by a fat, smiling Creole cook.

"Bon Mambo, please fix this boy a hot breakfast right away. I'll go fetch Madame Violet. She's going to like this one. Boy, my name is Miss Rosie, so how do you get called?"

"Elexander, Miss Rosie," I says, Elexander being a name that has served me well in the past. Then I add for good measure: "Elexander George Phillip Blodgett."

"Fine then, Elexander George Phillip Blodgett, you eat your fill and I'll be back with good news by the time you're done." And with that, Miss Rosie sweeps out of the kitchen through a fancy beaded curtain, leaving me alone with Bon Mambo, who has already begun to crack a couple of eggs and turn up the flame under a pot of greens. Now in case you don't know, a Mambo is a lady priest of the voodoo people, whose priests ain't nothin like the frenchy catholick priest I near brained over the street at Our Lady of Perpetural Sorrows. I heard tell that Mambos could turn you into a zombie if they wanted to, and you'd have to do everything they tell you to. Bon Mambo set a plate of eggs and greens down in front of me, and I fell to it like a dog.

"Mistah Elexander," she says to me while I devours the victuals, "you ain't really no Elexander, and if you stay in this house much longer you ain't gonna be no mistah either. But they's good news for you too."

Now, the short hairs on my neck was standing on end but I kept silent and went right on eating. It's best not to innerupt Mambo ladies who are tellin your fortune so she kept on a-tellin mine: "Come tomorrow mornin, you gonna be not one but two dixies richer than you are right now. An you gonna give Bon Mambo one o them two dixies as tribute, and fo me keepin you alive with these here eggs and greens."

"Yes ma'am, Miss Bon Mambo, ma'am," says I, for her greens were perfectly greasy and mighty tasty, and besides, I had no wish to be zombified. "Soon as I get me two dixies, I'm giving one of em to you."

This was the rightest thing I coulda said, for she smiled real big and added some awfully good spoon-bread and syrup to my plate and I fell back to breaking my fast. Bon Mambo and I had ourselves an understanding.

"Don't you be wasting all my profits on every rag-tail scallywag what sets down in this kitchen, Bon Mambo." And with that, the beaded curtain swooshes open and in marches the Madame of the house, followed close on her heels by my quadroon angel. Where Miss Rosie is tall and thin and long of limb, Madame Violet is short and stout and about as stubby a woman as I ever seen.

"Stand up, boy, and let's have a look at you," says Madame Violet. So I do.

"Turn around." I do that as well.

"Take off your shirt and trousers." I don't do *that*.

"Boy, this is not the sort of house to be shy in."

I am at a loss for words, which as you know I am not often.

"Go ahead, Elexander," says Miss Rosie, "we seen it all before."

I finish chewin the bite of spoon-bread that's in my mouth and look over to Bon Mambo, who gives me a wink and a nod. So I shrug my shoulders and in no time I'm standing in this kitchen in my underwears.

"See, what'd I tell you, Madame Vi? Jest what the Major's been asking for: right size, right face, even the right hair. Ain't he perfect?"

"I wouldn't call him perfect," says the Madame, "and it depends how good he'll look in a dress."

The power of speech having returned to me, I reply: "Madame Violet, I look durned fetchin in a dress, my hair cleans up real good, but I'm afraid nuthin can be done for this pug ugly face of mine." All three women laugh out loud, and Madame Violet looks at me a lot closer then, pretty near to like a butcher who's inspectin a not-too-rancid side of bacon.

"So you like to wear dresses," she says, "but did you

ever lay down with a man before?" Well, it all fell in place for me right then and there what they wanted from me and what I'd most likely be doing to earn myself that dixie or two.

"My pap brought me to his bed more than oncet or twice, ma'am," I told her, "but layin there was all I did. Ef'n you mean did a man ever love me and did I ever love a man right back, then yes'm, I have and I find it to my likin. Might I put my shirt and trousers back on now?"

Did I ever tell you that about my pap, Tom? I don't think I ever did. I don't talk about those times all that much because when I do, I pretty near always start in cryin, which is what I started to do right there in the kitchen all over my greens. Miss Rosie leans down next to my chair and wraps her long arms around me and squeezes and squeezes. When she'd done with that, I get myself dressed and set back down to eatin and this Madame lays out exactly what I am to do, with whom I am to do it, and what words to say while I'm a'doin it. She has plenty of time to tell me all the details because I am eatin a great deal of Bon Mambo's delicious greens and spoon-bread.

What followed then was pretty near a day full of bathin and dressin and girl lessons. Pretty near every one of the wild women in that house took a whack at gettin me ready. They fussed all over me like I was they little sister gettin ready for her debyootant ball, which in a way was what I was. One of em curled my hair all up, and I ain't never felt anything softer against my neck, cept once I spent a night with a cranky old tom cat who liked to suck on my ear. One of em sprayed me in parfum all the way from France, every part of me except my feet and my toes, which they left all road-dusty and I'm sorry to say a bit ripe to the nose, but they explained that the Major perferred odoriferous feet. Next, a tall handsome nigger showed up. He is the piano player and barber of the house by the name of Perfesser, and he shaved me with a straight razor but he didn't stop at my neck.

By this time, I am feeling mighty fine. I am surrounded on all sides by scanty-clad women and they are touching me, stroking me, poking me, and sponging me, and soon enough a part of me has come to attention. A skinny little thing named French Annie says: "Sugarboy, you want me to take care of that little soldier of yours?"

"Miss French Annie," I replied, "I would be most obliged."

But instead of what I expected her to do, she flicks me across that very tender part of me with just one finger, and down I go to half-mast again, and they bust out laughin all over again.

"You remember that move," says French Annie to me. "It may come in handy someday."

They was pretty much all generous and good-natured like that. I was a bit embarrassed. Not shy, I wasn't shy. I was embarrassed I couldn't pay them for all the work they were doin makin me pretty and presentable. Madame Violet was givin me just one dixie for the whole night. Looked like Bon Mambo wasn't that much of a fortune-teller, for with no second dixie I couldn't pay her tribute. But ef'n I did good enough tonight, and this Major who was from Massychoosetts liked me and all, well, I could move into the house. I'd be a regular, and I could work there and get the same pay as the other girls. That's what she said: "the other girls," like I might could be one of em. I didn't mind much the idea of lyin down with the Major. Boys and men can be just as lovely as the ladies ef'n you're lyin in their arms.

By now we was getting down to the finishing touches. Little French Annie places her palms just over my nippies and pushes em one toward the other, giving me little boobies. And while she's holding my new boobies in place like that, another of the girls applies a sticking plaster, and some minutes later I am the proud bearer of a fine set of womanly bosoms which shook like the real thing, especially when I laughed. But then they commenced to apply feminine underwear to me and this was truly torture. Tom, I have beared up with ticks and chiggers and fleas and skeeters. I have braved snakes and even once't I faced down a mad fox was fixin to bite me. But I have never come to grips with anything so diabolical as the womanly torture of hooks and eyelets. Hunnerts of them on one little piece of skimpy underwear and they helped me hook each and every one of em. I always been most comfortable with niggers, and these girls were just another kind of nigger, so we all got along.

By now it is evenin time and all the girls and women

are in their finest frippery, and Tom, I am one of them, waitin down in the parlor, flirting with all the gentlemen callers. Miss Rosie, my tall quadroon crooks her little finger at me and that is my signal to meet my Major in the parlor. He is the attashay to General Butler hisself! Takin the Major's arm like I was teached, I wait while he counts out the cash into Madame Violet's hands. Only then do I let him escort me up the stairs.

"What's your name, lovely lady?" he asks of me.

"Miss Sarah Elizabeth Amy Potterfield Grangerford, suh," I reply, "of the Jackson, Mississippi Potterfields and Grangerfords, of course."

"Do I detect a hint of Southern aristocracy, Miss Grangerford?"

And here I lifts my chin into the air and squints my eyes at him like he was a bug, just like Madame Violet teached me, and I say, "Major, suh, there is no Southern belle as aristocratic as I, and I will thank you to remember your place as the crude barbarian invader that you are." The fine Massychoosetts Major writ them words, not me, and now he turns all red and commences to sweat like a plow horse. Did I mention the Major is easy on the eye? Well, he is. We reached the top of the stairs and we were standing in front of our room for the night, and the Major gives me a wink of his eye that makes me blush like a girl.

Inside the room, I remember the words I am spected to say, and I start saying them. I call him all sorts of worm and coward. "You ain't even fit to lick my toes."

"Oh, Mistress Grangerford, ma'am," says he, "I am, I am fit to lick your toes."

"Oh no you ain't, you catawumptious weasel," says I, just the way I been schooled.

"Oh yes I am. Allow me to prove it to you."

"Oh no you ain't, you gritless varmint, and if you push me one step further, I'm gonna whoop you with this here cowhide like the monkey you are."

Now, I should tell you that women in Nawlins are not in any way permitted to call Union soldiers monkeys, nor are they to spit on em in the streets, much as they may want to, for otherwise they are to be taken as common whores and subject to their whims, and all this by the order of the boss general of my very own Major, General Butler hisself!

But here I am, calling this Yankee officer a monkey, and then I hawk a fine gob of spit right down into his face. Well, you woulda thought I'd fed the man a spoonful of sweet potato pie the way he slobbered it up. This was gettin to be fun. Then I whoop him. I whoop him really good, and once't I done that, I tell him: "Now lick up my toes, you chatterin monkey. Clean up these here Southern belle toes of mine, you Yankee scum." I made that one up myself, and he seemed to like it. "Go on, use that ill-bred tongue of yours."

He goes down on his knees, and I'm afraid his smeller is gonna get more than he bargained for. But no sooner do I finish this thought when I feel that bristly moustache and that warm tongue of his workin their way over my toesies. He pauses right there and looks up at me, and I'm afraid he's got hisself some misgivings.

"Miss Sarah Grangerford," he gasps, "your feet are the most delicate flowers of the South," and he falls to further lickings and suckings for the better part of half an hour. I have learned myself a good lesson, and that would be: Beauty is in the eye of the one payin for yer services.

Then, just like the Madame said he would, he starts workin on my ankles with that prickly, tickly moustache of his. I am biting my lip so as I dasn't laugh, but then his moustache is ticklin the calf of my leg, and next the back of my knees. Seemed like I'd die if I couldn't laugh, and all the time I'm tryin *not* to laugh, he's shoutin things like, "Long Live King Cotton," and, "Ulysses S. Grant is the Devil incarnate!" and, "I believe in states' rights!" which is the signal for me to pull his head up between my legs and say, "Use that mouth of yours to show me how sorry you are for despoiling our gentile South with your oafish manners," but as I'm pullin his head up, that troublesome moustache of his tickles me where I can't stand it one moment longer and I bust out laughin. And he's lookin up at me all astonished, and then he busts out laughin hisself! But he takes me into his mouth anyways and I didn't know you could do that so good and be laughin at the same time, but that's what he's doin. He's doin it so good that pretty soon I stop laughin and commence in gaspin. And then I'm not gaspin but I'm jest cryin out: "Oh, oh, oh! Oh! Oh!

Ohhhhhh!" And without thinkin and without bein teached by Madame Violet, I ask him does he want me up between his legs with my mouth on him.

"Girl," he says to me real soft like, "I can think of nothing I would cherish more." No one ever talked to me like that before. He ackshully used the word *cherish* and it wasn't till then I noticed what a nice smile the Major has. We spend the better part of the night wrapped up in each other's arms and legs and tongues and other parts. The way he's treatin me I think to myself maybe just tonight I am a little bit of a woman.

He has to get back to his barracks before the bugles blow revelly, so he gets outta bed just before dawn. I pretend to keep on sleepin, so's I can enjoy watchin what he's like when he's not actin out the words he writ for us to use the night before. He gently tucks something in between my bosoms, which by now have come partly unstuck one from t'other, and then he walks out the door, pullin it closed real quiet behind him. I just watch the door through half-closed eyes fer maybe ten minutes. Then I remember to reach in between my bosoms to see what he left me. He had tipped me another dixie. Bon Mambo was gonna get her tribute after all.

Well, my Massychoosetts Major is uncommon fond of me, and I of him, so I been stayin here at Madame Violet's since that night. A true adventuress, that's me. The war is over and he has told me he is returning to Massychoosetts where he has a wife and four chilren, the oldest is my age near exactly. But the city has been fillin up with carpetbaggers and scallywags for some months now, and with the war over it is sure to fill up more. So there's gonna be a whole new crop of men who are gonna want to buy themselves some evenings with girls like me. I got nowhere in particular to go, and besides, I sort of like it here.

Bon Mambo is ringin the dinner bell, and I am uncommon fond of her cooking so I'm gonna close up this letter now. Write me a letter when you have a chance to, will you? It would be so very good to hear how you're gettin along. Or better yet, come to Nawlins and allow me to show off our lovely city to you. That would be ever so much better. Jest make your way to the frenchy quarter and remember if you please to not ask for Huckleberry Finn. You kin just ask any kind stranger where is Sassy Sarah, and they will lead you right to my door.

Fondly,
(your) Sassy

1884

THE WATERBURY

by David Rees

IN THE LATE 19TH CENTURY, America found itself going apeshit for **THE WATERBURY**, universally hailed as the best watch for bicyclers. Why was it the best watch for bicyclers? *Because it was the least liable to get out of order.* And for the type of **BAD-ASS GENTLEMAN** who rode bicycles with his legs crossed, it was vital to wear **THE MOST SIMPLE** of watches. Indeed, of all the pleasures running rampant in the 1880s, **THE WATERBURY** was perhaps the most simple of all. And the least liable to get out of order. And all in nickel-silver case. And every watch warranted.

ASK YOUR JEWELER FOR IT.

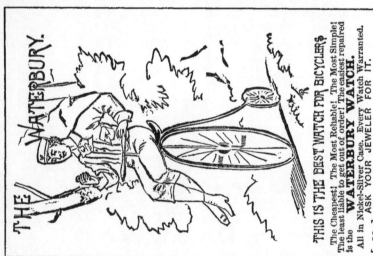

THE WATERBURY.

THIS IS THE BEST WATCH FOR BICYCLERS

The Cheapest! The Most Reliable! The Most Simple! The least liable to get out of order! The easiest repaired is the **WATERBURY WATCH.**

All in Nickel-Silver Case. Every Watch Warranted. ASK YOUR JEWELER FOR IT.

[1884]

1905

A True and Faithful Account of Mr. Ota Benga the Pygmy
Written by M. Berman, Zookeeper

by Adam Mansbach

A True and Faithful Account of
Mr. Ota Benga the Pygmy
Written by M. Berman, Zookeeper

I am Mordecai Berman, a zookeeper. Morty, they call me at the zoo. Also shit-shoveler. Of the two, shit-shoveler I prefer. Monkey shit is my specialty. I have been keeping clean the Primate House eight years now, and though I have no fancy education to prove it, I know more about the animals than probably anyone. Simply from spending time. What else I got to do? Sit in my cold-water flat, smelled up the same way every night from the wilted carrots and chicken fat of my neighbors? Chase after dames, on a crap-carrier's salary? Maybe sit in synagogue? To this I say: Ha ha, good one, my friend.

I bought tonight this notebook, and in it will keep record of what is to begin tomorrow at the zoo: a very curious affair. Who knows, perhaps I sell my story, if I make one, to the *New York Times*. Probably not, I think—already I am babbling on like a babushka, saying nothing.

So: Tomorrow arrives at the Bronx Zoological Park
Mr. Ota Benga the Pygmy, the great success (I wonder
whether he would say so) of last year's World's Fair in
St. Louis. He is brought by the great explorer Samuel
Verner, the same man who took Mr. Benga from his
home in the Belgian Congo, together with some others of
the Pygmy's tribe. As reported by the *NYT*—which is
daffy for both Benga and Verner, so you see my plan is
not entirely absurd—Mr. Benga returned from the successful hunting of an elephant to find his whole village
destroyed, including, sad to say, his wife and child. Thus
was he agreeable to Mr. Verner's entreaties to board the
great ship. Just how the village was destroyed, and what
form of entreaty was employed by the Man of Science,
the *NYT* leaves to the imagination of the reader.

In St. Louis, Mr. Benga was displayed in the Fair's
Anthropology Department, as part of the Exhibition of
Savages. Those who believe like Mr. Darwin that we
come of the monkeys have lately decided that the different races of man derive from different races of monkey.
They hold the Negro to be of the Gorilla, an animal considered strong of body but weak of mind. The Oriental,
they have paired with the Orangutan, and the White
with the cleverest of apes, the Chimpanzee. They further
believe that under Mr. Darwin's idea of Evolution, man's
inferior species will die off, and in particular the Negro.
When slavery ended, they were certain this would right
away begin. I do not know how they square the fact that
it has not with the continuation of the theory, but then

true Men of Science are in many ways a mystery.

I will now put aside Mr. Benga for only a moment to record my own lowly opinion of these ideas: It is clear to me that the men behind them have never been to a zoo. If they had, they would not be so eager either to compare themselves to Chimps, or Negroes to Gorillas. The Gorilla, you see, is the most lovely of all Apes. He is quiet, thoughtful, he takes care of his babies and his fellows. His eyes, when you look into them, you see yourself there. The Gorilla knows sadness. He knows he is a prisoner, and yet does not hate his jailer. Perhaps you cannot know what I mean if you have only, like most people, been to the zoo for an afternoon's fun with your girl or children.

The Chimpanzee, meanwhile, is by nature an asshole. He throws his feces by the handful—does not pluck them from the ground, mind you, but defecates directly into his palm for this purpose and no other. He attacks his cohort without reason, quarrels with him all the day. Alone among Apes, he has been known even to murder. Sometimes, it is true, he seems the most human to me, but only on days when my landlord has threatened to shut off my heat, or a pretty girl, when I smile at her on the subway, turns away, or prankster kids break into the zoo's sanitation room and knock over my shitcans.

To resume: In St. Louis Mr. Benga was tested in his intelligence, to see how he rated against defective Whites. He was tested also for the speed of his reaction to pain, and for his athletic ability, which was found to be in severe lack. Of this last experiment I remember reading with some confusion, for the Pygmies were made to compete in games we here have made up: the shot-put, the javelin, and other such contests of track and field. How a man who has killed an elephant could be in so bad a shape, I cannot fathom. But I imagine Honus Wagner might fare just as badly if he were stripped naked, dropped into the middle of the jungle, and told to kill dinner for himself and his family.

When Mr. Benga was not being tested, he sat in a mud-field, outside a shack constructed for him. Occasionally the anthropologists arranged between the Pygmies a mud fight for the enjoyment of the public. Of this, the *NYT* gave a picture. Verner was quoted in the report that followed, wondering whether the Pygmy was highest ape or lowest man. He then suggested that the Bushmen of Africa be collected into reservations and the continent colonized and run by Whites, as the Bushmen have no religion, no tradition, and can neither remember the past nor contemplate the future. Verner was described in the report as an exceedingly Christian person, a lover of all creatures, and one of the few men who can accept the ideas of Mr. Darwin and of Scripture both, no problem. He will make a speech tomorrow, I am sure. A man like Verner, that is what he does. I expect I may meet him, as Mr. Benga is to make his home in the Primate House.

The Pygmy is four feet eleven inches tall, twenty-three years of age, and weighs one hundred and three pounds. He was presented today by Verner to our Director

Hornaday; the word around the zoo is that the explorer has fallen on hard times, and lacks the money to keep Mr. Benga himself. To this, at least, I can relate.

The crowd was the biggest we have ever drawn, I am sure in great part because of today's *NYT* headline: *Bushman Shares Cage with Bronx Park Apes.*

Verner I did not meet, though I did shake the hand of Mr. Henry Fairfield Osborn, an Evolutionist who made some opening remarks. I have copied into my notebook one of his statements. Through Mr. Benga, he said, Modern Man will have "access to the wild in order to recharge itself." This I liked, as I have often felt recharged through visiting with the Apes and other animals. Then Mr. Osborn declared that, "The great race"—he means the White—"needs a place to turn to now and then where, rifle in hand, it can hone its instincts."

I myself understand this to be merely a lofty way of speaking, but still its effect on me was discomforting. I do not hope to see rifles in the hands of any visitors to the Bronx Zoo, and I'm sure even Mr. Hornaday, although he nodded his head all throughout the speech, would agree.

My own first glimpse of Mr. Benga came together with the crowd's. He was brought forward by Mr. Verner, and at a signal from the explorer, the Pygmy opened wide his mouth so as to show off to the crowd his teeth, which are filed down into sharp points. This the crowd seemed to relish, for Mr. Benga's teeth were met with loud applause.

Mr. Benga's contact with Whites has contaminated

him in the eyes of his people, Mr. Verner said, for when
he brought the Pygmy home from St. Louis, his tribes-
men would not speak to him. They believe he stands
with the race of white warlocks who separate men's
voices from their souls. This is what Edison cylinder-
phonographs mean to them: that the body sits and lis-
tens to the soul speak.

Mr. Benga watched the explorer closely as he held
forth, and if I had not known different, I would have
sworn he understood the words, and pitied himself. He
is to me a strange-looking fellow, the darkest and tiniest
I have ever seen, with hairless skin and an odd sense of
balance about him, as if he is leaning always forward
into a strong wind. But I do not look at Mr. Benga and
wonder what he is, for that is clear. He is a man. A man
who is in a very bad way.

It was not until this morning at 7 a.m. that I was able to
make the acquaintance of the Pygmy. He has been provided, as companions, with an African parrot and an
Orangutan named Dohong, the both of them also donated
by Verner. I found all three asleep when I arrived, each
in a separate corner of the cage. It is furnished lightly,
and contains a sleeping pallet, a blanket, and some bales
of hay.

Mr. Benga did not stir as I went about my morning
duties, no doubt worn down by yesterday's crowds,
which stayed on well after the zoo would normally have
closed. Verner, Osborn, and Hornaday set out to lead

him on a tour of the grounds when the speech-making was concluded, and the visitors swarmed around them in such a density that the trip took hours. Great laughter boomed forth often, at what I do not know. Today, Mr. Benga is to be kept locked up, and if he seems able to handle it, he may be walked again in the afternoon, accompanied by several keepers.

But when I entered his cage, the Pygmy was immediately to his feet, and the Orangutan as well—both of them regarding me with no small fear. Mr. Benga's hands stayed to his sides, an odd thing for a man if he feels threatened. Unless he has learned that raising them will make the danger worse.

"I mean no harm," I said, and found myself bending at the knees, in the manner almost of a lady's curtsy, to speak to him. "It is an honor to meet you, Mr. Benga."

I do not know what response I expected. The Pygmy looked to the Orangutan, the Orangutan to the Pygmy. First the one, and then the other, bared his teeth. On the Orangutan, I have seen the gesture many times and know it to be harmless. On the man, I decided to believe it was a smile.

"I am Mr. Berman," I told him, and reached out my hand. He took a step back, and so did I. In a cage, there is only so much room. "I am a Jew," was my next remark. I cannot say why these words leaped out of me.

Mr. Benga made some response in his own language. The effect of my presence had diminished, for his body seemed to loosen, to relax. The Orangutan Dohong, at this point, swung himself over and wrapped his arms around my legs. I scratched his head, as this the Orangutans enjoy.

Mr. Benga watched, and again his lips peeled back and the teeth came into view. This time, I was certain it was a smile.

"Are you cold?" I asked, for Mr. Benga had, when I entered, been wrapped in his blanket, and now the cold air of the morning was causing him to shiver.

I just now read back my account and realize I have failed to discuss Mr. Benga's attire: He is clad only in a sort of loincloth, to which has been added a canvas vest and a straw hat. It is a wholly insufficient costume, and the vest and hat are badly oversized, making Mr. Benga appear even smaller. Whoever gave these items to him, Verner I suppose, gave little care to the matter, or else little care to the Pygmy's comfort.

"I will get you some better clothes," I told him. "They will be too large, but better than what you have got." With that, I disentangled from myself the Orangutan and repaired to the sanitation room, where I fetched for Mr. Benga a spare uniform. It is a one-piece, such as I wear, due for the laundry but not badly soiled.

I returned to the cage and presented him with it, but Mr. Benga could not be convinced to put it on. It took me the better part of an hour to demonstrate to him just how stepping into the suit might be accomplished. I do not know whether his reluctance was due to mistrust. Perhaps he simply found the garment confining and prefers to be cold. In any event, no sooner did he have the thing on than I was called away, to attend to shit-related matters in the smaller primate cages. When I returned to Mr. Benga, another keeper, a man called Stanton, was in the cage, yanking roughly the Pygmy's limbs from the jumper.

"What's the big idea?" I called. "Hey, Stanton! What gives?"

Stanton looked up. He is a big, red-faced man, a drinker. "This your idea of a joke, Morty?" he replied. "I been trying to get him undressed fifteen minutes already."

"He's cold," I said.

"The people don't wanna see him dressed up like a zookeep!" Stanton shouted. "Hornaday's fit to be tied. You might as well start puttin' dinner jackets on the Chimps."

It was at this moment that Mr. Benga, having reached his limit after a morning—a life!—of being pulled and prodded about, managed to free his arm from the suit, and swinging it clumsily through the air, elbow Stanton squarely in the eye. I do not think it was delib-erate, but Mr. Benga, seeing what he had done, scam-pered away and, grinning mightily, hid behind Dohong across the cage. He then removed the suit himself.

"Jesus Christ," said Stanton, holding a palm over the eye. "That nigger bastard hit me."

Then the gates opened and the crowds began to stream in. Shouts of, "Where's the Pygmy?" and, "In the monkey house!" filled up the air. Stanton ducked out of the cage, and behind me surged a mass of eager visitors.

Mr. Benga peered out at them and then, to my surprise, he emerged from his cover and walked straight to the front bars of the cage.

"The Pygmy!" And up went a cheer. A hand grabbed at his leg, and Mr. Benga pulled back, though he did not retreat. Soon hands were poking through the bars all over. Someone threw inside a shoe, and Mr. Benga picked it up and sat upon the floor, turning it over in his hands with fascination. This prompted sustained laughter, and soon more objects were being tossed between the bars for his consideration: compact-mirrors, handkerchiefs, even an empty billfold. Mr. Benga's every action produced great response, and this frantic attention continued, without pause, throughout the day.

Things at the zoo are taking a sinister turn. Today's *NYT* reported on the objections of two parties to the exhibition of Mr. Benga. One is a delegation of Colored ministers. Their leader is a Reverend Gordon, who told the *NYT*, "Our race is depressed enough without exhibiting one of us with the apes. We think we are worthy of being considered human beings, with souls." They have asked Director Hornaday to call off the exhibit, and he has put them off, saying that the Zoological Society supports his efforts. They have requested also to meet with Mayor McClellan, and he has responded that he is too busy. Meanwhile, a separate body of White clergy has also taken exception, on the grounds that the exhibit of Mr. Benga promotes Evolution at the expense of their

Christian beliefs. Director Hornaday will meet with them tonight.

It may be, though, that the exhibit comes to an end for reasons distinct from all of the above. This morning Hornaday gave Mr. Benga a crudely fashioned bow and arrow, and encouraged the Pygmy to shoot it at a target set up in his cage, for the enjoyment of the tourists. This in addition to the rubber balls, mouth organs, and other toys now piled in Mr. Benga's cage, gifts from zoo and visitors alike.

Can Hornaday truly be so doltish? It was no great surprise to me that Mr. Benga, by afternoon, had begun to use the bow to fire arrows at the most obnoxious of the visitors standing before his cage, molesting him and making him the butt of jokes at every turn. He is an excellent shot, and clever enough to stand at the back of his cage when he shoots so that the missiles have some time to build up speed before they meet their targets.

A great outcry has gone up, and though no one was seriously injured, the bow and arrow have been seized. Many take the Pygmy's aggression to be proof of his savagery, but to me it is something quite different: proof against those who hold that Mr. Benga is mentally deficient, that he cannot learn. He is learning very well. He is learning to hate them.

Hornaday today gave in somewhat to the pressures of the ministers, both White and Colored, and allowed Mr. Benga to spend much of the day out of his cage. He was this afternoon dressed in a white suit and taken for a walk. Myself, Stanton, and two other keepers were responsible for holding back from him the crowd that followed. Mr. Benga was brought first to the Elephant House, and there photographed for the newspapers with a newly born Pachyderm. We then proceeded to the house of the lesser primates, where Mr. Benga, with evident joy, helped us feed the small monkeys. He also took the chance to feed himself, to the crowd's great jeering delight, though it was only some vegetables such as any one of them might himself eat for dinner.

Managing the crowd was a job more suited to police than shit-shovelers. The tourists poke relentlessly at Mr. Benga, try to trip him up when he walks. Some gather pebbles from the pathways and pelt him. Others simply want to touch his skin or rub his woolly head, which is level with most men's chests and thus difficult for him to protect.

At the Primate House, Mr. Benga grabbed off of a table a small knife, and with it in hand dashed out of doors. The crowds fell back as he swung the blade before him in great arcs. It is a dull thing, used by us for cutting through twine rope and such, but still the spectators fled in panic. Mr. Benga ran aimlessly about the grounds for thirty minutes, as keepers and crowd followed. Finally, seeing him desperate, I walked slowly up to Mr. Benga and removed the instrument from his hand. He gave it willingly, as if thankful to be relieved of a burden, and collapsed to the ground at my feet. This earned me great praise, and a fellow from the *NYT* asked me my name and position. Which is a considerable thing, but little did I enjoy it.

I imagine, as I write this, the fuss tomorrow's newspaper will make over the incident, and fully expect to wake up to a headline of the order of, *Bushman Tries to Kill.* When the truth is that the only person Mr. Benga would have hurt, had we let him keep his weapon, is himself.

It is now morning. The exhibit is to be shut down, and Mr. Benga will this evening be turned over to the custody of the Howard Colored Orphan Asylum in Brooklyn.

My name appears twice in the *NYT*, and I am identified as "courageous."

It is one and a half months since Mr. Benga left the zoo, and today I had my first news of him, courtesy the *NYT,* in a short account, some pages removed from any position of prominence: *Ota Benga Now a Real Colored Gentleman; Little African Pygmy Being Taught Ways of Civilization.*

He is said to be learning English, slowly but with promise, and to have taken up Christianity. His teeth, a dentist has capped.

It is my intention to visit him tomorrow. I hope he will remember me, and not too harshly.

Mr. Benga received me in the sitting room of the Howard Asylum, a well-appointed brownstone located in the neighborhood of Fort Greene. He greeted me attired in a shirt and a short necktie of the type worn commonly by young boys. His hair has been shorn close to the scalp, and his first words, upon recognizing me, were, "Friend. God bless you." I shook his small hand, which he surrendered calmly to the purpose, and we sat down to tea served by the house matron, a handsome Colored woman by the name of Robinson.

"Friend," Mr. Benga said again, smiling. The difference affected by the tooth-capping was striking and agreeable.

"Yes," I said. "I am your friend."

Mr. Benga nodded, then shook his head from side to side. "Zoo," he said. "No God bless zoo. No God bless."

"I'm sorry," I said. "You should not have been there, Mr. Benga."

"No God bless."

"No," I said. "I suppose not."

We sipped our tea, Mr. Benga using both hands to bring the cup to his mouth.

"Tea God bless," he said.

I nodded.

"Ota go home," he said after a moment. "My home God bless."

"Your home is beautiful, I am sure."

"Yes," said Mr. Benga. "Friend."

We sat together one hour, me asking Mr. Benga various small questions and the Pygmy answering with different combinations of the words he knew: zoo, home,

God bless, no, yes, Bible, please, thank you, friend, and so forth. The bar of chocolate I had brought him he had no use for, but after I removed it from my coat pocket, he embarked on a thorough investigation of my person, and was happy to find a package of the cheap cigarettes I am accustomed to puffing at.

"You smoke?" I asked him.

"Smoke," the Pygmy agreed. He reached into the pack and extracted a cigarette with a nimbleness to his fingers that was quite impressive, and we sat smoking. Mr. Benga held his fag with all five fingers, blowing into the end as often as he inhaled from it and taking much interest in the clouds we two created. I blew a smoke ring and he leaped up from the couch, delighted. I tried to teach him the trick, with little luck. His laughter made me laugh, and mine him, and so smoke and laughter replaced conversation until Matron Robinson reappeared to escort Mr. Benga to his next engagement. A Colored minister had arrived, and was waiting to see him in the study.

Mr. Benga was taken last week to Lynchburg, Virginia, there to work at a tobacco factory and be further tutored in religion and the English tongue at a local seminary. His departure was sudden, so sudden that I learned of it from Matron Robinson upon arriving at the Howard Asylum to call on my friend—in advance even of the *NYT*, which only yesterday published an account.

There had been an incident, Matron Robinson informed me, involving another of the Howard charges. Creola, the young lady is called. She and Mr. Benga had become close friends—here Matron Robinson gave me a queer sideways look, to be sure I understood what she meant by "friends." The only thing for it was to remove one of the parties, before the two parties became three. Mr. Benga, it was decided, would benefit greatly from the open air and natural beauty of the South.

I have spent all day attempting to locate this notebook, and finally unearthed it from a steamer trunk in the basement of the house in which I now keep an apartment, in return for my services as superintendent to this and other properties. I have written nothing here for some nine years, as there has been little in that time to report of the life of Mr. Ota Benga the Pygmy. It is my sad duty to say, that is no longer the case. Today, at an age of thirty-three, my friend ended his life.

By all accounts, Mr. Benga's mood had for some months been quite black. He had learned to read and write, and had taken up research on the cost of a steamship ticket to Africa, finally concluding that he would never be able to afford one. He could not speak of this without beginning to cry.

This despite the fact that the Colored community of Lynchburg had accepted Mr. Benga as one of their own. He was often entrusted to look after their children, and enjoyed leading groups of young people on forest expeditions. He was a great favorite of theirs, although the children considered him over-protective when it came to shepherding them through the wild.

The moments preceding his death, the *NYT* describes as follows: Mr. Benga, after an excursion, refused the urging of his small companions to take them back into the woods, and instead sent them away. When the children were out of sight, he removed the caps from his teeth, brought to his chest a revolver borrowed from a neighbor woman, and sent a bullet straight into his heart.

The article concludes with a quote from Director Hornaday, who remains in place as the top man at the esteemed Bronx Zoological Park. It is a shame, Hornaday says, that the Pygmy would rather die than work for a living.

1924

APRIL 9, 1924

by Amy Bloom

April 9, 1924

On April 9, 1924, Senator Ellison DuRant Smith of South Carolina makes a speech in the halls of the Senate, calling for—begging—America to shut the door on immigrants. "Let us breed pure American citizens," he says. "We do not want to tangle the skein of America's progress by those who imperfectly understand the genius of our government. Let us keep what we have . . ."

In the fifty-seven blocks of the Lower East Side, just that day, there are 112 candy shops, ninety-three butchers, seventy saloons, forty-three bakeries, and 500,000 Jews, and just that day Lillian Leyb arrives in America. She has two pieces of paper inside her blouse, for safekeeping, in addition to the usual, which isn't much.

She had sold her mother's red silk petticoat, sold the one goat that had wandered free and safe, sold the Kiddush cup, and given away the things for which no one had the money or the interest. A neighbor had given her their daughter's coat; the dairyman had given her a satchel that had belonged to his brother. Lillian had stood in a dead woman's coat, holding a dead man's leather bag, and her mother's half-sister had limped over to press a flyer into Lillian's hand: *Come to America, the New World. 45 rubles a ticket.* Beneath the words there had been a drawing of workers; you could see they were workers because they were short and bowlegged, with caps on their heads, and instead of a chicken under the arm, or a bolt of cloth, each little man had a bag of money, with the American sign for money on the bulging sack, and they were running, running, with their bags of money to a pillared building across the street, marked *BANK*. The puffs of smoke from the factory, the street-lamps and workers' shiny black shoes, all had a round, friendly quality to them.

"This place is cursed for you now," Aunt Mariam had said, waving her hand at the empty yard and the dark house. It had sounded as if she was also suggesting that the village was now cursed by Lillian and her unlucky, eviscerated family. "Go to America, you have a cousin there, Frieda. My other sister's daughter. My niece. Here's her letter."

Lillian hadn't said, *But I don't know them.* She hadn't said, *Will they be kind to me?* She hadn't said, *You have always wanted our house.* She had to go. She had buried her parents and her husband and made a grave for her daughter, whose body had not been found (Mariam swore she saw Sophie's body floating in the river out of reach, and Lillian could not ask her if she said that to comfort Lillian, put an end to her uncertainty, or to hasten her departure.) She was twenty-two, she would go to

America. She had read Frieda's letter every day. They have room, Frieda says, for family or dear friends. They have a little business and can provide employment while people get on their feet. It is a great country, she writes. Anyone can buy anything, you don't have to be gentry. There is a list of things Frieda has bought recently: a sewing machine (on installment but she has it already), white flour in paper sacks, condensed milk, sweet as cream and doesn't go bad, Nestle's powdered cocoa for a treat in the evening, hairpins that match her hair color exactly, very good stockings, only ten cents. They have things here that people at home cannot even imagine.

Lillian cannot imagine, even as she's walking through it, the noise, the crowds, the filth that is nothing like mere dirt, a dozen languages, market day times a million, a boy playing a harp, a man with an accordion beside a terrible, patchy little animal, a woman selling straw brooms from a basket tied to her waist and three more strapped to her back, making a giant fan behind her head, a colored man in a pink suit with black shoes and pink spats, singing something loud and cheerful, and tired women, who look like women Lillian would have known at home, smiling at the song, or the singer, a very old man and a very young girl selling shoelaces and shiny twists of dough on a stick, and the smell rises up through Lillian's chest and under her chin, making her swallow and swallow again, so she has to wipe her hand over her mouth and pull hard, she is that hungry. She did not imagine that as she approached cousin

Frieda's apartment building—having held up the letter and the block-printed address a dozen times to faces that were blank, or worse than blank, knowing and dubious, and held it up to some people who could not themselves read, who pushed her aside as if she had insulted them— that a woman would be standing across the street, dressed only in her nightgown and a man's overcoat.

Lillian watches the woman open a folding chair and take a china plate from her pocket and hold it on her lap. People pass by and put a few coins in the plate. Frieda comes down the stairs and hugs Lillian. "Dear little Lillian," she says. Frieda is thirty. Lillian remembers her from a family wedding. Frieda took Lillian into the woods, and they picked wild raspberries until it was dark. Lillian watches the woman across the street, sitting stock still in the chair, tears flowing down her face, onto her large, loose breasts, splashing onto the plate with the coins.

"Eviction," Frieda says. "You can't pay, you can't stay." She says in Yiddish, *"Es iz shver tzu makhen a leben"* ("It's hard to make a living"). She wants to make sure Lillian understands what she's saying. She doesn't want Lillian to be frightened, she says, everything will work out fine between them, but there is nothing wrong with Lillian seeing, right away, how it's nothing to go from having a home, which Lillian does now, with her cousin Frieda, to having no home at all, like the woman across the street who was thrown out that morning. Frieda takes Lillian by the hand and crosses the street.

She puts a penny in the wet plate and says, "I'm sorry, Mrs. Lipkin." Going up the stairs to her apartment, Frieda says to Lillian, "Poor thing." The lesson is not lost on Lillian, still holding everything she owns in Yitzak Nirenberg's leather satchel.

At the end of her forty-fifth day in America, Lillian understands that Judith is offering her something. "Hey, Lilly. Let's get us a . . ." Lillian doesn't quite catch what Judith says they should get. Judith is on her way to being an American girl. She gave away her shawl, she told Lillian she *gave* it away, she wanted so bad to be rid of it, and bought a little blue jacket at Kresge's. She has the American shoes, the green blouse she bought from the vendor, irregular but very good, and she is learning English, very fast. To Lillian, her English is good already; it is like something you hear on the radio.

What Judith has in mind is hot dogs and mustard and sauerkraut, and the man gives them extra because Judith has a way about her. That's what she says to Lillian: "As one might say, I am right-handed, I have a way about me." Lillian might have a way about her too. In Breslov, there were people who thought she had a way about her, but not here. In English, she is the ugly stepchild; people are not inspired to give her things, they want her not to even be where they are looking. There is a free class that adults can go to in the school on the corner, and Lillian goes when she can, sometimes on Tuesday, if she is not too tired, and she goes sometimes on Thursday, when she cannot get Joseph—who makes the most money of anyone in Frieda's apartment and stammers badly and smells like smoke and rotting leather, and is therefore most in need of companionship—to take her to the movies, which Lillian feels is also an education. Each time she enters the classroom, on the blackboard there is the same list: the noun (the thing), the verb (the action), the adjective (the kind of thing), and the adverb (how it is done). Judith says, "Just talk."

To go to the English class for adults (Miss Eriksen teaches, and her English is to Judith's as Judith's is to Lillian's; it is white satin, and there is not a bump or tear or bulging thread in it), Lillian passes the Fishbein family and Mrs. Arbitman on the stoop.

The Fishbein boy blinks at Lillian slowly and then bawls like a goat, "Ma, Ma, Ma," yanking on his mother's dress until the hem is almost down over her slippers, and then Mrs. Fishbein's great arm comes up, blocking the sun. Louie is not afraid; it would be wonderful if Louie was afraid. "Ma," he says, "why is the stove hot?"

"Hot?" she says. "It's hot because there's a fire inside. It's hot to cook the food, and if you touch even the door it will cook you—like a chicken. It could burn up a little boy, that fire, jump out, the flames, and burn you to a crisp."

She lifts her skirt to her thigh (she does this when the subject of stoves, or children, or tenement conditions, comes up) and she shows her son and Mrs. Arbitman and Lillian a large webbed triangle, dark red and wide as an iron, where she was burned. They have all seen it before; it is her treasure, as Mrs. Arbitman has her husband's death certificate and Frieda has her one blue eye and one brown and her boarders—Mrs. Fishbein has her terrible scar.

The social worker comes up the steps, carrying clothes for the Lipmans. She particularly likes the Lipmans because they are so grateful. They thank the social worker when she comes up the stairs, they thank her when she takes the clothes out of the bag, and when she hands out the clothes, and when she goes down the stairs, and when she is walking away from the building, Mrs. Lipman yells out the window, "Thank you, thank you, God bless you, lady." The Lipman girls wear old ladies' black bombazine skirts, the bottom flounces torn away to make them for schoolgirls; their brothers wear men's plaid knickers, so big they fall to the boys' ankles, like they are handed down from giant giddy children.

The social worker says to Mrs. Fishbein, who is still waving her arm over Louie like the wrath of God, "I think you are frightening your son, ma'am." Louie buries his face in his mother's leg, his hand covering the scar, not from shame and certainly not from fear. Her whole body is a comfort to him: her wide, fat white arms, strong as a man's, her cracked, dirty feet, and her fierce Ukrainian eyes. Everything she has, everything she is, is his. Louie moves his hand up to his mother's neck and pets her chest.

Mrs. Arbitman laughs. "The frightened boy," she says.

The social worker gathers up her little red jacket around her (it is very like Judith's and Lillian makes a note to tell Judith that; it will please her), and, knowing she is overmatched, opens her mouth to answer and closes it.

Mrs. Fishbein tells her she had two children die in a fire, because of no heat, and they turned the stove on and the building burned with them in it, and when this lady becomes the mother of dead children, then she can tell Mrs. Fishbein what's what.

The social worker leaves, like that, pink as sunset, and it is a great day for Mrs. Fishbein; she will tell this story to everyone, for months to come, how she told off Pearl Lipman's social worker. This is what Lillian's days are like. But in the night, she dreams of the deaths of her family. She wakes to the sound of her own screaming and to Judith's warm body. She eats bread and cabbage with strangers in a small, dirty room. She puts in and takes out stitches to make clothing, puts together blue petals and takes apart flawed silk flowers, and she does it all badly. She learns the language of a country she hates, so that she can dig deeper into it and make a safe hole for herself, because she has no other country. She walks with Judith down Essex Street every Saturday night at 8 o'clock, to watch the modern world, to move like an ox among Americans.

Judith's collar and sleeves and waistband are stuck with pins, and two straight ones dangle in the corner of her mouth. They bob up and down as she works, and they move—only a little—when she whispers to Lillian that they are hiring seamstresses, tonight, at the Goldfadn Theatre. Every girl in the city, that is from Flatbush to Franklin, will go. It is very generous of Judith to tell her. No one tells Lillian anything and she could spend a whole evening wandering the streets looking for the Goldfadn Theatre and find nothing. If Lillian knew where gold might be buried, would she tell Judith?

The crowd at the back of the Goldfadn Theatre is like an all-girl Ellis Island: American-looking girls chewing gum, kicking their high heels against the broken pavement, and girls so green they are still wearing fringed brown shawls over their braided hair. Two older women, pale and dark-eyed, are pulling along their pale, dark-eyed children. That's a mistake, Lillian thinks. She would ask a neighbor to watch the child. She would leave the child in Gallagher's Bar and Grille, at this point, and hope for the best—but she knows that is the kind of thing you say when you have no child. Lillian walks away from the women with children; they reek of bad luck.

Lucky girl, Lillian's father told her, told everyone, after she had fallen in the river twice and not drowned and not died of pneumonia. He said that smart was good (and Lillian was smart, he said), and pretty was useful (and Lillian was pretty enough), but lucky was better than both of them put together.

Lillian and Judith push their way to the middle of

the crowd and then to the front, and then they push themselves into the sewing room of the Goldfadn Theatre, soon they are standing inches away from a dark, angry woman with a tight black bun ("Litvak," Judith says immediately and happily; her mother was a Litvak), and also from two men, who are, even to the dullest girls, stars in the firmament of life, visitors from a brighter, more beautiful planet. Mr. Reuben Burstein, the Impresario of Second Avenue, is a little wider, with gray hair brushed back like Beethoven and a black silk vest, and Mr. Meyer Burstein, the matinee idol, the man whose Yankl in *The Child of Nature* was so tragically handsome, so forceful a dancer, so sweet a tenor, that when he romanced the gentile Russian girl Natasha, women wept as if their husbands had abandoned them, and when Yankl killed himself—unwilling to marry poor pregnant Natasha and live as a Christian—everyone wept, not unhappily, at his beautiful, tortured death. Meyer Burstein is a little taller, with a smart black fedora, a cigarette, and no vest over his silk shirt.

The men are moving through the crowd like gardeners inspecting the flower beds of English estates, like plantation owners on market day. Whatever it is like, Lillian doesn't care. She will be the flower, the slave, the pretty thing, or the despised and necessary thing, as long as she is the thing chosen from among the other things. Mr. Burstein the elder makes an announcement, and the voice is such a pleasure to listen to, the girls stand there like fools, some of them with tears in their eyes at its rich, thunderous quality, even as he is telling them only that Miss Morris (the Litvak) will pass around a clipboard, and they are to write down their names and their skills, or have someone write it for them, and after Miss Morris speaks to them she will indicate who should return tomorrow evening for more interviewing. There is a murmur at this last declaration; it was not so easy to get away for even one night, and Lillian thinks that the bad-luck mothers and the women who look as if they walked from Brooklyn might not return.

Miss Morris approaches. Lillian has rehearsed her remarks with Judith. "Very well, thank you," if the question seems to be about her health; "I am a seamstress, my father was a tailor," if the question contains the words "sew," "costume," or "work"; and "I attend night classes" (said with a dazzling smile), in response to any question she doesn't understand. Judith will get the job. Things being what they are, Lillian knows that a girl who can sew and speak English is a better choice than a girl who can only sew. Lillian watches the profile of Reuben Burstein; he looks like a man from home. She heard his big, burnished English voice and, like a small mark on a cheek and a tilt in the little finger on a hand injured a long time ago—the tilt and the injury both forgotten—underneath, she hears Yiddish.

Lillian runs to Reuben Burstein and says, "My name is Lillian Leyb and I speak Yiddish very well, as you can hear, and I also speak Russian very well" (switching into

Russian), "if you prefer it. My English is coming along," before adding in Yiddish, *"Az me muz, ken men"* ("When one must, one can"), and when Reuben Burstein smiles, she adds, "And I am fluent in sewing of every kind."

The Bursteins look at her; Miss Morris, who did have a Lithuanian mother, but was born right here in America and graduated the eighth grade and speaks standard Brooklyn English, she looks at Lillian without enthusiasm. The crowd of women look at her as if she has hoisted up her skirt to her waist and shown her bare bottom to the world; it is just that vulgar, that embarrassing, that effective. The elder Mr. Burstein pulls Lillian closer to him and waves his other hand toward Miss Morris, who directs the women to form groups of four to make it easier for her to meet them. There are instantly fifteen groups of four, and Lillian loses sight of Judith. Lillian feels like a dog who has leapt over the garden wall. She smiles up at Reuben Burstein; she smiles at Meyer Burstein; she smiles, for good measure, at Miss Morris. Lillian has been through a bad Breslov winter, the murder of her family, an ocean-crossing like a death march, intimate life with strangers in two rooms that smell of men and urine and fried food, and Lillian smiles at these three people, the king and queen and prince of her new life, as if she has just now risen from a soft, high feather bed to enjoy an especially pretty morning.

Reuben Burstein says, in Yiddish, "Come back tomorrow morning, clever pussycat." Meyer Burstein asks, "Really, miss, how is your English?" and Lillian replies, very carefully, "I attend night classes." She pauses and adds, "And they go very well, thank you."

Lillian has washed out her underwear and lain her cami-knickers and her slip and her hose on the radiator which has gone stone-cold in the night. She slips out past Frieda in the kitchen and walks to Second Avenue in cold damp underthings. She stands at the door of the theater, trying to feel a warm sun beating down on her, drying her knickers, and she imagines herself doing whatever either Mr. Burstein wishes her to do. She doesn't know much, but perhaps that will appeal to them—more than something else, something Lillian imagines prostitutes do (and if she knew what it was, she would be rehearsing it right at that moment).

Miss Morris opens the door. "Oh," she says, "you're on time. In here," she says, and Lillian is not unzipping the younger Mr. Burstein's pants and not sitting on the lap of Mr. Reuben Burstein; she is putting on a neat black smock and taking her seat next to a fat, pretty girl with brown curls and a pink, friendly smile. Miss Morris hands her a gold velvet tunic and tells her to take in the waist two inches. Mr. Reuben Burstein walks by when Lillian's hands are filled with gold velvet, and he winks at her.

Jerusalem surrounded, Jerusalem saved.

1932

THE STORY THAT REFUSES TO DIE

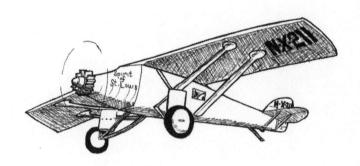

by T Cooper

The Story That Refuses to Die
Interview by T Cooper

From *Gay Aviation Today*, January 2004
(Reprinted with permission, ©2004 GAT Media Inc.)

*O*ver seventy-five years after making aviation history with the first solo, nonstop transatlantic flight from New York to Paris in 1927, Charles A. Lindbergh has sent shockwaves through the aviation world yet again. In December, a trio of siblings in Germany claimed that they are in fact the children of Charles Lindbergh—and they have the DNA test results to prove it. The aviation world has always feted Lindbergh as a quiet, traditional family man, happily married to one woman, Anne Morrow Lindbergh, until his death. The world-famous couple had six children (including Charles Jr., who was, as is well known, kidnapped and killed in 1932), and while subsequent books published by both husband and wife have revealed that the marriage was less than perfect, there were certainly never intimations of an indiscretion of this magnitude.

The three supposed German Lindbergh heirs—Dyrk Hesshaimer, David Hesshaimer, and Astrid Bouteuil—waited until the 2001 death of their own mother, a handicapped Munich hatmaker named Brigitte Hesshaimer, to go public with the news. The children, raised in the 1960s by what appeared to friends and neighbors to be a single mother, remember a tall, graying American man who came to visit them once or twice a year. According to one account, Dyrk remembered the man "cooking eggs, pancakes, and sausages," and sitting with the children for long breakfasts when he was in town. He would tell of his travels across the world, but the children assumed he was a writer because he was always carrying papers and reading books. The man was introduced as the children's father, but their mother told them his name was Careu Kent.

It was only after Lindbergh's death in 1974 that the children began suspecting otherwise. The aviator's familiar face was once again splashed across newspaper front pages all over the globe, and there was a striking resemblance to at least one of the two illegitimate sons. When cleaning out the attic after their mother's death, the children discovered over a hundred letters from someone named "C," consistent with a romantic relationship and referring to the three offspring as "our children." Lindbergh biographer A. Scott Berg confirmed that the letters were probably written by Lindbergh, and that it was "chronologically and geographically possible" that Lindbergh fathered these children. But the Pulitzer

Prize–winning biographer emphasized that he didn't believe it consistent with what he knows of Mr. Lindbergh's character—that he was by most accounts a fairly chilly, exacting man who eschewed all forms of physical intimacy.

Most of the Lindbergh family in America has not warmed to the news either. One Lindbergh grandchild, however, Morgan Lindbergh, reportedly visited with his alleged siblings in Munich recently. Upon his return, Morgan was quoted as saying, "There's certainly a haunting resemblance there." The German Lindberghs aren't seeking any money. They are simply telling their story to a German journalist, who is expected to release a book in 2005 which will detail Lindbergh's multiple affairs and children. The three children insist that all they want is to set the record straight, so to speak.

But will the many Lindbergh mysteries ever be set straight? Did Lindbergh have affairs, as well as multiple children out of wedlock? Was the wrong man, Bruno Richard Hauptmann, executed for the murder of the Lindbergh baby? Was this ultimate American icon gay, as some have suggested? Was there something wrong with the Lindbergh baby? Did the nursemaid have something to do with his kidnapping? Was Lindbergh a spy for the Nazis? To comment on some of these and many other unresolved Lindbergh questions, here, exclusively in Gay Aviation Today, *we have secured an interview with one man who claims to be the famous Lindbergh baby, all grown up—not to mention alive and well.*

Charles Augustus Lindbergh Jr. (as he is now legally

named), says that he was indeed kidnapped, but clearly, never actually killed—and that through extensive hypnosis and other memory-recovery techniques, he was able to recall what happened to him on that fateful night of March 1, 1932, when he was stolen from his crib inside the plush Lindbergh estate in Hopewell, New Jersey.

Charles Lindbergh Jr. is joined by his longtime friend Mr. Donald Smith, who also has "family ties" to the Lindbergh saga—though in an admittedly very different manner from his friend Charles. Smith's mother was one of a handful of women who wrote Charles and Anne Lindbergh during the days after their child's 1932 kidnapping, offering their own children as a possible replacement for the one that had just been stolen.

The two men, both seventy-four, have struck up a lifelong friendship, grounded in their decidedly odd connections to the Lindbergh legacy. They co-own one of the world's only two known working replicas of the Spirit of St. Louis, *though only Smith still holds a valid pilot's license to fly it. Lindbergh and Smith live in a residential retirement community located between Boca Raton and Delray Beach, Florida. "Above the Clouds," as it is called, is the only aviation-themed retirement community in the country. Residents house their planes in hangars beside the development's first-rate private airstrip, and staff pilots are on hand when residents are no longer able to fly their ships themselves.*

I caught up with the two septuagenarians at Norm's

Coffee Shop in West Boca, just a few days before Christmas. As strings of multicolored lights twinkled and flashed in the palm trees outside the window beside our booth, Charles A. Lindbergh Jr., Donald Smith, and this inquisitive reporter chatted about past and present Lindbergh revelations—as well as their own unique perspectives on this still-captivating, world-famous aviator's complicated history.

—T Cooper

GAY AVIATION TODAY: So where did you two meet?

CHARLES AUGUSTUS LINDBERGH JR: We met under the arch in St. Louis on the fifty-year anniversary.

GAY AVIATION TODAY: Of?

DONALD SMITH: The flight. The transatlantic flight that started it all.

GAY AVIATION TODAY: So what happened that day under the arch?

DS: Well, I'd traveled to St. Louis for the fifty-year anniversary, hoping to see someone from the family, and after the ceremonies started, I noticed this gentleman who looked stunningly like Lindbergh. He was so handsome and stately, just sitting on a concrete barrier outside the tent where the festivities were taking place. I thought it strange that we were both outside, when everything was happening inside.

CAL JR: They wouldn't let me in.

GAY AVIATION TODAY: What happened?

DS: Tell him.

CAL JR: Well, I sent letters and called for months before the celebration, but nobody would return my calls. I thought I should be allowed to be an official part of the celebration. You know, after all those years, and my father had just passed a few years before. I thought maybe it would be water under the bridge, but . . .

GAY AVIATION TODAY: Why do you think the family was so hostile?

CAL JR: They didn't want me. They'd already dealt with me and moved on.

GAY AVIATION TODAY: Dealt with you how?

CAL JR: Well, the alleged kidnapping.

GAY AVIATION TODAY: Could you explain?

CAL JR: Whole thing was a setup. My mother Anne didn't

want me. She was quite depressed—you know, the post-departum *[sic]* baby blues that some ladies get? Well, my mother had it real bad. And my father felt I was putting a cramp on their world-travel schedule. So they figured out a way to get rid of me.

GAY AVIATION TODAY: What about the "trial of the century," the dead body of the baby found by the side of the road? The fact that Anne had another baby just a few months later?

CAL JR: All a setup. The FBI was in on it with my father. He was so popular then, people would do anything for him. Even resettle an unwanted baby.

GAY AVIATION TODAY: Forgive me for asking, but why didn't they just have you killed?

CAL JR: It's okay, people ask this very question all the time. Well, the answer is that my father just couldn't do it, although I know my mother wanted it done. But he just couldn't bear to kill his first-born son, his namesake.

GAY AVIATION TODAY: How could the whole world be fooled?

CAL JR: How could they not?

DS: What he's saying is that he knows Lindbergh like nobody knew Lindbergh.

GAY AVIATION TODAY: So let's start from the beginning. When did you realize you were Charles Augustus Lindbergh Jr.?

CAL JR: It's really hard to pinpoint one single moment in time. I would say that from what I've read of the men who turn into ladies later in life . . . It's sort of like that, where you always knew there was something wrong about your body, who you were. Like you were someone else. Only with me it was my name, not like wanting my penis to be lopped off or anything. No, that name just never felt right, even though I tried to ignore the haunting feeling, I tried to make it fit. I never could, because all these fragments of memories I couldn't place kept tugging at me.

GAY AVIATION TODAY: Can you remember what happened that night of the kidnapping?

CAL JR: The *alleged* kidnapping.

GAY AVIATION TODAY: The night of the alleged kidnapping?

CAL JR: Well, it was only after a well-known hypnotist, someone with a Ph.D., you know, a real expert, took me into his care for a couple of years. Three days a week, he would take me back, you know, just doing all these relaxing things—look at the watch, look at the pencil, look at my finger. Finally I started remembering what happened. Which was basically that Betty Gow, who I sort of felt closer to than my real mother, well, I didn't know anything was wrong, because after she put me to bed, she came back a couple hours later and pulled me out of the crib and carried me down the back stairway and out to a car which was waiting at the bottom of the driveway with its lights turned off.

GAY AVIATION TODAY: There was no ladder, no climbing out the window from the nursery?

CAL JR: No, nothing like that. Just as normal as if we were going out for an late-evening stroll. I wasn't feeling too good that night, and I remember the scent of Vicks VapoRub wafting in the air around my head as she carried me down the stairs and out to the car.

GAY AVIATION TODAY: So who was driving the car?

CAL JR: Well, all this will be revealed in the documentary I'm doing with a very well-respected young filmmaker from New York. But I guess I can say now. Basically, there were a couple of Capone's gangsters in the front, and a pale lady with curly black hair in the back. Betty handed me to her, and off we went.

GAY AVIATION TODAY: How do you know they were Capone's men?

CAL JR: I found out years later. I stayed with them in a tenement in South Chicago until the supposed Lindbergh baby's body was found. That lady from the car had been caring for me the whole time. I don't believe she was a very nice lady. She was just doing it for the money. I remember being hungry a lot. I missed my mother's breast and the gentle touch of Betty, my nursemaid.

GAY AVIATION TODAY: So you stayed there in Chicago?

CAL JR: No. After the news died down a little after the police supposedly identified the dead body, the gangsters took me to Iowa, where I lived with a man named Jones. That's how I got my original name—Jonathan James Jones II, which was the name that never felt right as I was growing up. I don't even like saying it.

GAY AVIATION TODAY: So that was it, you never saw Lindbergh again, and this man became your father?

CAL JR: I grew up with Jones—I don't call him my father. He was an awful man, treated me just horrible. He drank, and he put out lit cigars on my stomach. He hit me and the various ladies who lived with him in the house. He never worked, but he did always seem to have enough money. But one time when I was about six, I was going to buy a bottle of milk from the corner store for the lady who was living with us at the time, and all these men in black cars pulled up beside me and dragged me into one of the cars. I remember feeling dizzy and strange, and then everything went black. When I woke up, I was in a dark and dusty barn with horses kicking the dirt, and light coming in little strips through the wooden roof. I was sitting across from my father, who was looking very worried and nervous.

GAY AVIATION TODAY: Jones was—it was Jones who took you here with these men?

CAL JR: No, my father, Lindbergh.

GAY AVIATION TODAY: So what happened?

CAL JR: Well, he didn't touch me or come very close, but he stared at me a lot. I could tell that he wanted to embrace me, but he didn't. The FBI men were all talking quietly to the side, and I was terrified. I think what was happening was that my father wanted to make sure I was being taken care of. But the state of my clothes and the fact that I hadn't bathed in a week, I think this troubled my father, so the men were trying to figure out if I should be left with Jones or maybe resettled in another family, which was risky.

GAY AVIATION TODAY: Did you go with him?

CAL JR: No, that was the last time I saw my father in person. He gave me a bag of marbles though. I still have them. I always carry one with me wherever I go.

[Reaching into his pocket.] See? *[Opens palm to reveal small black marble.]*

DS: I've never seen him go anywhere without a marble.

GAY AVIATION TODAY: What happened next?

CAL JR: Well, the government men carried me to their car and took me back to town and deposited me in front of the same store I was about to go into. I remember turning to try to look at my father as they carried me. I swear I saw a tear fall from his blue eye, but the FBI men didn't hesitate. And you know, they followed me all throughout my lifetime—it was only after the hypnosis that I realized it wasn't normal for a boy to be constantly followed by a black car with two men sitting in the front seat. But this was my father's way of watching over me. And I think these guys went and roughed up Mr. Jones a little after this incident, because he had a black eye when he got home later that night, and for a few months after he was nicer to me.

GAY AVIATION TODAY: So where does Hauptmann fit into all this?

CAL JR: They set him up.

GAY AVIATION TODAY: Who?

CAL JR: All of them.

GAY AVIATION TODAY: Who's "all of them"?

CAL JR: Jafsie, Schwarzkopf, and the rest of the New Jersey police, the NYPD, the judge, all those lawyers. And of course my father—everyone was in on it.

GAY AVIATION TODAY: Why Hauptmann?

CAL JR: Oh, he wasn't completely an innocent guy, but I do know he had absolutely nothing to do with my abduction. I think they got him involved in some scheme where when he got the marked ransom bills, he thought it was for some racket he was running—so he knew he had to hide the dough in his attic, where the police discovered it later. With great fanfare, of course.

GAY AVIATION TODAY: And the ladder found at the Lindbergh home, that was planted too?

CAL JR: Sure was. The NYPD pulled that one unique piece of wood from Hauptmann's attic and had a carpenter with skills like Hauptmann construct a ladder with it—one that would perfectly reach the second story window of my nursery. My father provided them the measurements so it would be conclusive that Hauptmann had made the ladder specifically for the kidnapping job. That's why

Hauptmann never confessed—even when they offered him a stay of execution in exchange for an admittance of guilt. He never admitted being involved. Because he just wasn't. *[Shaking his head.]* That poor man didn't know what had hit him. But that's what happens when the entire U.S. government is stacked against you.

GAY AVIATION TODAY: So where'd they find Hauptmann?

CAL JR: They just wanted an anonymous German immigrant who didn't speak English very well—someone with a few petty crimes on his record and living nearby in New York, just greedy and stupid enough to get himself involved in a scheme that sounded too good to be true. They were also taking advantage of the anti-German sentiments going around in those days.

GAY AVIATION TODAY: That's interesting considering Lindbergh's stated admiration for all things German.

CAL JR: It's one small sacrifice. Plus, it makes it all look even less suspicious when my father later sits up there on the witness stand in that courtroom in Flemington and testifies that Hauptmann's voice is the one he heard in the Bronx cemetery when Jafsie was handing the ransom money over.

GAY AVIATION TODAY: Do you think Lindbergh was a Nazi sympathizer?

CAL JR: He just said what he believed. Nothin' wrong with that. *[Looks at Donald.]*

DS: Nope, nothin'.

CAL JR: He didn't think entering into a foreign war was right for our country at the time, and he felt it was his duty to go public with his sentiments. I tend to agree with him—but I know it's not a popular thing to say these days. *[Silent for a few moments.]* You know, everyone was so worked up over what my father said about the Jews, but he wasn't anti-Semitic. He was a principled man. He spoke the truth. The Jews *did* control the movie industry and the banks. They still do. That's why I can't get my film made, besides this one art school fellow in New York who's going to do it.

GAY AVIATION TODAY: Well, a lot of people might take issue with those views.

CAL JR: But if they're true, then they're true.

GAY AVIATION TODAY: But that's what I'm saying. Some don't believe they're true.

CAL JR: I don't really know.

GAY AVIATION TODAY: Don't you think he might have at least

apologized when he figured out what the Nazis were doing?

CAL JR: My father wrote in his journals that he was horrified when he first found out.

GAY AVIATION TODAY: But he never apologized publicly.

CAL JR: But when the time came, you know, after Pearl Harbor, he wanted to fight. Because he knew then it was time to get involved. He had a wisdom, you could say, that your average everyday people simply can't and won't ever understand. This is essentially the first man who traveled the world like that, hopping around from country to country in his plane. He saw things people at that time couldn't imagine . . . He knew what he was talking about. This country might've been better off if we listened to him, but at the end of the day, I don't know, it's really the visionaries who get screwed because they're the ones sticking their necks out for the world to hack away at.

DS: With a blunt blade.

GAY AVIATION TODAY: Okay. Maybe we can move on to the present revelations. What do you two think of the news of this German family?

DS: Not entirely surprising.

GAY AVIATION TODAY: Why?

DS: Well, given the guy's track record with deception.

GAY AVIATION TODAY: Charles?

CAL JR: Well, I'm a little less jaded than Donald, but then, it makes sense, because boys always idealize their fathers and don't want to believe they'd do anything like that—fooling around on my mother and having three bastard children with this German lady. But I guess it technically makes sense, when you think of how he spent all those years of his life flying back and forth to Europe for long spells. No, no more! *[Holds palm over coffee cup to indicate to waitress he doesn't want a refill. Waitress turns on a heel and yells "Happy Hanukkah" to an elderly couple just about to leave through the jingling front door to the restaurant.]*

DS: It's Hanukkah?

CAL JR: It's *always* Hanukkah around here. *[Laughing.]*

DS: That David Hesshaimer, he's a dead ringer for Lindbergh.

CAL JR: Yeah, my brother David in Germany, he looks just like my father, same smile, same eyes. It's uncanny.

GAY AVIATION TODAY: Have you tried to contact the Hesshaimers since they announced the news?

CAL JR: I've had a friend send a couple e-mails, a fax. I called a newspaper in Germany to try to reach them. But they haven't responded. Why would it be any different? No Lindberghs want to know the truth about me. They can't handle it.

GAY AVIATION TODAY: So you tried to contact Charles and Anne?

CAL JR: You betcha. I spent the better part of my life trying. But nothing. They'd tell their guards to send me away.

GAY AVIATION TODAY: Guards?

CAL JR: One time I did go to the Lindbergh home in Connecticut. This was after my father had passed, and I thought maybe now that he was gone, my mother might feel some sense of regret and want to see her first-born son again. So I went with my wife to—

GAY AVIATION TODAY: You're married?

CAL JR: I was—just for a year or two, and then we parted. I met her at the annual New England Lindbergh Society Luncheon in Hartford—you know, every year on May 21 they hold it. *[Sighs, looks at hands and rubs them* *together.]* I think she was just, well, taken by me as soon as she figured out who I was. Chasing a star, as they say.

DS: That's not exactly what they say.

CAL JR: *[Whispers.]* He doesn't like me talking about those years.

DS: No, I just say, call a spade a spade. A star-f*cker a star-f*cker.

CAL JR: So Ann and I—my wife's name was also coincidentally Ann, but without the *e*. Her mother supposedly was the lady who gave Lindbergh the mirror to put in the *Spirit of St. Louis* cockpit before he took off from Roosevelt Field. Anyway, so Ann and I go to Darien to try to see Anne Lindbergh, but the guards said they were expressly told not to allow us onto the property. Ann burst into tears.

DS: She thought you were her ticket inside.

CAL JR: She was just very worked up about the whole thing, like ladies get. She had also tried to make contact with Lindbergh after her mother died, but besides a couple local newspapers where she told her story of her mother giving him the makeup mirror and some gum to stick it onto the panel, there wasn't much else.

DS: You still don't see how she used you?

CAL JR: Not now, Donald.

GAY AVIATION TODAY: Okay, can you guys tell me a little about your plane? I'm sure *Gay Aviation Today* readers will be interested in the specs.

CAL JR: I don't want to talk about the plane.

DS: *[Whispers.]* It's, you know, your typical nine-cylinder reciprocating radial—223 horsepower.

CAL JR: Shut your hole. You're not even blood. *[Looks hurt.]*

DS: He's still a little touchy about having his pilot's license revoked. Aren't you? *[Pokes CAL JR. playfully. CAL JR. doesn't respond.]*

GAY AVIATION TODAY: So, Donald, can you tell me a little about your past, and how you came to feel so connected to the Lindbergh saga?

DS: Basically, on the morning of the third day after Charles was kidnapped, my mother went to the Western Union downtown and offered me to the Lindberghs as a replacement baby.

GAY AVIATION TODAY: Really?

DS: Yeah, yeah. I was about Charles's age, blond-haired and blue-eyed. We lived outside Birmingham, and my folks had eleven kids; I was the last of the lot. I guess my ma figured one less wouldn't kill anyone, but it might help the Lindberghs a whole bunch. So she sent a telegram expressing condolences for the loss and offered that if they didn't find their baby, she would bring them me.

GAY AVIATION TODAY: That's quite a story. Did she ever hear back from the Lindberghs?

DS: No, but my ma sent a total of something like ten telegrams and letters. And we didn't have that kind of money for postage and stuff like that. When my pa found out, well, let's just say Ma wasn't cooking the meat for a few days—she was putting it on her face.

GAY AVIATION TODAY: Did anything else ever come of this?

DS: Just that as I grew up, all my siblings always teased me that I was the kid our ma wanted to get rid of. It happened, well, anytime Lindy was in the news—which was all the time up to the beginning of the war. So it was kind of like Charles—I grew up always knowing something was wrong. I guess you could say I wasn't really loved. But who am I to complain? Everyone had it hard then. You know, that's why it was such a brilliant scheme, with the kidnapping and ransom and stuff. Kidnappings happened all the damn time then—everyone was so desperate.

GAY AVIATION TODAY: What was it like growing up in the shadow of the Lindbergh kidnapping?

DS: I don't really know. My ma shot herself through the jaw when I was about thirteen, and she died. Then I left town when Pa had to move out of the house and didn't let me come with him. I'd always felt like New York was calling, so off I went with the money I earned working on a neighbor's farm. I guess I started drinking like Pa . . . You know how it is, just a bunch of years go all hazy. Then you look up and you're an old man, and you don't know where it all went, all that sweat spent just trying to stay alive.

CAL JR: You got yourself into some trouble there, didn't you? *[DS doesn't respond.]*

GAY AVIATION TODAY: Care to explain?

DS: Naw.

GAY AVIATION TODAY: Sure?

DS: Just a little trouble with the law, is all. I was, well, you know—getting money any way I could.

CAL JR: Till he finally figured out he never quite got over the thing with his mom.

GAY AVIATION TODAY: You sort of hit rock bottom? *[DS doesn't respond.]*

CAL JR: And then he met me at that fifty-year reunion, and all of it started making a little more sense, both of us being kind of, you know, orphaned because of the Lindberghs. It seemed at first like it was just me helping him. But he helps me too. He helped me.

DS: I would be dead if it wasn't for this man. *[Turns to face out the window, looking up at lights in palm trees.]*

CAL JR: I don't know where I'd be without him either.

GAY AVIATION TODAY: So you've been lovers ever since, what, 1977?

CAL JR: I didn't say that.

DS: No, no, no. Nobody said anything about that.

GAY AVIATION TODAY: I'm sorry, I—

DS: We agreed to do this interview for the sake of aviation, for Lindy, but you can't say that. Don't say that. We're not fairies.

GAY AVIATION TODAY: My editor—I thought . . . I'm sorry. Well, so you just live together there at "Above the Clouds," and share the replica plane and—

CAL JR: We live in condos, next door to each other.

DS: They're adjoining, we got a double door put in between them. But it's two entirely different, totally separate places.

CAL JR: Yeah, you should see this guy's housekeeping. Are you kidding me? [*Jabs thumb toward DS, laughing heartily. Summons the waitress with the universal gesture for "Check, please."*] Sometimes I go into his condo and I think to myself, was this guy raised by wolves, or what? And then I remember, yeah, you know what? He kind of was.

•

T COOPER is a writer and aviation enthusiast who has a private pilot license with a single-engine rating. Cooper's last interview for Gay Aviation Today *was with Linda St. John, President of GLBTIBHUNA, the Gay, Lesbian, Bisexual, Transgendered, and Intersexed Baggage-Handlers Union of North America.*

1937

FIVE AND DIME VALENTINE

by Felicia Luna Lemus

Five and Dime Valentine

Patti lured me in with promises of a little extra something if I called her in the next three minutes. "A
special surprise just for you," she whispered, and
caressed the heart locket Angela wore strung on a gold
chain around her failed-swan, too-long neck. The camera
zoomed in extra tight as Patti's long manicured finger-
nails grazed Angela's flesh. Nestled right above Angela's
pert tits, the gold locket caught light and glistened. I
shivered.

Same as the endless call girls pictured on glossy little square advertisement flyers—their outsized curves
and skinny shaved bodies strategically blacked out with
jagged Sharpie pen lines in accordance with some newly
enforced and entirely misplaced Pilgrim ordinance—just
like the lassies littered on the sidewalks outside our
casino, Patti was pretty, but not exceptionally beautiful.
And even better than those interchangeable disposable
girls, Patti was an excellent whore—more geisha than
streetwalker. One look and I was hooked so hard I was
certain whatever she could offer would actually edify me.

I was depleted. I'd already spent the twenty dollars of gambling money credited on the plastic card all the other tour folk wore looped around their necks, but that I insisted on clipping to the inside of my jacket. Half an hour at a dollar slot machine, bored out of my skull, I'd given my two free drink coupons away and headed up to my cruddy economy room. I'd only agreed to come to Vegas because Marjorie had begged. She said it'd be fun, that it'd take us out of our normal routine. I liked our normal routine. Always had. But even more than our routine, I liked making Marjorie happy.

So there I sat, alone on the north end of the Vegas strip in a third-floor room with no view, in a horrid crumbling hotel that boasted of having a roller coaster inside, and that employed tired clowns with dirty shoes. Quarter of a peanut butter sandwich lunch wrapped back up in its wax paper wrapper (hell would turn icy before I'd shell out for snacks between the three buffet meals a day included on our tour), I wiped my hands on the edge of the bed, glad the crumbs disappeared, lost evidence, into the scratch-ugly polyester comforter.

Patti on the TV screen winked at me. She said I'd better call real soon, that she had something very exciting just for me. Still seated at the edge of the bed, I surveyed the hotel room. Marjorie's bottles of arthritis and heart medicine sat in neat rows on the crummy nightstand. Her clothes hung in the closet, organized by type and color. Marjorie was a tidy girl. Me, coated with a slight layer of crumbs, I stood and sat at the little round table next to our room's one smudged dark window and picked up the phone. The call alone was going to cost more than I'd allotted myself in spending money for the entire trip. No matter, I dialed 9 for an outside line and called the number listed on the lower left corner of the television screen.

The operator who answered my call asked for my credit card number. I'd gotten so goddamned caught up in Patti and her come-on hustle that I'd forgotten I would need to pay for more than just the call itself. And pay I would. Gladly. She kept smiling at me from the screen. I swear I saw the pink tip of her tongue flick Angela's neck. Was that possible? Would she really do that? For free? By the time I retrieved my credit card from my wallet, any price would have been fine by me. I'd never given the number out over the phone before; the situation seemed fraught with potential for fraud, but this was different. This was urgent. I gave the operator my credit card number and expiration date.

"Would you like to talk to Patti?" he asked.

How stupid was the kid? Of course I wanted to talk to Patti. Why else would I be calling? I told him as much. He asked my name. I gave him my full name. I thought it was for the credit card.

"Please decrease the audio volume of your television," he said in an awkward monotone from what seemed to be a very poorly written script. "There is a delay on the broadcast. It will only confuse you if you hear yourself on the television, ma'am."

Ma'am. That's when you know you're closer to the grave than the cradle, when absolute strangers with no need or desire to be respectful call you *ma'am.* He already had my money. He didn't have to be polite. And he wasn't. In fact, he was almost rude the way he said *ma'am* in acknowledgement of the way my voice shook old-woman-tired vocal chords. To hell with him. I *was* old. I'd be eighty-five in June. So what? It frustrated me beyond explanation how young people assumed I was easily confused.

"I'll mute the television, son," I said, over-enunciating the word "mute" so he'd know I wasn't a complete techno-imbecile. I surfed the Internet, for Pete's sake. I had CD music at home. I owned a digital camera. One thing I didn't have was any children, thank God. Milking the patronizing saccharine potential of the word *son* was a skill I'd perfected long ago. I used my power sparingly, but without hesitation.

"Please stay on hold, ma'am. Patti will be with you momentarily."

Muzak played. I didn't recognize the song. But it was too jazzy and loud. My mouth was dry. Why hadn't I gotten a glass of water before calling? All that peanut butter and now I was going to try to charm Patti? I stared at the vanity counter near the bathroom. Two plastic-wrapped plastic tumblers sat next to a padded ice bucket no one in their right mind would ever trust. I knew if I put down the phone to get a glass of water, the music would stop and Patti would pick up the line, and by the time I'd make my way to the vanity and actually manage to unwrap one of those damned flimsy cups, let alone fill it with disgusting rusted tap water from the bathroom sink—in the time it would take me to do all that, Patti would have come and gone off to the next admirer.

"Hello, Luisa." An overly cheery female voice intruded on my wandering thoughts.

I jumped, startled, and almost dropped the telephone. Three-second-delay, a muted Patti on the television mouthed, *Hello, Luisa.*

"Oh, hello," I said with a clumsy parched tongue.

"Very good to meet you, Luisa," Patti said, the static nature of her enormous lovely smile hinting at impatience.

I liked that she knew my name, and I liked how she said it. She took her time with each syllable and sang the final letter slightly. She smiled bright for me. Her cardigan hugged her pretty curves and showed off her slim shoulders. I took in every detail and noticed she kept her left ring finger folded back as it grazed Angela's neck. There was a cut on the middle joint of Patti's finger. Nothing more than a paper cut or maybe a nick from shaving those pretty little hands of hers, nothing dire, but she had to hide the cut. Patti wasn't allowed human flaws.

"Are you buying this lovely heart locket for someone special, Luisa?" Patti asked.

"No, dear, just for myself," I lied.

"Isn't that wonderful? Good for you, getting yourself a little Valentine's treat. We should all do that, get ourselves a little Valentine's treat, don't you think?"

Patti could pitch with the best of them. As much as I wanted to like her, as much as I *did* like her, there were no two ways about it—the heart locket Patti hawked was only part of why I was calling. Sterling silver. Or white gold. Didn't matter if that heart had been solid platinum, I knew it wouldn't be as elegant as she promised when it arrived in the mail. Not even for three easy payments of $35.75 each. But that barely mattered. Light bounced off Patti's bleached teeth. Angela's heart locket sparkled.

I said: "Once, I shoplifted a locket just like yours for a girl I wanted to be my sweetheart. That was during the Woolworth's sit-down strike. We had a committee that was supposed to keep track of what girls 'shopped' during the strike, but it was too easy to pocket things. No security cameras or any of those little magnetic strips back then, not in 1937. That's long before your time, Patti, but have you heard of that strike, dear?"

Okay, so I didn't tell Patti any such thing. But did I wish I could confess that and so much more to her. Maybe she would have been impressed how we made it into the papers and even *Life Magazine* when we shut down all of Woolworth's five floors, lunch counter and all, for more than a week. Great Depression to the birds (what was so fucking *great* about depression, economic or otherwise, I'd never understood), we didn't give an inch until the owners met each and every one of our demands. I wanted to tell Patti how splendid those days we lived in the store had been. I wanted her to look at me with her big brown eyes while I told her about Marjorie. Mercy, Marjorie's eyes had been an even bigger and prettier brown than Patti's.

"Marjorie sold candy upstairs. The cutest girls always got the sales jobs. Long legs and penciled eyebrows and glossy lipstick made for the best money," I wanted to say.

Patti beamed those perfect teeth at me and I wondered if she liked peanut butter sandwiches with thin-sliced bananas layered inside. Bread cut into triangles. Crusts sliced off.

Peanut butter with banana on white. Brown pasty stuff smeared on squares of bleached wheat was foreign to me, but I played like it was my very favorite. I packed three extra sandwiches the morning of the strike because I knew Marjorie would be hungry. She always was. Voracious kitten, she had hollow cheekbones and skinny wrists. She spent all her money on store-bought clothes and fancy perfume. She never ate lunch. No one had enough money back then, especially us on Woolworth's payroll. Marjorie sorted and sold Necco Wafers, Kits Taffy, and Choward's Violet Mints, but, damn, did she ever look elegant as she did just that. We all had our priorities. Hers included sheer silk stockings with cocoa-brown seams up the back to emphasize slim calves Betty Grable would have envied. Yes, we all had our priorities. Mine was packing sandwiches to share with Marjorie.

Peanut butter with banana on white.

"What are we going to do with that, Luisa?" my mother said, her tired face confused, as she pointed to the groceries I'd tried to hide from her. I bit my tongue and didn't admit that I too wished I'd brought home the cornmeal and tomatoes and meat she knew how to make into dishes we both understood and preferred. I stood at the cutting board over the sink and made sandwiches.

"I might need to stay at work late tonight," I said.

"Be home by dinner."

"Mamí, the strike starts today."

I wasn't sure if I'd be home for breakfast the next morning or even the morning after that. I had reliable inside information on this matter. Marjorie worked with Vita Terrall at the candy counter and Marjorie told me Vita had organized plans for the strike down to the very smallest detail. Vita told Marjorie to spread the word that we girls better come prepared to stay the night if we had to. I didn't tell my mother this exactly, but she knew if I didn't come home, she'd just have to accept it. It wasn't like she had much choice. I earned all our money. Thirteen-fifty a week plus tips, at least fifty hours each week. A girl of sixteen and I was in charge at home. For all of my mother's wrinkles and giving up hope, she knew as well as I did that it was a miracle I'd gotten the lunch counter job downtown.

The bosses had looked at my green eyes and rosy cheeks and they'd had no inkling that my family came to Illinois from Mexico to work on the railroads. My name changed from "Luisa" to "Louella" en route from my mouth to their ears. My English accent carefully perfected, how would the bosses know I'd learned to speak their language from the evening dramas that played loud on our neighbor's radio, most likely their one-room apartment's only luxury?

I spoke little beyond taking customers' orders and saying "thank you" and "yes sir"—mostly because I had few English words to use. They liked quiet girls. They liked us interchangeable and anonymous. They never inquired about my home life. So long as I worked hard, smiled, and deferred like a polite little mouse eager to please, they didn't care anything about me. And so they never knew my mother and I only moved to Detroit because my father had been killed in Chicago. They never knew about the derailed car that collided with the defunct boxcars beside the tracks, the makeshift steel shantytown we'd lived in as we worked. They never knew about the small stack of twenties, a large fortune for us, the company had given my mother and me to make us disappear after they put my father's remains in a simple coffin and into the ground. Nobody at Woolworth's knew anything about me, least of which that I'd never made or eaten a peanut butter white-bread sandwich, thin banana slices or no thin banana slices, ever before in my life.

I knew the sandwiches would congeal into disgusting lumps before dinnertime, let alone lunch, but I'd over-heard Marjorie tell another shop girl she loved peanut butter with banana on white, so I packed for the strike prepared to impress. Strike was scheduled to begin at 11, but Vita made it very clear we were to work as if nothing at all was different until she told us otherwise. So for five hours I wiped tabletops and carried heavy plates and suffered pinches on the ass by regulars who most definitely didn't tip enough to compensate for the pounds of flesh they skimmed with all their thick paws.

A tired mother with her young son sat at my section of the counter. I handed her a menu.

"This menu is sticky. Don't you know how to clean?" She sneered at me.

In fact, the menu was clean. I'd just wiped it down with a damp white towel folded into a tidy square smelling faintly of bleach. The way the woman looked at me, I knew her pointer-dog skinny nose had detected something in me she couldn't quite understand but that she knew her husband and his Friday clubhouse buddies might chase down in a truck and string up in a tree. I hesitated speaking for fear of a trace of any accent other than Midwest peeking through. Didn't matter, she didn't want to hear my voice. I wiped down her menu again and handed it back with a small smile.

"Give me ice cream," Junior said.

"It's too early for that," his mother said.

"Give me a triple scoop. Chocolate, vanilla, and strawberry," Junior demanded—of me, of his mother, most likely of each woman he'd come across his entire life through.

"You heard him," Junior's mother said, and thrust her menu at me.

10:37 a.m. I served the ice cream. Refilled coffees. I delivered greasy hash browns with slimy cubed ham and American cheese omelets. I prepped tables with pristinely arranged paper napkins and scratched silver settings. I filled creamers and dusted pepper shakers. 10:59. Junior's mother impatiently waved me down as she wiped her monster's smudged face. 11:00 a.m.

"Strike, girls, strike!" Hark, the angel sang.

Vita blew the silver coach's whistle she wore on a cord around her neck and repeated the call to arms.

"Strike, girls, strike!" she screamed. And smiled.

The hustle and bustle and the clanking of trays and the barking out of orders to the short-order cooks stopped. Junior's confused mother snapped her fingers at me. In vain. I followed Vita and all the other girls upstairs to the very center of the first floor. We stood against the counters with our arms crossed. The real work had just barely begun.

We stated our demands. I forget what they were exactly at this point. Okay, maybe I do remember them, but does it really matter anymore? I'll play the Senile Old Woman card here. Our laundry list of demands included something like: union recognition, a ten-cent-an-hour raise, an eight-hour workday, time and a half for overtime after forty-eight hours a week, free laundering of our required uniforms, blah blah blah.

What was important was that we shut down Woolworth's. We shut down the entire operations of the biggest and most important store in all of downtown Detroit. People don't seem to know this anymore, but back then Woolworth's was like Wal-Mart, K-Mart, and Costco combined. For seven days we ruled that store, got the entire nation on our side, and made Woolworth's squirm. Workers in New York and Chicago and Los Angeles and all over the entire nation watched us and threatened to do the same. Sure, there was that big sit-down going on at General Motors at the same time, but our strike was even more important—it was 1937 and we were girls. Literally. Most of us were barely in our twenties, if that. Our parents had been Victorians, for God's sake. We were 108 girls standing with our arms crossed, refusing to obey, screaming, "Strike, strike, strike!" at the top of our lungs. We were previously unthinkable.

12:30 p.m. We escorted out any customers still lingering. We locked the doors from the inside. We lowered all the blinds. Waving at supporters gathering on the sidewalks, we blacked-out the street-level windows with butcher paper. We covered the counters and goods with the same paper. Shop was closed.

Marjorie wore the biggest smile I'd ever seen on her.

That glow only got brighter when Vita came around and shouted out: "Lunch downstairs is on the house, girls!"

Ice cream, hot dogs, jelly donuts, pies, pancakes, sandwiches, sodas. My peanut butter and banana sandwiches sat lonely. A giddy and full-bellied Marjorie put her arm around my shoulders and nestled her heliotrope-perfumed hair against my shoulder.

"Isn't this the most amazing time, Louella?"

Indeed.

She looped her arm with another shop girl and they marched the floors singing trench and saloon songs they'd learned from their soldier brothers after they came back from the war, changing the lyrics to fit the occasion. "Mademoiselle from Armentieres" became:

> We slave at Woolworth's five-and-dime,
> The pay we get is sure a crime.
> Hinky dinky parlez-vous.

Marjorie was a natural for the strike's Cheer-Up and Entertainment Committee. I was, of course, on the Food and Store Clean-up Committee. I kept my sandwiches handy as a matter of responsibility. As Marjorie organized impromptu "entertainments" and kept spirits light, I swept and watched for rats. I would have laughed to know the roles we played those seven days would define our relationship for decades to come. She and all her frilly friends sat around giving each other manicures and giggling over tall stacks of awful dime books with titles like *How to Get Your Man and Hold Him,* books destined to be pulped, books that promised to reveal earth-shattering revelations such as "Secrets to Flattery." I could barely tolerate how froufrou girls could get in pack mode. It was hell how long into the night past our 11 p.m. curfew they chitter-chattered and laughed and threw pillows across the dozens of mattresses the cooks' union had delivered earlier that night and that we'd set up on the store's first floor with one pillow and one small blanket to each girl. Vita had finally gotten everyone to hush it when one of the girls with a bed in an aisle screamed bloody murder.

"A rat! A rat!"

This was no strike metaphor. An actual rat the size of a possum made its way across the mattresses, touching base on nearly every one. Every girl was up and screaming, and then the rat was gone and still the screaming. Vita blew her whistle.

"Upstairs, girls. We're going to the second floor."

We dragged our mattresses up the stairwell, one level further from the kitchen downstairs. It must have been 1 a.m. before we were lying down again. I started to fall asleep when I remembered my bag of sandwiches. They'd been downstairs next to my mattress. The rat. I was certain that if he hadn't already eaten them, he would. I couldn't get up. Vita was beyond strict at that point. The only thing that made that first awkward night livable was that Marjorie had set her pillow beside mine when we'd settled down. Three girls per mattress, me right up against Marjorie as she breathed steady, quiet little darling. I stayed awake to listen to her sleep, to enjoy the warmth of her small frame snuggling up against me to take the body warmth I would have formally offered to her along with my very soul if only I'd known how.

8:00 a.m. Curfew lifted. I sat in the main stairwell and found the Sunday paper someone snuck in for the Scrapbook Committee. The girls had already torn out the page I guess we were on, but they'd left the rest. I read the paper. Or tried to, anyhow. Each page took at least an hour with how slow my brain translated English. But unlike having to listen to spoken word and respond without preparation, with reading I could take all the time I wanted. And during the strike, time was what I had the most of.

That morning, girls gathering on the stairs around me to knit and crochet, I found the first article about the geisha girls: *Geisha Prepare for Battle*. All the way over in Osaka, Japan, three hundred geisha girls were holding a sit-down strike. They wanted a union. Their strike had started the same day as ours. At 11 a.m., same hour Vita blew her whistle for our strike, they prayed to Buddha for victory. They were singing songs and shouting protests just like we were. They were sitting strike in a temple on the top of a mountain. Just like we were.

I kept reading and half-listened as the girls around me gossiped about what a bitch Mae was. More accurately, Mae was a girl of rigid principles. Apparently,

Mae, who worked downstairs with me and had a peculiar fondness for operating the shake machine, had caught a few girls trying to sneak out the basement exit the night before to meet their boyfriends for Saturday night dates. Rumor was she'd taken the chewing gum out of her mouth and stuck it in the locks on the back doors. Those doors were locked for keeps. Marjorie was kinder in her response to the girls' needs. That second day of the strike, Marjorie and the Cheer-up Committee set up the Love Booth.

Girls worked themselves into frenzies at the three pay-station telephones.

"Honey, come by the store. There's a booth. We can go in it. But only for five minutes."

God knows what happened each three hundred seconds in that booth, the "booth" really just a curtain set up in the corner of the third floor for a small triangle of privacy. Who knows how many extra Detroit babies were born nine months later. Even the geisha girls didn't have a Cheer-up Committee setting up love booths. At 1 p.m. the geishas did write love letters and postcards to their patrons to flirt up support for their strike, but they didn't let their admirers come for make-out sessions. Our strike's Cheer-up Committee was instantly popular, as if the cheery girls on that committee hadn't been already.

Marjorie, the most cheerful and popular of them all, set her pillow next to mine the second night of the strike. And the third. And the fourth.

By the fifth night, rumors were starting up that a settlement was being negotiated. Of course, none of us girls were directly involved in the negotiations; the Hotel and Restaurant Employees Local 705 was taking care of that. Our job was to keep the reporters entertained when they came around. Our job was to refuse to work. My job required me to sleep next to Marjorie on the second floor of the downtown Detroit Woolworth's. I was the happiest of the workers for that alone, but for everything else, I felt justified in what I decided to do on the sixth day of the strike.

8:00 a.m. Most of the girls still yawning and lazily stretching their makeshift-bed-cramped limbs, I wandered to the third floor. Past woven pastel Easter baskets and stuffed Peter Rabbit dolls decorating the seasonal-amusements section nearest the stairwell, I made my way to floor four, Jewelry.

A few weeks before the strike started, I'd seen Marjorie admiring something in the display case there. It had been Valentine's Day—the only time of year the store brought in actual silver and gold niceties to supplement the standard cheap-costume crap. Fancy girl, Marjorie had pet the case glass as if a small kitten purred at her from the other side. The salesgirl had taken a necklace out for her to try on. They'd giggled as Marjorie stood in front of the mirror and preened. Her break ended before mine, and I watched as she sighed and gave the necklace back. I walked over to the counter.

"I need to buy a gift," I'd said.

"Marjorie downstairs dresses like a star and she loved this one," the salesgirl said.

She reached into the case and retrieved a light-gold necklace chain with the most delicate of heart lockets.

"Would you like me to wrap it for you?" she asked.

"I'll be back next payday."

"It might not still be here," she said.

Nearly three weeks passed.

That sixth day of the strike, I prepared myself not to find the necklace. Heavy brown butcher paper covered the case same as all the other cases in the store. Nobody was keeping watch on the fourth floor. No one saw me walk behind the counter and reach in to where I hoped the necklace would still be. Not a soul saw me slide the tiny twinkling of gold into my sweater pocket as I walked back downstairs to find Marjorie at the second-floor bathroom sinks, planning the day's first "entertainment" with another girl.

"We could set up a salon and have a beauty day pageant, the girls would love—"

"Marjorie . . ." I interrupted.

"Oh, good morning, Louella," she said. She blushed. That was all I needed.

"There's something important," I said.

"Is something wrong?"

"Just important."

I hated how truncated and redundant my English was. I smiled and gestured for her to follow me. She did.

With all the girls still putting on their faces and smoothing their clothes in front of mirrors on the first and second floors, the third floor was empty except for Marjorie and me. Her arm looped in mine like she did with all the girls—such a friendly doll. I led Marjorie toward the northeast corner. Then she saw the Love Booth. She hesitated. She took her arm from mine. What had I been thinking? I was such an idiot. She looked up at me with the strangest expression. Confusion? Fear? But then she smiled. A shy smile. A quiet smile. A "please do it" smile.

My hands shaking, I reached into my pocket.

"For you," I said, and offered the heart locket.

Until the day I die, I swear the kiss she gave me that day was sweeter than any other. Love Booth to hell, the entire third floor of Woolworth's couldn't contain that kiss. Marjorie tucked the necklace under the neck of her sweater. "Just to be safe," she whispered. She was smart that way. We did need to be safe. 1937. During a strike. Flashing that stolen sweetheart necklace wouldn't have been the most self-preserving of moves.

That night, Marjorie again put her pillow beside mine. Very close to mine. The next day, 5:30 p.m., Woolworth's and the Local 705 came to an agreement. Each of our demands was met. Plus we were paid fifty percent of our usual rate for the time we'd occupied the store. Employees at all forty Detroit Woolworth's received the improvements. Marjorie was wearing the heart locket I'd given her. Victory was sweet and far-reaching.

The headlines read:

Stand-Up Win for Sit-Down Girls;
Rich Success for Five and Dime Valentines

Two days later:

Geisha Union Recognized—
Osaka Teahouse Girls Back to Work

And then, February 5, 1960, nearly twenty-three years after our sit-down strike:

Klan Objects to Negro Lunch Counter Protest

Two days after that, reported from Greensboro, North Carolina:

Negro Protest Closes Woolworth's

Indeed, victory was sweet and far-reaching.

Patti was done with me. The operator promised the heart locket would be delivered to my home address with a gift card enclosed. I hung up the phone just as Marjorie walked into our hotel room waving two crisp hundreds in her hand.

"I won!"

She'd probably flirted up the roulette dealer. Or not. She was just charmed, that girl was.

"There's some sandwich left if you want," I said.

"I am hungry."

Of course she was.

"Baby, don't forget you need to take your heart medicine at 4:00," I said.

"Lou, you are such a bore." She walked over and sat on the bed next to me with a sweet little kiss on the cheek. "Nothing changes, does it?"

No, nothing does. And yet, everything does.

Marjorie. My Marjorie. She was even more stunningly lovely in her eighties than she'd been at twenty. All her delicate beautiful bones had worked themselves to the surface of thinned old-woman silk-soft skin. And her still-heliotrope-perfumed hair was silver. Truly silver. I detested how so many of our friends died their blow-dried helmets in impossible shades of black and red and brown. My own short no-fuss hair tended toward sulfured tinges of yellow, but Marjorie's was the silver stuff angels would weave stars from—if they only could.

"Happy Valentine's Day, darling," she said and smiled.

I wiped a white bread crumb from her wrinkle-free polyester blouse.

"Yes, Happy Valentine's Day."

1946

ONE MORE OLD HAT

by Darin Strauss

One More Old Hat

J ust as I was getting up to leave.

"Hey, hold it a minute," Mr. Olishansky called to me.

Olishansky (a seventyish real-estate lawyer) had a soft custard voice, and a dark, horizontal wrinkle across his hairless scalp. "Listen, mister," he said, "if you're the young man I'm thinking of, I got a story for you."

Olishansky and I had come, separately, to sit shivah for my Uncle Harold, who had died of a brain tumor that week. All around us in what had been Harold's house, the mirrors were covered with black cloths of mourning.

"So, Bella tells everyone you're a writer," Olishansky said. "If I can trust you, I got a book idea that's a million-seller for sure. Can I trust you?"

I'd seen him talking to my Aunt Bella earlier, his hands over hers, his honeydew head dropped in sympathy.

Now he was looking sideways at me: a gaze of disquieting intensity. *I know a lot of people say they have stories,* this look seemed to say, *but the story you're about to hear is nothing like the so-called stories you hear from those other schmucks.*

It was a look people had thrown at me before.

"Well, um," I said, "the thing is . . ." I had my coat and gloves on already.

"If you're not interested, fine," Olishansky said. "A busy young fellow like you." He was judging me as he spoke, cocking his blemished face—as if trying to suss out a faint noise in another room, a neighboring house, a far-off country.

"How old are you?" he asked at length. "Thirty, thirty-two?"

It wasn't that I didn't want to hear his story, I told him, but I was kind of in a rush.

"It's the life of my father," he said, winking at me.

Here's the story.

My father came from the old country. Russia, I'm talking about. Matter of fact, he was a poet. You ever heard of Osip Mandelstam? No? He was very famous in Russia, Mandelstam. My father was not as famous as Mandelstam. But close. Until 1929, he had a big following, my father. Then one day his works were no longer published. My father's name was Isaac Olishanski.

You know the name Anna Akhmatova? Another famous poet. She was my father's girlfriend for a time, sort of. *Was your image flickering sweet in the theater of my brain / Before you were even born?* That lovely poetry line was my father's. Well, it sounds better in the original Russian. He and another poet, Mikhail Bronstein, were leading elements of the Zenithist school of writers; *that* I'm sure you've heard of. No?

My father was thrilled by the Revolution when it came. Don't judge: A Jew back then, even if he was not religious, he was still a Jew in the eyes of the Cossacks, and that spelled trouble. Communism offered a change. My father, he was just twenty in 1917, started writing journalism that praised Lenin. Not that he stopped doing his poetry, but this journalism was taking up his time. He and Mikhail Bronstein had a lot of fights about this. "Olishanski, you're giving your art short shrift"— that kind of thing. Bronstein, who welcomed the February 1917 Revolution but not the October 1917 Revolution, called my father a propagandist. That's a word that really hurt my father, *propagandist,* because he was a poet above all else. All else. So my father stopped speaking to Bronstein.

When Stalin came to power—God shit on that monster's head—my father's friend and rival Bronstein disappeared. Most likely to Siberia, or worse. (Bronstein had written this epigram, *Murder must be fun/For Russia's Attila the Hun.*) Anyway, some loudmouths in the poetry world thought that my father betrayed Bronstein to the authorities. Ridiculous! But he wasn't deaf, my father, to that kind of gossip. He understood there was this talk. All untrue, of course. Totally untrue! Because, you have to understand, Stalin then stopped my father's work from getting out, too. I mean, would Stalin have done to my father what he did if my father was on his payroll? No, Stalin would not have done to my father what he did if my father was on his payroll. So, then came the hard times. No more poetry from Isaac Olishanski from now on, said the Soviets. This made no sense! Because he'd been in the circle of officially approved poets, my father.

Anyhow, after eight months of this silence, my father became desperate. He wrote a history of Stalin, a long poem I mean, very favorable; still nothing. He was "doomed to silence" is the way he put it. Doomed. I guess if you writers can't write, then it's all doom doom doom.

Anyway, from bad to worse—my father got a call from a government official by the name of Andrei Andreevich, a cockroach from the Soviet Security Bureau. My father was to come in and answer "concerns about the bourgeois, overly cerebral nature" of his work, or some such nonsense.

Now, the Soviet Security Bureau had been the agency that had gotten rid of my father's friend Bronstein. Probably Andreevich had killed that poet himself.

Understand, my father was very isolated by then. Thirty-five, thirty-six years old, he had no friends, no wife at this time, and he was estranged even from his parents, because he'd called them reactionary and spat in my grandmother's eye. In other words, he was all alone for what he thought would be his last night alive. Andreevich was going to have him killed for sure. The thought of certain wrongs he had done to placate the Soviet government, certain moments of cowardice, came at him now like a woodpecker pecking at the inside of his head. Peck, peck, peck.

When he went the next morning to the offices of the Soviet Security Bureau at the Spasskaya Tower, wearing his only suit (a blue one) and a rope for a belt, my father had to wait for six hours outside Andreevich's office. Nothing to read, just listening to the *thump thump thump* of his heart for almost a whole day. Thump, thump, thump; peck, peck, peck. Hours of this! Finally, at ten after 5:00, the cleaning workers started to turn off all the lights. My father didn't know what to do. *Is this a trick?* he thought. Someone must have been testing him, he thought. So he stayed there in the dark. Just sat there alone, sweating (he was a big man and often sweated like a milk cow).

After two more hours of nothing he just left, and you know what? He never went back.

Get this. Turns out, the bureaucrat cockroach Andreevich had himself been arrested that same morning, for a supposed lack of allegiance to the Five-Year Plan. Imagine! The drama—my father missed death by a whisker.

"So, Mr. Writer," Olishansky said. "You write this, they'll call you a new Chekhov!"

The nature of his eagerness was familiar to me.

I smiled at him, the sort of narrow smile I thought appropriate for the moment. We were standing close enough that I heard his sport jacket rustle as he began to nod. Meanwhile, someone unseen had started to weep in my Aunt Bella's living room.

"Missed death by a whisker," Olishansky said, and he smiled as if he were telling me his father had bequeathed him millions, or a comparable treasure.

I told him it was a wonderful story. His nods got more vigorous. And the weeping in the other room was growing louder. I turned to see if it was Bella who was crying. It was. Her old face had been squeezed by grief; the dark vigor of her wrinkles bespoke the terrible lonely fear of a widow who'd never before lived by herself. I turned away so that she wouldn't see I'd been staring.

Olishansky was still nodding at me.

Was he thinking of writing the story as a book? I asked.

"Me?" he said. He fired a toot of irritability from the cannon of his nose. "Just listen, Mr. Writer," he said. "There's more."

That whole thing with Andreevich spooked my father, of course, and he decided to get out of Russia. Not an easy thing to do after the war. Some people in the West, however, powerful people, still remembered the name Olishanski.

We ended up in Budapest for a month, waiting in what my father called a *camp*—but it wasn't a camp; it wasn't that bad, he was a writer, with a writer's imagination, remember—and then we made it onto a steamer bound for New York in 1946.

Oh—that's right: *we*. My father had met my mother in St. Petersburg in 1942. She was a milliner, very pretty. I was born in Russia in 1943, not that I speak that particular language.

Anyway, it was hard for him in this country, my father. We lived for a while in Little Italy. Of course, not many people knew Russian there in 1946. It was an unpopular language in the later '40s and '50s, put it that way. My parents stopped speaking it altogether, like a purge, and changed the *i* at the end of our name to a *y*.

My father got a job making deliveries for the Ansonia Pharmacy on Sixth, in the Village. Yeah—pharmacies used to make house calls back then. Where were the powerful people who'd told him to come to America? "Blown off like loose papers in a wind," my father said.

In any case, he started trying to write poetry in English. Just a little at first, he hoped to do some more as his fluency improved. And my mother worked in Chinatown, she was the only non-Chinese girl in this factory on Canal Street that made knockoff leather gloves.

So, here's where the story picks up again. One day my father has to make a delivery to this fancy Fifth Avenue address, headache salts or something. Right near that park that's by NYU. Anyway, who's ordering this stuff—who lives behind the fancy door to the penthouse apartment—but Mikhail Bronstein, the Russian poet who was supposedly dead back in Russia.

Locks unlocking, click click click, and then Bronstein

opens the door with, "Yes, hello?" At that point they recognize each other for who they are, and he and my father
stand there, silent as two old dogs going face-to-face.

It was not an easy moment, I can tell you. My father
lost his breath as he looked at the face of this man who
had been his friend and rival. Was it him? Had to be.
The old-fashioned glasses over the old-fashioned nose.
Those watery-blue eyes. (My father described this scene
to me so many times I, an eleven-year-old boy, could
recite it along with him.) Anyway, my father took an
unthinking step backward, and so did Bronstein. For a
full minute neither could believe what he saw, though
life should have taught both of them to believe everything. Bronstein in a silk robe? My father thought his
eyes had lost their mind. Bronstein in this big-shot
apartment?

Twenty feet behind Bronstein there was a bay window
that looked down on the whole city—from this height, it
was a view that my father rarely got to see in his life. By
the window, a shiny piano had its lid lifted. And here was
Bronstein, looking at my father without blinking, or
speaking. Would he say something about their past? My
father hoped not. A hatred grew tangled in my father's
chest. He thought he'd punch Bronstein if the guy was
tactless enough to bring up their shared past and their
different presents. But my father wanted to punch
Bronstein if he'd be rude enough *not* to mention it. So you
can see my father's dilemma. Here's where a good writer
could do it justice. But only a good one. I put it to you.

So, finally my father just said, "You ordered this, mister?" with that syrupy accent of his.

"Yes," Bronstein said with the very same accent. "Well, my wife ordered it."

Funny how the eyes are drawn to things sometimes. Is it the Talmud that says people have a sense that tells them where to look, what to see? Maybe it was a poem I read. But over Bronstein's shoulder, my father caught sight of a new book jacket that was written in English, a book of poetry with the name *Bronstein* big across the spine. That hurt, you can probably imagine.

"Seventy-five cents, please," my father said.

Bronstein gave the money, but—and my father always pointed this out whenever he told the story—he didn't look my father in the face; Bronstein's eyes were facing the floor when he thrust the money into my father's hand. Both men knew the real poet was now delivering headache salts. My father, a goddamn delivery boy! No, he was not that!

They didn't cross paths again, my father and Bronstein. But the old woodpecker started up again. The woodpecker that he'd known in Russia once more started pecking and pecking at his brain. And it did this for the rest of his life. He talked about it to me. "That goddamn woodpecker," he'd say. "That goddamn woodpecker never takes a day off." Which is very poetic. But he never wrote a word of poetry in English and lived very poor until I bought my parents a house in Florida six months before they died, one right after the other. The end.

* * *

"Wow, Mr. Olishansky," I said. "That is a story, all right."

"Of course it's a story. What else would it be, a show tune?"

Olishansky stared into my face with humid, deliberating eyes. He was waiting for me to say more. He put the tip of his tongue to his upper lip. The old man actually bounced on his toes a little, but slowly. The skin around his lips tightened. I wanted, of course, to say something about the story; something encouraging. I didn't. And at that moment I couldn't have said why I didn't.

By now Olishansky was pulling unhappily at the cuffs of his jacket. Sizing me up.

"Don't patronize," he said in a peculiarly calm way, blinking. "I'm aware of how evocative it is. I said it needed a *good* writer. Maybe I have to look somewhere else."

His air of outright displeasure lent him a certain dignity.

"Well, maybe that's right," I said. "I just don't think that I'd know how to tell it." I wasn't lying. I thought it an interesting story, but one that I wouldn't know how to shape into a narrative. As often happens with life, the structure was nonexistent. The middle part had its own dramatic peak, and then, all that time later, a single moment of pathos. But how to handle the years in between?

"What the hell do you mean, *how to tell it?*" His eyes bulged out, as if from a force inside his head. "What kind of a question is that? You would just tell it. God in heaven. Straight! You'd tell it straight! It's a beautiful story, what's so hard?"

"There would have to be some kind of framing device. Some imposed architecture, or—" I couldn't find the word I wanted. "Anyway, it's not mine; it's yours, this story."

He wasn't listening. "Writers," he said. "They go through life not recognizing gold when it falls in their hands."

And then he waved me off with a gesture that meant *phooey,* and walked past me toward the door and out of this story.

I didn't go anywhere. My Aunt Bella was still crying in the next room, not hysterically, but like a tired child. I was pretty sure I was the only person in my family who knew that my Uncle Harold had cheated on Bella for the last twenty years of his life. Who would tell that story, the life of Harold and Bella? Or the story of my own father, who'd made a fortune as a young man, lost it all, earned a second fortune, and then lost that fortune, too? There are innumerable stories in the world, even in my own family, stories that belong to me, they are mine, and yet the feeling to tell any of them is crumpled up inside me like an old hat.

I waited a minute until I was sure I wouldn't run into Mr. Olishansky outside. And then I went home.

1955

THE COURAGE TO LOVE

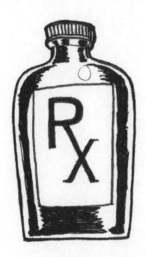

by Sarah Schulman

The Courage to Love

New York City

Anna Fuchs had a hot plate. She boiled coffee and soup. There was black bread, real butter. She stewed fruit. Anna ate toasted corn muffins with that butter, and she bought jars of fruit salad and some cheese. She sliced a tomato. She bought cold cuts from the German delis and strong mustard. Two bottles of beer sat in the refrigerator for months. The moment was never right. There was a bottle of sherry somewhere. Two nice glasses. Occasionally, a piece of cake. That summed up her domesticity.

To cook would never be.

There was classical music on the radio. This had become a habit. It was civilizing. She loved her chair. It moved her, emotionally, the comfort of that chair. Its love, in a way.

Someone had phoned that morning to see if she was the same Anna Fuchs who had been murdered at Baba Yar. But no, that one was Russian, ironically also a doctor. This one was German. Same name. The caller still had hope. For his sister. He was a laundryman from the Ukraine. Charlie Yevish. *Was this productive,* Anna wondered, *imagining that the dead had lived?* Occasionally there were stories. She knew that her husband was dead, and she hoped he was dead. She didn't need him and she didn't need to see him. If he had lived, he would have hurt her even more. Their son. Leo's troubles were coming to the surface now. He was irrational. Angry. Was this caused by Leo's years of exile in Turkey, the torture and death of his father? Or was it his father's cruelty before he himself had become the victim? These distinctions would become more and more difficult to draw. Would Leo have been equally conflicted if he had grown up quietly in an educated home with a sadistic father? Or did it take the Nazis to make him this sick? There, she said it. Her son was sick. She knew it. Does the cruelty of others transform one's mental health, or simply reveal existing problems? Now he was training to be a psychiatrist. He could have a brilliant career in America. Even if his symptoms deepened. The controlled atmosphere of the therapeutic relationship might help. The authority. The power might help her son. The power to help others. Sometimes the mentally ill can improve by caring for a pet, or an aged grandparent. Or, perhaps, a patient. A child.

She loved her chair. The tight feel, to be so close to something physical. Its smell. The relief, the perfect lamp, the smell of the rain, and the sight of it out her window. She loved the wooden table next to the chair.

The reliable presence of her reading glasses, the opened book. An article waiting to be seen. The gorgeous presence of new ideas being created, offered. There was room on that table for a book, glasses, a cup of coffee, and the lamp. It was perfect. The reach was perfect. The relationship between chair and table, perfect. To both see and hear the rain. The radio. To hear the radio and the rain, the inner life and the outer world. To know and see.

Anna prepared.

When the doorbell rang, the tea kettle was on the hot plate and slices of *mohnkuchen* were laid out on an old china serving plate, two matching saucers and cups. Two forks and linen napkins. There is intention behind that kind of gesture. It took an effort, a prethought. Anna had had to go to the bakery and choose the right thing, poppy seeds something clearly not American. She tried to be acknowledging in that way. It should be associative to Larry, the taste of his parents' house. That was kindness, thinking about the other person and what they would like. Mendelssohn was on the radio. She loved this recording. Mendelssohn used this sonata form for his "Hebrides Overture" because it has a fairly strict pattern to follow in terms of form, key, and temperament. The combination of passion and discipline. Freedom with responsibility. Another thing of beauty not destroyed. She loved that. It moved her. Anna cried, inside. The doorbell rang again.

Larry walked in, and they habitually smiled without speaking because the music was so wonderful and she had turned it up. Why speak? He sat in his chair while they listened together for three full minutes. Then the kettle whistled. Anna lifted it off the hot plate, poised, until the piece resolved, poured the water into the teapot, and turned off the radio. There was the sound of the steam of moving water, the shifting of the tea leaves, and a damp, living city purposefully turning from below. They were safe.

"Today is your last day."

"And tomorrow will be my first. As 'Graduate of New York Psychoanalytic.' That is, if you passed my final paper."

"You pass, of course you know that."

This is what Anna Fuchs could give to others. She could teach them, and then acknowledge their achievements. This was that moment when success was realized only because they had both succeeded. She at teaching and the other at learning. He had received constructively, and she had given individually. The consequence was a new person equipped to do for others what she had done for him. A triumph of human negotiation. This was what her teachers had left behind in her hands, before their humiliations and deaths. It was a successful realization of the passing down of human gift. A successful realization of the potential of human intelligence and compassion. Another defiance of the Nazis. Another reason to live and do. Another good day.

"Great. I mean, I knew you would like it." He was lank,

dark, the kind of young beard that can never disappear. Thirty years old and frantic, alive. The old-world Jewish panic of Eastern European peasants combined with the enthusiastic curiosity of Americans. Jewish brains, American entitlement. Germany had been Jewish minds and German rigor, producing great structural theories of explanation and forward-motion Marxism, Psychoanalysis, the Theory of Relativity. Here in America another combination was at play. Strategic intelligence in combination with opportunity. Would it be used for good or for gain? To cure schizophrenia or to create movie stars? Depth or surface? Both require management and similar degrees of effort. It was in Larry's hands.

"I don't know why I worried, but . . . I just didn't want you to be disappointed . . . at all. In my final paper. That it wasn't good enough, not that you'd punish me, but that you wouldn't hold me in the highest possible regard."

"And then what would happen?"

"I can't think about that. It doesn't matter now."

Good. He didn't need her anymore and it was important for them both to acknowledge it. She had taught him without taking away his self. Without creating ego worship or competition. Just simply expanding his heart.

"Let's celebrate. Some *kuchen*?" Anna took the carefully prepared plate casually from its spot on the bookshelf and placed it on the table where her book and glasses usually sat. It was small, this apartment. The same chairs and tables had to serve multiple functions.

"Did you make this?"

She had to laugh. "No." Did he think she had the secret life of a baking *hausfrau?* Americans were always surprised by professional women. Which still surprised her.

Larry stuffed a piece of cake into his mouth and spoke without swallowing it first. "Dr. Fuchs . . ." He was still young.

"I think you can call me Anna finally. Unless you want me to call you *Doctor* as well. That's what happens when you graduate and become colleagues. Of course, there is always a parental kind of caring between supervisor and trainee, but graduating you means welcoming you, sharing the practice with you. The practice of healing."

She poured the tea. Took a forkful of cake. Larry picked his up and dunked it in his drink. Tea dripped on the napkin and crumbs floated in the cup. This was their final supervision. After today he would be an authority. Suddenly she flashed on her husband, making his rounds at the Tegel clinic. Dr. Rabinowich. She was already Dr. Fuchs. No reason to give up a beautiful German name for an ugly Polish one. Why did she think of him? Larry Proshansky. That's why. Her student's last name and her son's last name. Proshansky and Rabinowich. Sounded like an accounting firm.

"Thank you, doctor."

"You're welcome. Well, let's begin our final supervision. How are your patients this week?"

"Can we talk about my paper?"

Anna was surprised and a bit annoyed. It was her job to organize the session, not his, and he knew that. But she spoke kindly to allay anxiety. "We'll get to that."

"I'm so excited, I feel so happy." He was smiling. Proud.

"Good. Let's start with your Thursday 2 o'clock, Larraine."

He drained the cup and sat back in his chair, then on its edge, then back again. "Larraine. I . . . I do . . . I . . . I do have some over-identification there because of the similarity of our names—Larry and Larraine. And in some ways I also identify with her childish impulse to blame her first husband for her failings. I too—I mean, I know I suffer from a weak ego, don't you think so, doctor? We've discussed that. And I still often find myself projecting my inadequacies onto my wife and our daughter. Which troubles me. I don't want to do that." His foot was wagging. That would be a distraction for any patient. Too revealing. They need to be thinking about themselves, not the doctor's anxiety.

"But you're working on this in your own analysis?"

"Of course."

All right then, thought Anna. *As long as Larry is facing and dealing with problems, he will improve.*

"That's the main thing I talk to Dr. Rechtschaffen about. He says that I am so afraid of treating my wife and daughter the same way that my father treated me that I want to push them out of my life forever, to avoid the tragic repetition that I feel is inevitable."

"That makes sense." Rechtschaffen was a good referral. He had always been a good doctor. He was the only person Anna still knew who had been at the ball where she waltzed with Jung and made Freud jealous.

"I know. It does."

Probably an unresolved childhood fear, Anna thought.

"He says that I have fear that is unresolved from my childhood. And that when I am filled with love for Ruth and our daughter, I suddenly become terrified. But this terror is rooted in the love I felt for my father, and how he abused it. The love. Because I feel a deep familial love for Ruth and Franny, I am afraid that they will violate me the way my father did, and then I act out in the moment, blaming them for my fear. I feel afraid, I see them, and I make them be the cause of my fear. But Dr. Rechtschaffen says that by fully facing and understanding the real source of that fear, I can stop punishing my wife and daughter. And I feel that the same is true for Larraine, my Thursday 2 o'clock."

Her tea was finally cooled and Anna raised the cup to her lips. She knew that Larry could become a good doctor. But he would have to stop narcissistically projecting onto his patients. Identifying with them was inevitable. But he also needed to be separate from them. Just as he must from his daughter.

"Are you able to enact this understanding in your daily life? Really make change?"

"Not yet. But I want to."

She believed him. "Good. If you want to, you will." All her life Anna had believed that people could tell each other the truth. And in her profession she had found the handful of others with the same wish. They would sit together and carry out their dreams of confessing their simple mortality. It was a safety. The knowledge that one is not alone.

"Like last Monday night," Larry said, pouring more tea. Two sugars. "Last Monday night I came home late, hoping to be alone with Ruth, but Franny was still awake."

"Were you disappointed?"

"Yes."

"Were you jealous?"

"Yes."

She waited. He had more truth to tell.

"I felt like the baby was in the way," he said, looking down and then back at her. "And then I felt angrier because Ruth wanted me to look in on Franny. I hate doing that."

"Why?"

"Because I'm not good at it. I'm not good with infants."

When Anna was a girl her mother read to her every night. She read Goethe, Schiller, Shakespeare. Her father came home from the university where he taught philosophy. He came home late due to romances with young female students, wives of students, daughters of colleagues. He'd come in to say goodnight, anything to avoid her mother's accusations. Her father would sit in the chair at the foot of the bed and say over and over, *"Schatzi, meine leibling. Meine tochter.* Anna." All her first life, in Berlin, Anna was somebody. She was Leo Fuchs's *tochter.* Here, in New York, she was a refugee with an imagined past. Only Dr. Rechtschaffen had seen her father's face. Only Dr. Rechtschaffen knew that she had broken with Freud. That he had denounced her. The American colleagues at New York Psychoanalytic had no idea of these details. Only that she had trained with the great man. Touched his sleeve.

"I'm not good at it . . . infants. I hesitated in Franny's doorway, then took one step into her room. Suddenly, then, it was as if . . . I was terrified. I reached out one arm stiffly to touch the child, and put my hand on her head. She started to cry. I said, *There, there honey. There, there Franny. It's Daddy. Daddy. RUTH!* She wouldn't stop crying. *RUTH!*"

Anna felt sick. She realized that her son was mentally ill because she never loved her husband.

"So Ruth comes running in. And she said what she always says—*Just pick her up when she cries. You have to jiggle her a little. You know, like you really mean it. Didn't your mother jiggle you?*"

"Did she?"

"She patted me on the back. That's the whole problem, you know. We've discussed this. My parents. I mean, they were, you know, *grubayink*. You know. *Grub*."

"I don't speak Yiddish."

Then Anna remembered that this was not the reason why her son was mentally ill. It was because he was traumatized, either by his father or by Hitler or by both. He could still recover.

Larry was sweating. He was nervous, starting to feel insecure, and his foot was bopping up and down, up and down. "It means *common*. That's it, doctor, you know that's it. That's what I'm worried about." His speech was rapid now, the speed of discovery and the desire to get it out. "You and Dr. Lublin, Dr. Rechtschaffen, all of you German Jews. You're all so well educated, you speak languages, you play instruments. You studied with Freud! With Freud! I mean, look at me. Your father was a professor. My father . . . my father . . ."

"Yes?"

"My father took a hundred pounds of butter and added a hundred pounds of water and made two hundred pounds of butter."

"Are you ashamed?"

"Yes." Of course he was ashamed. His father was a greedy Jew. Taking the money of people as poor as himself and giving them water to spread on their hard-earned bread. "Yes," Larry said. "I am. And you, your husband was killed in the camps. And your little girl."

He was retaliating now. Projecting his shame by trying to hurt her. Anna was disappointed. Larry should be beyond this by now.

"Your child died and mine lived. Mine lived. And now I don't want to jiggle her. Is that right? What do you think about that? What do you think? Died. Lived. Died. Lived. Died. Lived."

"Do you wish your child had died?"

"Why do I feel that way?" he asked, open-hearted. His hands were open, his eyes. "I don't deserve to have a child."

"What do you deserve?"

He stared up at her, from his slouch. "I'm drawing a blank. I'm just drawing a blank." He needed her help.

"If you were my patient," she said, reminding him that he was not her patient, while instructing him about how to relate to patients. "If you were my patient and not my student, I would tell you to just *free associate*. But because you are my student, I am telling you to *free associate so that you can discover where your responsibilities lie*. So that you can be proud of yourself, for being self-knowing." This was Anna's generosity, to be clear. She didn't trick people by withholding information, and she didn't try to make them guess what she thought or felt. She took the chance, she told the truth. "I am being explicit with the technique," she said. "Because you are my student. Just free associate."

"Let's see." He was relieved. He didn't have to guess, just relax into being himself. "Medical school on the G.I. Bill. I applied to ninety graduate schools and got into one. Blah, blah. I repeated my first year three times and got the highest score in the country when I took my first year anatomy comprehensives for the third time. Now I can carve turkey at anybody's Thanksgiving and win praise."

"What else?"

"Tuesday morning I stopped off at Romanoff's Coffee Shop for an American cheese on white bread with some mustard and coffee . . ." Larry was comfortable now. It's a kind of trance, free association—for the speaker and the listener. A trance of comfort. Anna looked out the window. They say that gray covers a city like a shroud, alert in its sadness, like a cello. The tones of a cello mimic exactly the range of the human voice, which is why it speaks to us with such conviction. These are the kinds of afternoons when New York City is in gray and white, like a television show. She had a small television. "I see Mr. Kelly, the counter guy. *How is your son doing? I ask him.*

"I don't know, doc, he says. *We're like strangers.*

"Try jiggling, I tell him. *Try patting him on the back and you'll feel that father/son bond."*

Larry was theatrical. This was part of his charisma and part of his mask.

"How did that feel?"

"It felt good," Larry said, smiling. Enjoying how excellently he free associated. He had learned this technique, submitted to it out of a desire to get better. "I felt like a doctor. I helped him. Sometimes you can help yourself and sometimes you can't. But a psychiatrist can help someone else, even if they can't help themselves. Just pass on the good advice. The compassion. It could help someone else. It could help them."

"You brought up medical school, your training."

"Yes, I did. Let's see."

Anna had learned and come to believe that all human beings, by virtue of being born, deserve acknowledgement, recognition, negotiation. To love is to listen. The more precise the listening, the more love. Then people will listen to themselves more, take more responsibility for what they promise others. What they themselves say, if they know you are listening.

"Uh." Larry was confused, then he remembered. "One of the requirements in our third year of medical school was to take a course in psychosomatics. I was hooked. During that course I realized something very important about myself—I realized that the cause of my lifelong fear of dogs had nothing to do with dogs. But actually, I was afraid of my father. Once I understood the projection, I lost my fear of dogs and developed a healthier relationship to my late father. Uh . . ." he was confused again. "I'm having a lot of trouble with Dr. Lublin."

"You mentioned your late father, coming to be able to feel love for him, the satisfaction of that achievement, and then you started speaking about Dr. Lublin."

"How am I going to be able to work with him at the Institute?" Larry was an impulsive person. He burst out with distressing feelings, didn't mitigate them. Many

SARAH SCHULMAN ❧ 1955

Eastern European Jews living in New York had this same tendency. It was somewhat vulgar. But they couldn't control it. It was a combination of lacking education and feeling constant panic. "As a colleague? Dr. Lublin despises me. He does not respect me."

"Why is that?"

"Why doesn't he respect me? Or why do I think he doesn't respect me?"

Good. He was trying to be precise. To tell the truth.

"You choose."

"Well," he settled back again. Anna knew this would be a theatrical storytelling. Another cultural artifact from his peasant roots. "Well, Ruth and I had him over for drinks Tuesday night. Ruth looked great. She wore a red cocktail dress and served Velveeta cheese on crackers, olives, and gin and tonics. She really had it under control and I felt very proud. Dr. Lublin and I were playing chess. I was telling him about Larraine . . ."

"Your Thursday 2 o'clock?"

"Yes. I was telling him that it was the most extreme form of transference I have ever seen. How her sexual obsession with me, and her desire to reconceive her dead child, led her to have actual intercourse with a substitute for me, my own patient, who she met in my waiting room at the clinic.

"Did you have an erection? Lublin asked.

"No. I told him that it was not erotic. It was more exciting from a therapeutic perspective. And right then, Franny starts to cry. And out of the blue, Ruth says, she

205

says, *Honey, can you get that?* And I know she's sabotaging me, right?

"So, of course Lublin asks, *Is that your daughter? I'd love to see her.*

"And we all have to go traipsing into the bedroom. Franny is crying, of course. And I pick her up. But of course I don't know what to do, so I start jiggling her. Patting her on the back. *Ahah baby. Ahah baby.* And Dr. Lublin, he . . . Lublin . . . he starts . . . he says, *No, no. Like this.* He takes my baby in his arms, while I'm standing there watching.

"You see, Dr. Fuchs, I mean, clearly, I mean. My unresolved competition with Dr. Lublin is interfering with my child's ability to bond with me. She's almost three months old now, and all of her patterns are being established for the future."

"At three months, of course, it's early, but in order for her to be a successful mother and wife, she will have to learn to bond with her father, so that the Oedipal period will be successfully conducted."

"Yeah, Dr. Fuchs, of course." He was insulted that Anna would imply that he didn't know that. "And here, at the crucial moment where I was given responsibility for my child, Dr. Lublin interfered. Precisely as he was beating me at chess and being served by my wife, while discussing an erotic transgression. I felt that I was being temporarily castrated and that I had to reassert myself as a strong father figure before the unhealthy symptoms of a compromised masculinity developed any further.

That night, after he left, I resolved to separate from Dr. Lublin.

"This is Tuesday night. Wednesday, I get two calls from Dr. Lublin, I ignore them. Thursday morning, I see him on rounds and cut him dead. Like I never knew the man. He leaves two more messages with my secretary and I throw them away. So, Thursday night, after the clinic, I come home and Ruth wants to have a talk. She starts telling me that she went to the pediatrician, and that Franny's early childhood development is progressing rapidly. She is a very aware, intelligent baby. She has independent response and a low level of suggestibility. Right then, the doorbell rings. Ruth answers the door. It's Dr. Lublin. He's enraged.

"You fucker, he says in that accent. *Why have you cut me off?*

"RUTH! I yell. *Call the police!* And she does. Which is good, because I asked her to.

"Coward, Dr. Lublin says. *Cutting off is a neurotic way to deal with conflict. What's so terrible about discussing your feelings? You know I'll listen. Cutoff leads to an aggravated conflicted relationship. Resolution is a healthier approach to relationships.*

"RUTH! I say again. *Call the police."* He paused. He wanted Anna to take it in.

"Why did you ask her that a second time?"

"The first time I asked her, she did it. I felt loved. Like everything was going to be okay. Can I have another piece of cake?"

"Of course."

He reached for the slice with his hand. Anna took a second forkful, got up from her chair. Refilled the kettle, put it on the hot plate. If she was with a patient, she would never have done any of those things, but even though he was behaving like a patient, Larry was her student.

"See, Ruth knew that I was really in trouble in that moment, and that in that moment I needed her support. Love. Loyalty. Whatever you want to call it. So, when he started encouraging me toward resolution, I felt so threatened that I called up the first thing of comfort that came to mind, which was the moment, a second before, when I knew that Ruth loved me. And in fact, I was right because she had called the police the first time, and didn't need to do it again. This support, this love, gave me the strength to face Dr. Lublin. I could stand up to him because someone loved me. Someone believed in me, so I could face and deal with problems."

"Good."

"I explained to Dr. Lublin that I did not want him to get involved in my child rearing, and he agreed."

"Good."

"The police arrived and I told them that I had over-reacted."

"Good."

"Dr. Lublin said that I had explained to him clearly and honestly what was bothering me in a way that he could understand. And so the problem was resolved. No need to escalate. No need. And I realized that it was better to talk than to act out impulsively, destructively, and then get rigidly fixed in a cruel and destructive stance. That doesn't help anybody."

"Good." Anna had praised him into a place where he could learn. This was the psychoanalytic project. To fully face the event in order to fully understand it. Only by saying what really happened—the sequence, the patterns, the conflicts—was what was being represented and denied revealed. Only this way could the nature of human suffering and cruelty be understood. Things happen for reasons, reasons usually located in the past that get misplaced to the present. "To know these reasons," she said, "is to be able to create communication, negotiation, reconciliation, and healing. To understand WHY."

"Some people don't want to know why. They just want to keep doing it."

"Yes, knowledge brings responsibility. Refusing that responsibility is to embrace the tragedy of repression, projection, and denial."

"Anna?"

Ah. He'd used her first name. He must feel deserving.

"Yes."

"Why are we the ones willing to do this work, the work that the rest of the world wants to avoid?"

"We? You mean psychoanalysts? We've made a commitment—"

"No. The Jews. Why are we willing to face what other people want to hide?"

The tea kettle whistled. She got up and lifted it off the hot plate. Refilled the pot.

"Because we have always been so vulnerable. For 5,700 years we have had no army. We were not made stupid by the poison of nationalism. We had no guns. We were at the mercy of those who do. No Jew ever marched into a village, committed an atrocity, and bullied a child. We have always been on the receiving end of the cruelty. It is the person who is being blamed and punished who wants understanding, wants some kind of conversation ending in truth. It's the other who clings to a static, disordered reasoning and refuses to discuss. He found a way to act out his pain and he does not care if the person on the other end deserves it or not. These are the Fascists. You see, I know them. I know them."

"I wish I understood my father's pain," Larry said, vulnerably but narcissistically. "Why was he so cruel? I need to understand so that I can be a better father than he was."

"To say what happened, and why. That is the only hope."

"Anna. I could not have understood my behavior toward Dr. Lublin without the help of you and Dr. Rechtschaffen, and without Ruth. Without her love. I want to be able to give that to a patient someday."

"I also wish that for you."

"I'm so afraid that—" Larry stopped. He looked up at her. He was selfish, but he had the ability to reason. Her son Leo was losing his ability to reason. That was a fact she had to accept. "I'm afraid that I won't know what to do."

"Listen with compassion and with an open heart. Don't tell them how to feel or what to do. Give the other a chance to speak, to say everything. Don't compare their life to yours or you will have a narcissistic projection onto their treatment. Just listen with compassion until you can say something helpful to them, not to you."

"Thank you."

He put the cake in his mouth. She poured the tea. It was almost time to bring up the paper. But she could still help him be a better father.

"Let's go back to Ruth."

"Okay."

"You were telling me about your love for her. Your appreciation."

"Yeah, that's right. So, Dr. Lublin and I reached an understanding and we're all friends again. We have more gin and tonics and he goes home. So then Ruth picks up the conversation she'd started hours before when I first walked through the door."

"About Franny's development?"

"Yeah. Only, I'm exhausted. But she insists. She has something to tell me."

"What?"

"Ruth tells me she wants to be an analyst."

"She's a . . . social worker?"

"Right. The Jewish Board of Guardians. So then she tells me, and it's like midnight. That *that* day she took the El back to Brownsville and talked it over with her father. Before we even discussed it. He washes other people's clothes for a living. He told her that he didn't have the kind of money for that sort of thing, but that he would help her any way he can. I was devastated. She did this whole thing before *we* talked about it. It reminded me of the time she cheated on me. I felt that same way. Like when I watch her play with Franny. I felt left out."

"When did she cheat on you?"

"When I was in the navy. Her father had a heart attack. I was overseas. I didn't know anything. She thought she was going to lose her father. He was in the hospital. I was in the navy, and she needed someone to take care of her. So she called up her old boyfriend, Tommy O'Hara. A real *sheygis,* let me tell you. She told him she was going to lose her father, so he came over and she gave him a blowjob. She told me a couple of years later and I flipped out. I kept saying, *You sucked off Tommy O'Hara?* I couldn't get over it."

"Why did she tell you?"

"She said it was explainable. She called it *explainable.* Here she was, doing it again. Going behind my back. Excluding me, really. Having something intimate with someone else and then telling me later. It hurts."

"Good."

"That it hurts?"

"That you can say so." Her tea was cool enough to drink now. "You can acknowledge the humiliation and disappointment. That is the first step toward healing.

Truthfully acknowledging the nuance of feeling. What did you say to her?"

"I said, *If you needed someone to help you, why did you end up servicing him sexually? He should have been caring for you.*"

"That's very compassionate. But I mean about her becoming an analyst."

"We have a three-month-old. But if she can do it, I'm all for it."

"Larry, I'm very proud of you." Anna had trained first. After her father died she married Rabinovich and had two children. Even when she and Leo had suffered through Istanbul, she tried to see other exiles in private practice. There was no point to thinking about what would have happened if what had happened had never been. It was an unknowable and stupid projection. "Larry, you have deep feelings. You feel ashamed, you feel inadequate, as all people do, but you try to understand these feelings. You want to know. By acknowledging your inadequacies, you make relationships with all people. You accept yourself, and then you accept others."

"No one in my family ever talked this way," he said, receiving her praise. Reveling in it. "I had to . . . I have to learn all of it."

"How do you feel?"

"Better."

"Good."

"Thank you, Anna."

"You're welcome. Now I will evaluate your paper."

"You failed me." He panicked.

She was disappointed again in his lack of grace. He would never learn this, to not be so affected by everything. "No, you pass. But the bad news is that you failed me." There—she assured him that his materiality would not be affected, but that regardless of lack of punishment she had an intellectual disappointment. Would he ever be able to hold that contradiction, or would everything always be so falsely black-and-white?

"What? You said you loved it."

"No I didn't."

She was disappointed again. He was not listening with precision, as she had for him.

"Doctor, you have been sitting here pretending to be on my side, but all along you . . . know. You tricked me."

"Don't overreact." It was an order. She had no time for that. "We talked about some things one way, and now we're talking about something else."

"All right, all right. Why did you hate it so much?"

Anna picked up a copy of his article. It was on her bookshelf. She needed another tabletop, but where? She switched her glasses, held the paper away from her face, and read out loud.

THE NEW DRUGS (CHLORPROMAZINE
AND RESERPINE):ADMINISTRATIVE ASPECTS
by Lawrence Proshansky, MD

Use of the "new drugs"—chlorpromazine and

reserpine—have been effective for large numbers of patients in large hospitals. A larger proportion of patients are being treated with them than we have so far been able to treat by other means. As a result, the whole hospital has to be reorganized.

First of all we need a new kind of doctor in a psychiatric hospital—one who is not afraid of medicine. Such problems require a new kind of attitude in addition to the psychiatric point of view, and this new attitude we might perhaps call a medical or pharmacologic understanding of what is going on.

"Right." Larry had come back to life at hearing his own words out of his teacher's mouth.

"Well, I profoundly disagree with you."

"Things change," Larry said. "New discoveries are made and they help patients." He was so energized. This was his game. She'd never seen him so masculine. This was the father and husband she'd only heard described.

"How does this new fashion help patients? This is an efficiency action. There is no merit to the medicalization of psychiatry." Rechtschaffen would have remembered these old arguments. They had been settled long ago.

"Anna, you know very well that there are patients who do not respond to talk therapy."

"I don't believe that, doctor." The tables were turned. She was *Anna;* now he was *doctor.* Funny how quickly medication distorted human relationships.

"But you've met them," he said. And for the first time all afternoon, Larry was standing, walking around the small apartment, finally looking out the window at what she had been watching alone. The rain on the street. "Of all the thousands of people you have treated, in Germany and here, in hospitals, in private practice, there must have been a significant number who did not get better."

Anna thought about her own mother, reading to her, sitting beside her, touching her face. A person never stops wishing for their mother to love them.

"That is because . . . either . . ." Thankfully, her mother's awful, painful, helpless deterioration from cancer preceded the Nazis. She died in a rage against God instead of numbed by human cruelty. "I did not listen closely enough . . . or the patient had not made a sincere commitment to getting better. And I agree, Larry, it is an evolving method . . . Not perfect. Filled with mysteries. But we are all human. We all have pain. And we all can resolve that pain. With compassion and understanding. Understanding."

"Some psychic pain is biological in nature. It must be." This made him happy.

"Not only do I disagree with that claim," Anna said, her words cast in iron, "but I would argue that much biological pain is psychic in nature."

"How do you know? How can you know that catastrophic anxiety can be brought to a place of comfort and order, by you and you alone?"

"It is not by me. It is by me and my patient. The two of us. Together."

"Some pain is just too large for the two of you."

This is where Larry was wrong, and would always be wrong. Anna knew that any pain that the experience of being human could create, could be healed—also—by human relationship. There were fundamental things that must be in place for someone to heal. Anna knew what these things were. The person must discuss—with another human being—the origins and nature of his pain. They must stay in relationship to another person. And, finally, that person must believe that he can get better.

"But what if he doesn't want to stay in the relationship?"

Anna looked up. Larry was vulnerable again, childish.

"Are you thinking of yourself or your patient?"

"Both," he said. "My wife."

"And your daughter." Anna flashed on her daughter's exterminated mouth, sucking, then she moved on.

"What if I don't stay? In the marriage? Then what? What if the family is the cause of my anxiety? That child? Some things cannot be corrected. If I have to stay, some medication that would make it bearable—that would be better than abandonment. Don't you think?"

"What is so unbearable?"

"That I'm not good enough."

Her heart opened now because he had told her the truth. Whatever the fears, if the patient faces them truthfully, he will recover. "It is in relationship that healing takes place. Only in relationship. No pill will ever compensate for a human relationship. Watching you, listening to you, is a process. Understanding what I am seeing. How can I know who you are unless I think about you? Regression . . . unlearning what you already know, unknowing, emotional amnesia, emotional rewriting—this is a desperate, albeit incapacitating, effort to feel more safe, even though it is actually very dangerous. Repression is dangerous. Bringing the fear to the surface makes a person's life better." Her daughter's sucking mouth. Leo's disorder. He seems irrational, in terrible pain. He babbles. Reads cultish writers obsessively. Quotes them. Lords them over other people's conversations. He is lost. "In order for the truth to come out, it must be faced, not medicated."

"What truth? That I'm not good enough?"

"Every human being is good enough."

"Even the Nazis?" This was Larry's low blow. When he wanted to unsettle her. She'd heard him say the word *Nazis* repeatedly with no reality behind it. "Would you sit down with Nazis and try to understand them?"

"Of course."

"Anna? Really? You would ignore all your pain to face your torturers with compassion, treat them as human beings?"

"They *are* human beings. Ignore? Never. I would treat them. Of course I've often thought of this. In German, *die Deutsche Sprach*. Our shared language."

"In German."

"That is the way that I reason, remember. I hope someday to work with patients in German again. It is in German that my life took place and in German it was destroyed. It would be a return for me."

"You would analyze a Nazi?"

She hated the way he said that word. Not knowing the difference between *Nazzi* and *Natsi*. "I would treat any brute. We have to. It is the only hope."

"That's ironic. They benefit from your grace."

"Grace and culture," she spit with bitterness. These were the basis for German values. Grace meant not responding no matter how cruel the other's actions. It was a disorder passing for etiquette.

"What do you fantasize teaching your Fascist patient?"

"That feelings are symbolic. They don't have to be acted out in order to be taken seriously. They can be spoken. You can say, 'I am afraid,' instead of fleeing, instead of demonizing, instead of killing. Find out first if the thing you are destroying is really the cause of your fear."

"That's what you would say to a Nazi?"

She was picturing Georg Osterman. The boy she had hated in first grade, who she later saw wearing a swastika. After the war he became a dentist, she'd heard. "Yes."

"And to me?"

"Yes." She knew he was using Nazis as metaphors for his own emotional life. An increasingly common distortion among Americans.

"Doctor," he said. "I really don't agree with you. It feels like you are . . . you are, in some way . . . romanticizing mental illness. Almost as some kind of historical emblem. It's not like loneliness, saved by love."

"It's a special kind of loneliness."

"But it's not just a feeling." Larry was pacing now. Gesturing. This was a speech he had probably given in his living room, to his social worker wife. Now he had a chance to deliver it to its intended audience. "Like God. God doesn't exist. It is just a feeling. But mental illness is real, like a molecule. You look at the pain and unhappiness, contradiction and conflict, in the person's life. You analyze the events in that person's past of which these breaks are consequences. You discuss and discuss, and the patient makes some headway. Perhaps a lot. But at some point, in some cases, understanding is not enough. The patient bravely faces all his truths and still he is haunted. Knowing, knowing is not all. There are biological sources of pain that cannot be cured by knowing. Knowing your arm is broken does not mend it."

"No." Anna was fed up now. This was beyond her responsibility to coddle. "It is the acting out of pain that is the illness. That is how the illness controls the person. Awareness, consciousness, the creation of choices. That is the healing."

"But then the patient doesn't get better," he insisted. Whining, really. "And you look like a horse's ass. You feel like one. A failure. You are a failure. Like my child, I want *nachus*. I want my child to marry a good man, to be a good mother, it reflects on me, on my manhood. I don't want to wake up one day and my child is a schizophrenic or homosexual or alcoholic. Some of these diseases may have biological origins. They may be equal parts the failure of parenting and bad genes. So, talking will never resolve them. The patient really needs medication to get better."

"No." Anna was facing the truth now. Larry would not make a good doctor. He was lazy, lazy about himself and other people. "It is not the trauma that makes someone psychotic. It is the repression of the trauma that causes the illness. A person must face the truth, not deny or repress it. They must, or there is no healing. Otherwise, the repression poisons all future relationships. He constantly causes more pain by trying to protect himself from dangers that aren't there. That lie only in his past."

"You." He was pointing now. "You expect that every person can simply have the revelation."

"Yes, through relationship." Anna was suddenly exhausted. She had invested so much in this man. But he was still a boy. He could not heal others. He was looking for a way out of himself, not a way to himself.

"You think that a person can just wake up one morning and *get it,* snap out of it. Well, Anna, they can't. Some of them are under such a cloud of pain that they can't see the revelation, even if it is staring them in the face. They need the medication to lift the cloud, so that they can see their own choices."

She had to put a stop to this. "Is that how you feel about yourself?"

"How do you feel?"

Anna had a choice. He was being a bratty child, trying to stand up to his parent, his teacher. She could indulge him by answering, or just refuse.

"I feel . . ." she said. "That my sadness is . . ." She looked into her own heart to be honest. "Is slowly . . . subtly . . . that it is . . . transformed every time I speak truthfully with another human being."

"I don't feel that way." He refused her gift. Again. No point then in offering anything else.

"Larry, there is so much sadness in you. This is our final supervision. I respect you. I trust your ability to face your limitations and overcome them."

"Don't manipulate me, doctor."

"You feel manipulated because I believe in you."

"Don't convince me that I can overcome something that can't be overcome. Then I will be a failure and you won't be. It's a setup. A trick. For you to remain superior, despite all your tragedy."

She sat for a minute. Quiet. Once the volley ceased, he didn't know what to do. He posed, then had to sit down. Now things were calmer.

"Let's not try to obstruct right now," she said softly. "We're at a crucial moment. The understanding is within reach. Larry, of course you're afraid of your wife and your daughter. Your parents didn't know how to love and support you. How are you supposed to know what to do? It takes courage to love. You can love them. It's just anxiety. Understand, and you won't need drugs."

"Anna, I'm surprised. You're panicking. You're desperately trying to manipulate me." He jumped up then. So quickly, she was startled. He was in a fury, a rage. He raised his arms and voice. He grimaced. "You're the one who is afraid," he insisted. "YOU!" He pointed. "You're afraid that your method won't work with me. And if you can't cure me with compassion, how can you save your family from the camps? If *I* need a pill, *talking* to the Nazis isn't going to get you anywhere, and then your little revenge fantasy goes down the drain, doesn't it?"

"You are very angry, let's—"

He grabbed his overcoat and stomped to the door, pulled it open.

"Larry, what are—?"

"I'm leaving." He looked like he wanted to hurt her.

"You can't leave," she said calmly. She feared nothing. "Not in the midst of the conflict. Talk it through and alternatives will be revealed."

"Don't tell me what to do."

"Healing is just around the corner," she said. "We're almost there."

He slammed the door behind him. She heard him stomp down the hallway and ring for the elevator. She heard him pound the elevator button and then stomp back down past her door again, to the staircase. She heard him flee down the stairs.

Anna sat in the chair for about twenty minutes. She

rested. In that time, the sky finally opened and lightning cracked over the gray rooftops. It rained down onto the roofs, splattering them with its cleansing weight. An hour after napping in her chair, she took out her Underwood typewriter and set up some carbon paper and three sheets of onion. She typed the words, *Manic Flight Reaction*. And stared at them for a while. Yes, this was right. Then she wrote the following:

> *The courage to love does not pretend away the truth of human experience through manic flight reactions. The courage to love endures the distress of disillusionment and frustration so that new value can be found. The courage to love is inexhaustible in its resources of general repentance, repair, and reconciliation, since this process of negotiation is the essence of dignity and creates the healing wholeness of the flawed and mortal we.*

That night Anna ate dinner in a coffee shop. She had brisket and a boiled potato. Canned beets. It was a lonely night. Too wet for a walk. When she came home she tried to listen to the radio but it depressed her. Her son was sick, but he could get better. Healing others was the key to his own salvation.

1968

THE RECRUITERS

by Ron Kovic

The Recruiters

When I was still in high school, about a month or so before I was to graduate, the Marine recruiters came down to my school with hopes of getting as many young men as possible from my graduating class to put on the uniform. I was so excited that day that for a few minutes before they arrived, I sat in my seat in the Massapequa High School auditorium wondering how I was going to react when they finally walked in. At first I thought I would stand up and salute, but after a while I figured that might look a little silly, so I then thought of maybe just sitting in my seat and humming a few bars of "The Star-Spangled Banner." I practiced a few, much to the dismay of a guy sitting next to me, who nudged me with his elbow to let me know it was time to stop. At about that moment, two smartly dressed Marines came marching into the auditorium.

"God, look at that," I said.

"Yeah," agreed a kid from the back row, "they're really something."

The Marines quickly walked to the front, climbed the

stage, and suddenly to our surprise began tap-dancing right there in front of all of us. After a furious little jig, they started singing a song about a young man who loses his penis in the war but is still alive.

"Oh, if you lose your penis in a war," sang the one Marine.

"Oh, if you lose your penis in a war," sang the other.

"And you can't make love with sexy girls no more," sang the first one.

"Then don't blame it on the old Marine Corps," sang his partner.

"Yes, don't blame it on the old Marine Corps . . ."

The entire auditorium began to boo.

"Hey, we don't want to hear that part!" shouted a little fat kid from the front row.

"That's not supposed to be part of the bargain," said another boy.

"Yeah," I found myself shouting from the back row, "I thought the Marine Corps built men—body, mind, and spirit!"

"I'm getting out of here," said another kid not far from where I was sitting.

"You said it!" a kid in the front row shouted, throwing his books and pencils up in the air.

At that exact moment, both of the Marine recruiters pulled their pants down.

"What are you doing?!" shouted one of the teachers who had put the assembly together and had bragged about serving in the Marines during World War II and killing so many Japs he couldn't count them all. "That's against regulations!"

But by now both Marines had their pants all the way off.

"Their penises are gone!" shouted a boy from the back.

"They've been castrated!" yelled another boy.

"How'd you lose them?" said a voice from the front row.

"In a pool game," said the one Marine.

"What kind of romantic battlefield wound is that?"

"It wasn't too romantic," said the Marine, pulling his pants back on.

"No penises," I whispered to the guy next to me, who was slouching deep in his seat, holding onto his penis to make sure it was still there.

"God," said the guy next to me, "I never thought the Marines were like that."

"What happened in the pool hall?!" the teacher then shouted.

"Well, we just went in there to shoot a game of pool—"

"We were confident as hell," interrupted his partner.

"Yeah, we had never lost a game of pool in our lives. We were Marines."

"WE HAD TRADITION!" screamed his friend.

"So we went in there swaggering, two drunken Americans with a mission."

"To win that pool game!" yelled a boy from the back.

"You're damn right!" shouted both Marines as they zipped up their flies in unison.

"We were pretty cocky. Before the game even started, we bought drinks for everybody in the place."

"Then what happened?" asked the teacher.

"Well, that's when this little Vietnamese guy walked in and told us we were fucked and he was challenging not only us but the entire United States to a game of pool."

"A championship match?" asked one of the boys in the front row.

"Yes," said the one Marine politely. "This little short shit who couldn't have weighed over ninety pounds is standing there in the bar telling everybody that he's sick and tired of being pushed around by bullies like us and that he's taking no more shit. We just laughed at him."

"He was such a nobody," said his partner, putting his hands on his hips.

"He was acting real uppity and arrogant."

"So we accepted the little gook's challenge. I racked the balls. We were playing eight ball. We grabbed our cue sticks, and that's when the guy said he wasn't using one."

"Wasn't using a cue stick?" said the teacher.

"Yeah, he whipped out this machete and announced to everybody in the bar that he was using it instead."

"To play pool?" said the teacher.

"That's right," said the one Marine, "and he promises in front of everyone in the bar that if he loses he'll be our servant for life. But if he wins . . ."

"He tells everybody he's gonna cut our balls off."

"What happened then?" asked a little boy in the front row, now standing up.

"Well, we just kept laughing at him."

"Everybody in the bar laughed at him," said his partner.

"Yeah, who did this short fucking shit think he was?"

"And besides, we had never lost a pool game. We didn't know what losing meant."

"So you bet your balls?!" I shouted.

"That's right, we bet them without even thinking."

"The crowd moved around the table and the game began. My partner broke. We had the high balls and the little Vietnamese guy had the low ones. For a while we were in the lead, but then the little guy started making these incredible shots with his machete that made everybody in the place become really quiet. I started to get a tingling sensation in my groin area."

At that moment, every boy in the high school auditorium grabbed hold of his penis.

"I had never felt anything like it before in my life. We had never lost," said his partner.

"It came down to one last shot. The Vietnamese guy had to sink the eight ball to win. It was an impossible shot. Everybody in the bar was betting against him. I'm telling you, nobody in the world thought he could make it. And then he just grabbed that big machete of his, closed his eyes—"

"Closed his eyes? He *closed* his eyes?" someone shouted.

"That's right, he closed them, and there was this tremendous hush in the bar. You couldn't hear a thing . . . and then it happened."

"WHAT HAPPENED?" yelled the auditorium.

"He sunk the eight ball."

"And then he made us put our penises up on the pool table."

"And after a couple shots of whiskey . . ."

"And the crowd roaring like crazy . . ."

"HE CUT OUR DICKS OFF!"

"You let him cut them off?!" screamed the teacher.

"We had no choice . . ."

"We made a bet. It was a COMMITMENT!" shouted his partner, now starting to cry.

The auditorium emptied very quickly after that, and when the final bell rang that afternoon, the Marine recruiters still stood crying on the stage of the auditorium.

1971

THE HARLEM GLOBETROTTERS

by Keith Knight

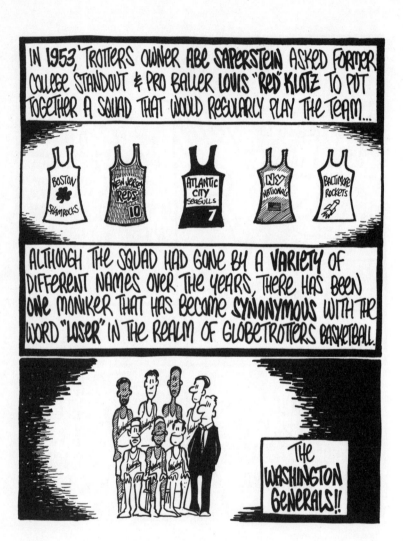

IN 1953, TROTTERS OWNER ABE SAPERSTEIN ASKED FORMER COLLEGE STANDOUT & PRO BALLER LOUIS "RED" KLOTZ TO PUT TOGETHER A SQUAD THAT WOULD REGULARLY PLAY THE TEAM...

ALTHOUGH THE SQUAD HAD GONE BY A VARIETY OF DIFFERENT NAMES OVER THE YEARS, THERE HAS BEEN ONE MONIKER THAT HAS BECOME SYNONYMOUS WITH THE WORD "LOSER" IN THE REALM OF GLOBETROTTERS BASKETBALL.

THE WASHINGTON GENERALS!!

SO MUCH PAIN... SO MUCH SADNESS... NOT ONLY DID THE GLOBE-TROTTERS LOSE THAT DAY.. OUR KIDS LOST. BUT WHILE THE CHILDREN MOURNED, ONE A.W.O.L. NATIONAL GUARDSMAN CELEBRATED.

1989

THE RESURRECTION MEN

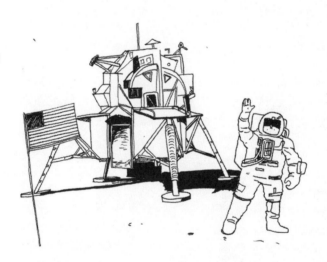

by Thomas O'Malley

The Resurrection Men

I have sometimes dreamed that from time to time hours detached themselves from the lives of the angels and came here below to traverse the destinies of men.
                    —From Victor Hugo, *Les Miserables*

Mother sang Elizabethan madrigals and Catholic hymns and Baptist choruses and the low blue notes of Muddy Waters from the bottom of the Mississippi Delta. And in all of this she searched for the divine, those notes and measures that could hold the soul, make the heart ache, and break it in two. These songs shared a special grace, for in them my mother found her way to God.

When I woke screaming in the night she soothed me with music. Listen to this, she would say, taking my hand. The antique Victor crackled in the corner, a record humming from the old speakers. What do you feel? And I would close my eyes and gradually sway with the sound until the humming filled me and there was no clamor or thought or worry in my head. Until I felt completely at peace, until all the monsters were gone.

Monsters, she said, was from the Latin word *monstrum,* meaning omen, meaning portent. A monster was a messenger, and in olden days they were considered to be divine messengers. A monster, she said, was something very special and important given to people, it explained that which could not be explained, and only the very blessed received such aid. A monster was not something that could hurt you. Next time you dream or have a nightmare, try to think of it as a message, it is telling you something, if only you can listen and hear what it is that it is trying to tell you. It is not always about bad things, she said, most often it is something good.

I looked at my mother and said: Like hearing God speak to you when you're born? Or believing Daddy is really alive, or hearing Elvis sing "Blue Moon," or watching Neil Armstrong take one small step for man and one giant leap for mankind?

I was ten and I feared greatly for the lives of the Apollo astronauts, never mind that they'd landed on the moon two decades before. In my dreams I saw Michael Collins, the astronaut left behind in the orbiting command module *Columbia,* as he turned his slow, lonely, vigilant revolutions around the moon, descending again and again, in and out of complete darkness, shooting, skimming, sixty-nine miles above its opaque and glittering gray pockmocked surface, spinning without end through the black vacuum, the integrity of his silvery

Mylar and Kapton suit compromised and he an eviscerated corpse within it; yet still he waited. The sad astronaut who could only watch from his small window and imagine what Aldrin and Armstrong were doing in those minutes, those hours after the landing, even as the command module passed into the shadow on the far side of the moon and into radio silence: wondering if he perhaps would ever get the chance to touch the lunar surface himself.

Day after day after week after month after year, waiting for the return of the lunar module *Eagle* while the bodies of Aldrin and Armstrong lay prostrate upon the moon's surface, the American flag held at eternal mast, the powerful sodium bulbs encircling the lunar module slowly extinguishing one by one and blackening into charred oblivion in the black starless night.

Shhhhh, Mother said, shhhhhhh. Be quiet, Duncan, and listen to the music.

On weekends, after Mother's shift at St. Luke's Hospital, we'd go to the Dew Drop Inn on Columbus where she sang every Thursday night. She'd buy me a Coke and order me the two-dollar cheeseburger with fries and I'd sit at the bar as Clay grilled the meat, and Mother danced with men—mostly friends of hers who I recognized—on the sun-bleached dance floor.

Mother drank her whiskey, Old Mainline 54, straight. And when she danced she held the glass tenderly, as if it were something incredibly fragile. If she relinquished her hold upon it and put it down on the bar, Clay always refilled it. But here my mother rarely seemed to get drunk, and though I saw her sip I could never be quite sure if she had ever finished a single drink.

Charlie Pride was playing on the jukebox, and "Kiss an Angel Good Morning" filled the bar. Mother was dancing by herself on the worn, amber-colored parquet. One of Mother's friends waved from a table and came to join her. Various flags and banners of regiments, divisions, and battalions hung like bunting over the back of the bar. Most prominent were the AAs of Army Airborne and the globe and anchor of the Marines.

The first time I met Joshua McGreevey he was singing, so softly and bent so low over the bar that at first I could not make out the words—there was only the melody, a haunting soothing music, and at once I'd felt at peace. Joshua had stared into the glass at the back of the bar and only paused in his singing to drink and wipe beer froth from his mouth. *O au o. The lights in Saigon are green and red, the lamps in My Tho are bright and dim.* It may have been the only song he knew but still I thought he had one of the sweetest voices I'd ever heard.

Now he stood next to me, and together we watched Mother. He wore an old olive-colored field jacket frayed at the upturned collar and cuffs, but there were no markings on it. The jacket did not even seem as if it belonged to him, and I was tempted to ask what outfit he'd fought with, what branch of the services he'd fought for. A dark blue bandana was pulled tight across his scalp and the long black hair at the back, wound into a ponytail, shone with brilliantine.

He stared down at me, glanced at the NASA/Apollo patches on my denim jacket sleeves.

You don't really believe that, do you?

Believe what?

That they landed someone on the moon. That was all done in Hollywood sound studios. It was all a stunt. I believed once, kid. I believed in JFK. I believed in doing for my country, never mind what my country did for me. I joined the Green Berets. Ever see John Wayne in *The Green Berets,* kid? What a load of shit.

Here are some facts, kid, and maybe you can tell me what you make of it all. Maybe you can explain it to me. During the moon landing they managed to beam a live-TV picture back to earth, from over 240,000 miles away. That doesn't strike you as odd? You know what television was like in the '60s? And get this, there were no delays in NASA's TV broadcast to the American public—we're talking 240,000 miles here, kiddo, and there's no delays in the transmission? C'mon. Look, we just didn't have the technology. NASA said it in '68 when they gave the odds of completing the moon landings a 0.0012% chance of success. They were speaking the truth.

Joshua tipped back his beer and banged the empty on the bar. He stared at me, and I stared back. He sighed. How do you figure top Hollywood execs being on NASA's payroll, including Stanley Kubrick? How do you

249

figure that many of the shots so closely resemble shots from Kubrick's *2001?*

And tell me, kid, if landing on the moon was so easy for us twenty-odd years ago, how come we haven't done it since? You know why? Because we can't.

He touched one of my patches with a finger.

C'mon, kid, don't be like your daddy.

You knew my daddy?

Of course I knew your daddy.

I glanced up the bar to see if my mother was within earshot. She was looking back as if she'd already caught me in a wrongdoing, a skill of hers which I'd always marveled at, and which always left me frustrated and yet somehow glad. But in that moment I wanted her to be elsewhere; I wanted to know what Joshua knew about my father.

Joshua, my mother said, and her jaws were clenched. Do you want me to call Clay and get you kicked out of here? Leave my son alone, he knows nothing about any of your conspiracies.

A smile played on his lips. He shook his head. Buy me a beer, Maggie, and let's forget about it. I slipped, that's all, my mistake. I confused your boy—what's your name son? Duncan, yeah, Duncan—I confused Duncan with someone else. It happens when I haven't had a drink in a while. Things come out of the walls at me. You know how it is.

Yeah, I know how it is. My mother gestured toward Clay, and as she did, she asked Joshua: Do you have your bike with you?

Sure.

If I start buying you drinks, you have to promise me you won't ride.

Joshua held two fingers to his breast. Scout's honor.

Why don't I believe you? I'm going to put some money in the jukebox, I'll just be gone a minute. Can I trust you with my son?

Sure, Maggie. You got it.

My mother strode toward the jukebox, and I was aware of men's eyes following her. I glanced at the sway of her hips, the straightness of her back. Joshua seemed to be the only man not watching. He was staring at me. Suddenly he tugged hard at the patches on my sleeve, leaned his mouth close to my ear and whispered: *Kid, don't be like your daddy.*

His beer came and he lifted it to his lips. To America! he shouted, and threw the beer back. The top was frothy and it spilled white foam down his chin and darkened his shirt. From over the rim of the large glass he winked. His Adam's apple worked up and down.

When he looked up his eyes were red and swollen; his breath came in deep gulps. Another beer, he said, and the bartender looked at him warily. C'mon, Clay, I'm fine, give us a damn beer, would you? This time, when the beer came, Joshua drank it slow, leaned forward on the bar.

My mother had put in her money and the jukebox began to play. The sound of Billie Holiday swelled around the room. When Mother returned she touched

him gently on the shoulder and squeezed. Joshua nodded, sipped his beer, and stared into the bar mirror. We
left before Mother's songs were done playing. When I
reminded her that we hadn't heard all her songs and
that she'd lost her money in the jukebox, she looked sad.
Finally she said, They weren't for me, Duncan. They
were for Joshua.

Every Wednesday during Lent Mother and I attended
Vespers at the Church of the Holy Eucharist and listened to the choir singing "De profundis," the psalm of
the holy souls in purgatory: *Apud Dominum misericordia
et copiosa apud eum redemptio.* And I saw astronauts, not
just Michael Collins but hundreds and thousands of men
adrift throughout the cosmos—faceless men with the
sun reflected in their golden, mirrored visors—all dead,
all desanguinated and floating through the heavens,
flashing through the crystalline, neo-chrome tails of
fiery comets a hundred miles long, and always, the star-
spangled banner across their left shoulder blinking in
the crimson and blue haze of stellar ash a hundred million years old.

I thought of astronauts who had been sent on space
missions we'd never heard of or been told about because
of their failures—and of all the astronauts thrust into
space upon the pinhead of the great Saturn V rockets
that were still out there somewhere, lost just like my
father and unable to come home.

I watched Mother mouth the words, the wet clicking

of her lips like a metronome. She smiled and reached for my hand, and when I took it, and closed my eyes, I heard the longing of all those exiled from heaven, all that pain and suffering for which our prayers, in the absence of God's embrace, offered the only succor. Later, during the mass, when the priest shook the aspergillum and sprinkled us with holy water, I turned to the back of the church and saw Joshua there, his head lowered on his forearms as if he were at the Dew Drop, and dusk had just fallen outside.

When Mother and I rose, Joshua was still sitting in his pew: head bowed, eyes closed; and looking so peaceful he might have been sleeping. But I knew it was the Librium and Valium that he took, that in the evenings he often lined up the pills on the bar and put them back with his beer. In the transept I placed coins in the prayer box and they clattered loudly in its bottom. I began lighting as many candles as I could, for suddenly I felt an emptiness so vast I could put no name to it. I thought of all the souls in purgatory lost to God and I knew that if we were to die in that very moment we would need such a powerful intercession of grace to be with Him in His Kingdom that I feared we might be lost as well. *Purgatory* resounded in my head as if my skull were the inner chamber of a bell.

Honey, who are you lighting all those candles for? Leave some for other people, would you?

I ignored her and set my knees on the padded rest, placed my forehead against my entwined knuckles, stared at the flickering flame muted through the blue glass, and began praying rapidly. I could sense her there, still at my side. Closing my eyes, I smelled wax and lead wick melting. The lingering odor of incense. Cool air rushing up the nave. I heard an altar boy practicing his swing of the censer for the blessing of the Eucharist. The chain taut through its pendulous stroke, and the slight rattle of the thurible at the height of that arc. Mother knelt beside me and began praying as well.

On the way out of church she took my hand in hers and swung her arm. That was nice of you, lighting a candle for Joshua.

I looked at her, and she smiled.

You always light five. I assumed the extra one was for him.

I nodded.

It's important that we pray for people, most especially for people who can't help themselves.

Why can't Joshua help himself?

Mother didn't respond, and when I asked again she sighed. It was the war. He's not the same as the Joshua I used to know. Sometimes he does things . . . It's not his fault . . . You would have liked the old Joshua.

I like this Joshua.

I know, honey, I know. She nodded and looked toward the rooftops but there was only the dark blue sky with night sinking down through it like ink. The last of the sun had sunk into the bay.

What happened to Joshua in the war? I asked.

I don't really know, honey, he doesn't talk about it. Sometimes, though, I wish he would, just so I could understand him better.

She swung my arm and our footsteps sounded on the tile as we skipped, but I knew that she was thinking of the Joshua she once knew and the man he was now, and in the space of those years, everything that had been lost between them.

At the bar I sat on the stool beside Joshua, waiting for Mother to finish her shift at St. Luke's. He'd bought me a second Coke with the promise that I'd make it last, and Clay had told me to go easy on the bowls of nuts— They're for paying customers, kid, I can't keep replacing them. Don't your mother feed you?

Joshua was humming to himself and tying a red cocktail straw into knots. In the backroom, a brawl erupted and a body thumped the floor. He paused in his knot tying.

My man, you ever rode a motorcycle?

I shook my head.

Come on, then. Charlies everywhere.

I nodded.

We climbed off our stools and I eyed Clay at the rear of the room with his Louisville. A man lay on the floor by the pool tables clutching his arms to his body, and sobbing. A dark stain spread across his crotch and then a rivulet of urine trickled from his pant leg along the wood. Joshua moved me toward the door, his hands pressed gently on the backs of my shoulders.

Joshua's bike was a hulking black Indian Chief from the early '50s that looked as if it had been left out in all manner of weather: The leather was torn and the chrome pipes oxidized, the metal of the gas tank stamped as if by a ball-peen hammer. I sat on the saddle behind him and held on tight to his field jacket as we sped through the streets, with Joshua leaning the bike at right angles as we took the curves. Relax, kid, he said, you want to take us both off the bike? Just enjoy the ride.

We crossed an old rusted trellis bridge, our tires thumping the dividers in trainlike cadence, and I peered down: wind in my face, and a slow moving gray channel streaked with iridescent oil smears passing into the bay.

Joshua parked the bike down by an empty lot that abutted the water. A rusted metal guardrail lined the wall. Behind us: industrial buildings and tenements waiting for the wrecking ball. Two large stacks blowing white smoke into the sky. A twenty-four-hour diner across the narrow cobbled street, and a bar. Paint-peeling façades. Adverts in the window from another generation. A faded poster for Chesterfield cigarettes. Kohl's beer. A handwritten sign: *Prescriptions Filled.*

Before us the water heaved out to the bay and there was the bridge with traffic moving like small matchbox cars across it. Joshua sat next to me. He pulled a cigarette from his shirt pocket and lit up. It was pungent and smoky and better-smelling than Mother's Claymores. He pursed his lips and glared at the horizon. When he looked at me his brow remained furrowed, gnarled like a knot of scar tissue. His skin shone like resin.

Y'know. I forget things sometimes. I forget that a lot of things have changed and that a lot of things haven't changed at all. I get all mixed up—the things I think everyone should remember, they don't. The things people talk about—it's all so much crap.

I nodded. It's the war.

Is that what your mother says?

I nodded.

What else does she say?

I shrugged. That you're not the same person you used to be. That you're a son of a bitch, just like my daddy.

Joshua caught and held his smoke, then exhaled slowly, nodding. He laughed, then slapped my shoulder. He kept his hand there, and the weight of it felt good and reassuring.

What's your mother cooking tonight?

Meatloaf.

Goddamn, I love your mother to death but her meatloaf is enough to make a man wish he'd never come home.

I know. I tried to tell her. She thinks it's her best dish.

Joshua tossed his cigarette onto the walkway, and, for a moment, as we rose, I hesitated, wondering if I should pick it up. The light had gone down and the street was lit by wide swaths of rectangular light cast between the buildings. Joshua was staring across the water, but his face was lost in shadow. I was suddenly seized by the expectation that he might tell me something real. Joshua, I said, what was the war like? Is that where you knew my daddy from?

War? Joshua bared his teeth and they flashed in the gloom. He seemed to be staring at something beyond the bridge, and out past the bay. But it was already dark and there was nothing to see but Venus shining in the east.

I was eighteen and I used to motor down to Big Sur on this bike. When I first got to 'Nam that's all I could think about: high twisting hills, the air dusty with wisteria, and the bristlecone pine hanging from the edge of those cliffs, with the Pacific crashing like thunder down below. That and maybe a girl or two.

He stared above the rooftops as night came down and pointed to a meteor that flared briefly across the horizon. He said: When I came back I didn't want to take no ride to Big Sur anymore. I'd left that boy riding his bike along Route 1 back in the jungles.

I waited but Joshua was silent. And my daddy?

Your daddy? He never did no tour. Joshua shook his head. No, that's not where I met him.

The streetlights were broken along the road and slowly the stars came into view as the clouds cleared. You could make out the Big Dipper and Six Sisters and most of the autumn constellations, all glittering in slow winking cadence.

Damn, Joshua said. Will you look at the size of that bastard sky?

When we pulled up on the bike my mother was standing at the curb with her arms folded stiffly across her chest. Her face was set and stern, yet with the flicker of shadow and light as dusk approached she was disarming in her beauty. Even as a ten-year-old I recognized this. Joshua's back stiffened and he gave a low whistle of admiration. There were tears in my eyes from the wind on the bike, and I blinked to take in the sight of her. For added effect, Joshua gunned the engine as we coasted toward her.

Joshua, I don't want my son riding motorcycles.

Joshua pushed out the kickstand and then turned to look at me. He grinned, and then shrugged.

You, she pointed to me. Get off that bike now. I don't want to see you on it again.

Maggie, Joshua called.

Get in the house.

Maggie.

What?

It won't kill him, you know.

Since when did you become his parent?

I'm just saying, let him be a kid.

I stood in the alcove watching and listening to them. Joshua blew my mother a kiss and began to back the bike away from the curb. Above him Orion and Ursa Major blinked into life.

Where the hell are you going? she said.

Joshua looked at her, surprised—it was one of those rare expressions of his: A veil was lifted and in that brief glimpse I saw no pain or rage, and perhaps something of the Joshua that was there before. What? he said.

I've got meatloaf on, and I was counting on feeding three mouths. Park that thing and get your ass in here.

And for a moment I thought he would just gun the bike and career off down the hill, but instead he smiled, relieved, it seemed, bumped the curbstone with his tire, swung out the kickstand, and shut the engine off.

On one condition, he said.

Yeah? Mother planted her weight firmly on a hip. What's that?

Let my man Duncan on the bike.

Sitting on his black motorcycle amid shimmering vapors from the steaming exhaust, Joshua was an angel and a messenger, a divine portent of things to come. He was an intercession of grace. Above the bay an amber crescent moon turned slowly in our direction. And I imagined myself 240,000 miles away, upon the moon, where there is no wind. If you were to step on it tomorrow your footprints would still be there, perfectly preserved, a hundred years from now. I liked the idea of stepping somewhere once and having your footprint remain forever—it would be a good way to keep track of people so that you would never lose them; their trails would never vanish or run cold; if you wanted to find someone you could, and if you were lost you'd almost always find your way home.

At night, during late autumn and into the winter, when the earth has moved on its axis and its most northern crown peaks toward the sun, there are bands of color bending their way across the sky in multihued striations of radiation, ultraviolet light striking the magnetic roof of the earth. There the vast, invisible magnetic field is catching the radiation like heavy raindrops upon a windshield and spreading wave after wave of them across its bowed surface. Passing like water across imperfect glass. I liked the idea that the sky above us, farther than I can see now, is like the windshield of a car, a car which my father might have driven—a Plum Crazy–purple, glittery swirl-painted 1970 Challenger with a 440 Magnum motor and Glaspak mufflers—and that it might offer a view by which I could see the galaxy, the universe, the stars beyond. I liked the idea of speeding somewhere, far far away, out into the cosmos, and that when I turned in my passenger seat, my father would be there at the wheel, smiling back.

It was Sunday, a warm day near the end of October, and Joshua and I sat outside on the steps as the light faded. He smoked a cigarette, threw it on the stone, and then lit another. He'd hardly touched his dinner and even my mother's singing couldn't soothe him. He was staring so hard that I looked away. Why are you still wearing that crap? I told you, it's all a lie.

I hugged my jacket and my patches tightly, and

looked up at the marble sky. In my head I recited a litany: The moon is 240,000 miles away. Apollo 11 mission commander: Neil Armstrong. Lunar module pilot: Edwin "Buzz" Aldrin. Command module pilot: Michael Collins. Apollo 11 was carried into space by a Saturn V booster rocket, the most powerful rocket ever built. Reaching speeds of 24,000 miles per hour, it took Apollo 11 four days to reach the moon. After thirteen lunar orbits, the lunar module, *Eagle,* separated from the command and service module, *Columbia.* On July 20, 1969, lunar module *Eagle* touched down upon the moon's surface, and Neil Armstrong took one small step for man and one giant leap for mankind.

How old are you?

Almost eleven.

Shit, you weren't even born. Joshua shook his head, frustrated. After a moment he rose and gestured for me to follow him to the curb, where his Indian angled its weight against the kickstand. Look, forget that crap and come here. He sat on the seat, moved the bike with his legs so that it was upright, and motioned for me to sit before him. When I struggled to get a leg over the gas tank, Joshua grabbed a handful of jacket and hoisted me up. My legs kicked air.

C'mon, get your feet over. Now rest your feet flat on the ground, jump up and down. Move from left to right, get a feel for its center of gravity.

The bike leaned to the right, and I felt the immense weight of it falling.

I turned to look at him.

I'm here, he said, it's not going anywhere. He placed my hands on the handlebars. Good. That'll do. Now watch.

He turned the key, pumped the kick-start with his boot three times. Can you hear that? he said, and I listened: like the sound of a heart wheezing. Compression, he said, not too much now, just enough to turn her over. He jumped on the kick-start, the bike shuddered, and the engine rumbled into loud, syncopated life.

Eighty-cubic-inch V-twin, he said, the last they made. She needs a lot of choke in cool weather, but if you're good to her she'll treat you right. I looked at him and he smiled, but there were tears in his eyes. His breath shuddered against my back. I held tight to the handlebars, and Joshua held tight to my shoulders.

He placed his hand over mine and revved the engine, and the motor turned faster and faster until it whined. Mother was coming down the stairs and she paused and looked at Joshua warily. She carried a pot of coffee and two ceramic mugs clutched in her hand. Joshua took his hand from mine and the blood rushed back into my fingers; the motor settled into a choppy rumble. He tugged at my jacket and I climbed from the bike.

An Indian, my man, he said, the best built American bike ever. He stroked the black enameled gas tank, then thumped the metal with his fist again and again. Yesss, my man. Made the last of them in the '50s, this same line, fucking Springfield, Massa-chu-setts!

Mother placed the decanter and the cups on the stone sidewall. J, you're drunk again. My son's not getting on that thing if you've been drinking.

Joshua shut off the motor and continued to stare at me. He climbed from the bike and pulled me tight against him, and I listened to the manifolds ticking as they cooled. Smelled his sweat, the brilliantine in his hair, the burnt-oil smell of his clothes. Duncan, he said, you trust me, don't you? Then don't worry, it's all cool. It's all going to be okay, my man. I promise. Then he looked at my mother for a moment. His jaws clenched and unclenched. A bubble of rheum burst from his nose. Quickly, he wiped his eyes with the back of his bloodied hand, and shook his head. Mother handed him a cup of coffee.

I'm not drunk, Maggie, he said. And I haven't taken my meds in weeks. I'm fucking alive is what I am. Fucking alive again.

On the last night that I would ever see Joshua, he rode us down to the empty lot overlooking the bay. Mother was working the graveyard shift at St. Luke's and Joshua had stopped by to look in on me. It was a full moon and the water seemed to be lit up all the way to the bridge. And in the dark places beneath the abutments, a shoal of fish spiraled in shining phosphorescence.

Joshua undid his field jacket, emptied the pockets into his bandana, folded it, and placed it on the seat of his bike. He dropped his jeans, removed his socks, and stood there in his grayed underwear. Going on a little recon, he said, and when he grinned, his teeth flashed. I won't be long. Keep the home fires burning, kiddo. His face looked lean and taut in the gray light, the skin pulled tight over his brow.

When he turned, shadow played upon his back, and as he walked toward the guardrail my throat tightened; below pale, rounded shoulders his back was scar tissue, the color of blackened meat. Joshua padded down the stones as if they were hard on the soles of his feet. He might have been a child at the beach about to take a mid-summer dip but for the arcs of the halogens, the cars humming over the metal dividers, the empty beer cans lining the wall, the smell of butane and gasoline exhaust, and his wound from the war.

He eased himself over the edge and slipped slowly down into the murky black. He began stroking his way out into the bay: strong, fluid strokes that seemed effortless. His pale skin shone bright as a beacon in the dark waters. He turned, and for a while floated on his back. He raised a hand and waved and the current carried him further and further out. Sound came on the air. He was singing. *O au o. The lights in Saigon are green and red, the lamps in My Tho are bright and dim. O au o.* High up and out over the bay, cars hissed over the bridge; high-density sodium bulbs glittered along its length. Upon its towers, airway beacons flashed on and off. A foghorn blew out in the bay and the top of the water bent with shuddering parabolas of silver.

I cupped my hands and shouted his name: *Joshua.* Once, twice, but there was no reply. The waters lay unbroken but for the sharp black edges of the towers emerging from the strait, as beneath the far bridge everything churned toward the Pacific.

The constellations turned slowly in their orbits; a satellite flickered at the close edge of space. In the light of the full moon, you could see its craters and its rippled hills, almost see where Neil Armstrong's bootprints remained perfectly preserved, just the same as when he'd first touched its inviolate surface two decades before. On the moon nothing changed.

Neil Armstrong sat at the bar of the Dew Drop in his spacesuit, drinking a Budweiser, and my father sat next to him. Joshua strode barefoot on the moon, and Michael Collins waved from the window of the command module as he passed above the Sea of Tranquility at the perigee of his orbit, but Joshua paid him no mind. He was all alone and far from God. My mother, locked in her bedroom, listened to "The Magnificat" on our Victor, finished her bottle of Old Mainline 54, and dreamed of a time when she sang like Maria Callas, and somewhere out in the dark, like a spark of dimming light, Elvis sang a halting version of "Blue Moon."

On Joshua's bike seat, wrapped in the centerfolds of his greasy bandana, he left behind six medals. Beneath the halogens, the tarnished metal gleamed dully. Only later would I learn that one was the Medal of Honor, one the Distinguished Service Cross, and another the Silver

Star, the highest commendations a soldier could be awarded: all for uncommon valor. The sixth was the Purple Heart. I folded them back into the cloth and held them tightly in my hands. In his field jacket pocket were the round vials of Librium and Valium, their seals closed, the date on the prescription a month before. When it grew cold I slid my arms into the jacket and zippered it to my neck so that I was lost in the size of it. I smelled engine oil and brilliantine and Old Spice; I smelled Joshua's tannic sweat.

I saw Apollo's lunar landing module being lowered via crane onto a papier-mâché moon crater. Set artists and designers and special-effects producers hollering above the sounds of whirring cable. Explosive directors firing explosive pins to suggest retro-rockets firing, while Stanley Kubrick, pale and disheveled, shouts film directions. And all the stars overhead glimmering from their greased track, hundreds and hundreds of Westinghouse filaments burning in 40,000 watts of pale phosphorescent brilliance.

I sat on the bike and watched the moon track across the sky and light bruise in the east. And still I stared out at the water, waiting. But there was nothing there. Joshua was gone. Dawn came slowly up over the rooftops of the factory, and when the lights on the bridge winked out, one by one, I walked to the twenty-four-hour diner and called my mother to come get me and take me home.

1998

THE NEW CENTURY

by Neal Pollack

The New Century

Everyone in the business was getting in trouble that summer: the *Time* intern and his fake genocide refugees, the *New Yorker* hatchling whose mother didn't, as it turned out, have an epistolary affair with Gabriel García Márquez in their mutual youth, and the *Washington Post* summer-stock player who invented an entire public-housing project. The *Nation* had a pretend Rhodes Scholar, and we all know way too much about doings at the *New Republic*. The fact-checkers were on strike or on vacation. And eventually, the plague struck my magazine as well.

They came through our offices ten a year in their light-blue, stiff-collared shirts and pressed khakis. One or two usually had a cultural bent, which meant hair past the ears, and, occasionally, down to the shoulders, with fashionable jeans on Fridays. Regardless, their eyes all glared with bland ambition. We fished from a narrow pool of Ivy Leaguers: a Dartmouth junior was our idea of minority hiring. I wanted to tell these guys (because they were always guys) to unclench a little.

This was only *The New Century,* after all, a publication of "ideas" that had split off from another magazine in 1900 over an obscure editorial dispute involving the Spanish-American War. Our best years saw a circulation of 35,000; a couple of Upper East Side multimillionaire octogenarian benefactors were the only reason for our continued existence. The fact that our most senior editors were on television every weekend had more to do with where they'd been eating lunch for the last twenty-five years than with any actual importance they carried in the world at large. But any path to TV was, apparently, a worthy one, and so the kids applied by the hundreds to make my coffee, research my columns, and write front-of-the-book items that criticized obscure trade policies and made fun of moronic junior Republican Congressmen from Arizona.

Jesse Hecht was just another of the herd, with pale, doughy, indistinct features, except for his eyes, which carried the spark of aimless ambition. We hired him off a clever clip file that lacked real content. He did a feature for the *Boston Globe* on "wacky" presidential candidates in 1996, and wrote an essay for his school magazine that compared the autobiographical works of Donald Trump and Benjamin Franklin—solid efforts that betrayed no life experience whatsoever.

He had a crisp, witty way of talking, full of contemporary references, and he often moved to the center of the conversation. But Jesse took care never to express an opinion that was more than one degree removed from conventional wisdom. He suited his ideas perfectly to their antecedent magazine pitches, and modeled his life on the same principle; his magnetism was utterly temporary. When he left the room, his pull vanished, and people immediately forgot what he'd said, even though it had appeared so interesting just minutes before. I envied him, for no good reason.

He waited about a month before he started pitching.

"I want to do a story on how we're becoming a VH1 Nation," he said one day.

"What does that mean?" I asked.

"It goes beyond MTV Nation," he explained. "It's like we're not only obsessed with celebrity culture, but with the *history* of celebrity culture. We write our own nostalgia even as we live it."

I hated the idea. But I had to admit that it was solidly conceived. We were always looking for some sort of ironic take on lifestyle issues to break up the monotony of our Washington-based cover stories. He got the assignment. A week later, he turned in a 2,500-word essay. Jesse always made his deadlines. A week after that, we ran it as the lead. By the next Saturday morning, Jesse was discussing his "thesis" on CNN *Headline News* and NPR's *Weekend Edition.* Overnight, he'd figured out how to win.

That Sunday, as I was making myself dinner and preparing to watch *60 Minutes,* I got a call.

"It's Jesse," the voice said.

"Jesse who?"

"Your intern."

"Oh, right," I said. "Nice job on TV yesterday."

"Can you come over right now?" he asked. "I'm having problems."

The request was so strange that I didn't respond.

"Please?"

"I'm kind of getting ready for dinner right now, Jesse—"

"I hate myself," he said.

Twenty minutes later, the Metro dropped me at the Foggy Bottom stop, and I walked three blocks to Jesse's apartment. It was in a big, featureless building that had a covered atrium between it and the next building, which was its identical twin. Like most of official Washington, it was a blank slate for sanctioned venality. Given its proximity to the State Department, it served as a kind of housing project for the world's most ambitious young people. On the South Side of Chicago, a complex like this would be slated for demolition.

Jesse lived on the top floor, in a 900-square-foot, parquet-floored one-bedroom that he shared with a Swedish diplomat who spent most of his time across the Potomac River in Arlington, at his girlfriend's house. I rang the doorbell. There was no answer. The knob moved to the touch, so I turned it and went in.

He was sitting on a futon propped up against the back wall of the living room, his face blackened by a scruffy half-beard. The only light came from a dimmed floor lamp. A Coltrane album was on the stereo. Jesse was sipping a glass of something. I saw a bottle of cheap brandy on the coffee table.

"You want some?" he asked me.

"That's okay."

"Washington is a terrible place," he said.

"No argument there."

"I'm having identity problems," he said.

"What are you, twenty-two years old?"

"Twenty-four."

"Of *course* you're having identity problems. Everyone does at that age. When I graduated from college, I sold my car and moved down to Mexico for almost two months."

"I'm worried about my career," he said.

The comment pissed me off. Damn these kids and their careers. It was time to deploy an elder's wisdom.

"Jesus, Jesse," I said. "Forget your career. You should be worried about getting laid!"

"What's the difference?"

We had an editorial meeting the day the Starr Report dropped. There were eighty different angles to the story, and we had to cover at least half of them over the next month if we wanted any shot at a third straight small-circ National Magazine Award. Ideas flopped around. Some of them were good, and some of them confirmed my suspicion that a couple of the staff dinosaurs were living up the vast right-wing conspiracy's ass. But none of them topped what Jesse said twenty minutes into the meeting.

"I dated Monica Lewinsky."

The room got quieter than a House Appropriations Committee hearing.

"What?" I asked.

"I was a Hill intern a couple of summers ago, and we met at a bar. We got along pretty well. We'd gone to the same summer camp."

Our literary editor, Albert Leibowitz, never one for the subtle touch, asked the obvious question that I never would have.

"Did you fuck her?"

"Of course I did," Jesse said, so matter-of-factly that it was almost pathological.

"Did she wear the blue dress?" asked another intern.

"No blue dress that I can remember," Jesse said.

"You've got to write about this!" the intern said.

After the meeting, I called Lisa Sherman, my trusted managing editor, into my office. She was somewhere between my age and Jesse's, and could therefore look at the situation with a reasonable amount of objectivity. Also, unlike me, she'd actually had sex in the last ten years. She understood the ever-shifting tectonic plates of gender politics.

"Do you think we should go with Jesse's Lewinsky story?" I asked her.

"It's pretty damn juicy stuff," she said. "And no one else is going to run something like that."

"But is it relevant?"

She didn't answer, because I was obviously asking myself.

"Goddamn it," I said then. "I got into journalism because of Watergate. We cared about things. All these kids care about are their cocks and their pussies and getting ahead."

"Uh-huh," she said.

This was not a new rant.

"Sex should be private," I continued. "I hate this whole fucking scandal."

I couldn't publish that piece. It didn't matter to me that Lewinsky had blown the *President,* much less some twenty-two-year-old blank-slate Washington nobody. The culture had coarsened almost beyond my recognition. But there was no way this magazine was going to contribute to it on my watch.

Jesse got the news. He was thoroughly gracious. That may have been because his summer job here was a week away from ending, but regardless, I appreciated his willingness to avoid direct conflict.

"It's been a pleasure learning from you," he said, his hand extended. "Thank you so much for the incredible opportunity."

"Let me know if you need anything," I said.

I was sincere, but Jesse needed a lot more than what I could give him.

Excerpted from "My Girlfriend, Monica Lewinsky" by Jesse Hecht, published September, 18, 1998, on Wink.com:

"I love your cock," she said to me, one rainy night after we'd eaten take-out Thai food and fooled around on the futon.

"Thanks a lot," I said, wondering how, exactly, I was going to tell her that I didn't want to hang out with her anymore.

"You're, like, the first rung on the ladder," she said.

"What do you mean?"

"The ladder that I'm going to fuck my way up."

I nearly spit out my Merlot. Monica's conversation, up to that point, had been limited to the following topics: alcohol, shopping, how much reading she had to do for school, and Dawson's Creek. *There'd been talk about sex, of course, but never with ambition attached.*

"Are you serious?" I asked.

She gave a merry laugh, and threw me the little heated look that the whole world would soon see in a photograph, from under a beret. It was definitely her best draw. I'd stayed around a couple of extra weeks just to see it again.

"No, silly," she said, "of course I'm not serious."

As if to prove her point, she planted her lips on mine. They parted; she moved her tongue inside my mouth slowly, deliberately. Monica was sexy.

"You know who I'd like to fuck?" she asked.

"Who?"

"The President," she said. "He is so totally hot."

The thing that galled me the most about Jesse's story was that it was later proven true. It's not as though it added to or subtracted anything from the scandal. I may be the only person left who remembers the piece at all. But Lewinsky never denied anything, and Jesse Hecht never had to move forward in the world under a cloud of plagiarism or falsification like so many of his compatriots did. He told all, and because of that, his path was unimpeded.

Eventually, I left *The New Century* to finish out my career in the Washington bureau of the *New York Times*. It was a depressing time to be a reporter, but no one could call it dull. The job ran seven days a week, which kept me from thinking too much about the fact that I was nearly sixty and hadn't dated anyone more than twice since my divorce in 1984.

One afternoon, I took a friend of mine, an old DNC hand named Webster Shoreham, out to lunch. As it usually did, the conversation turned to the moral hellbroth that had once been our polity.

"I can't believe how far it's gone," he said. "What we were pulling ten years ago was child's play. Even when we were at our worst, we weren't anywhere near what they are now."

"Yeah," I said.

"Remember when we tried to buy out that guy who worked for you?"

Now *this* was news.

"What are you talking about?" I asked.

"That kid. The one who fucked Lewinsky. Jason something."

"Jesse Hecht?"

"Yeah, Jesse," said Webb. "A real nothing kid. But when the White House was doing its own Lewinsky investigation, we found out they'd been an item. We paid him a shitload of money to write a tell-all."

"Are you *serious?*" I said.

"I told him you'd have too much integrity to print it, but he was certain you would," said Webb. "Stupid bastard couldn't get it printed anywhere but on some website that doesn't even exist anymore."

"That disgusts me," I said. "How the hell could you do something like that?"

"Oh, don't be such a scold, Matthew," Webb said. "These are dirty days."

Webb made me sick. Jesse made me sick. The whole goddamn city made me sick. We were living through the last days of the planet, and these people were still playing parlor games. I stood up.

"If you've got so much fucking money," I said, "you get the check."

I tried to go to the office, but I couldn't sit still. Instead, I headed for the gym. Five miles walking, and maybe a steam, would at least be enough to get me through the rest of the day.

VH1 was on in front of my treadmill and I couldn't

find the remote. Some loud show called *Best Week Ever* flashed in front of me. It was garish and current, and I had no idea what was going on. Then he came on the screen, billed as "Jesse Hecht, senior writer, *Entertainment Weekly.*" His hair was a little less thick, but his face still looked boyish and malleable. There were his eyes again, too, bright but utterly empty. Still, he didn't look any less happy than the rest of us—maybe a little happier, even. A mind devoted to one purpose rarely stays troubled for long.

Jesse didn't talk a lot. They never let people talk on those shows. And I sure as hell don't remember what he said. But what did it matter? He'd slept with the President's mistress, and now he was on TV.

2001

APPREHENSIONS

by Valerie Miner

Apprehensions

Does he have to turn it up so loud, Mom?" Jay whined. Her plaintiveness expressed more about the evening's stress than about her brother's music, which was, after all, a regular household feature.

"He's chilling," I said archly, hoping to raise a smile.

She sat across from me in front of the darkened picture window, picking raisins from an oatmeal cookie.

"Are you okay?" I asked.

She sighed heavily and stared at the empty fireplace.

From the study, I could hear her father on the phone, listened to the anger and incomprehension in his voice.

Just this morning I was complaining to Arjan about reliving Mom's typical American life—settled back in the Seattle suburb where I grew up, raising my own girl and boy, married to a loving but slightly obsessed man. Did I really need to travel to India, work there for ten years, in order to wind up in the same place? Okay, not quite the same place; while Dad was obsessed with the family budget, Arjan was obsessed by economic growth in South

A FICTIONAL HISTORY OF THE UNITED STATES

Asia. Still, there was an undeniable pattern. At least this morning, everything felt eerily familiar.

The phone rang as I got home from afternoon class.

"Mrs. Logan?" The man was brisk, edgy.

A telemarketer, obviously, because there was no Mrs. Logan here. Oh, Arjan and I married—several times in several countries and religions—but I kept my family name. And I gave it to my daughter, Jay Logan, just as Arjan gave his name to Gobind, Gobind Singh. "Unusual at best," is how his parents regarded the practice. And at times there *was* confusion. But I was *never* Mrs. Logan.

Dr. Logan. Professor Logan. Ms. Logan.

I guess you could say I married up. Construction worker's daughter snags economist. Certainly Arjan's family compound in Sunder Nager was classier than my childhood ranchette house on 82nd N.E. He was a third-generation academic from a distinguished Delhi family, and I was a second-generation American with two illiterate grandmothers from County Clare. How we wound up with teaching posts at Seattle University—a place I fled in favor of Berkeley and then graduate work in Bombay—how we raised two thoroughly American kids, can only be interpreted as ironic, or as Arjan's mother would have it, karmic.

"I'm afraid Mrs. Logan, my mother, doesn't live here," I snapped, lowering the receiver.

"Alice Logan, mother of Gobin, uhmmm, Gobind Singh?" The tone was urgent.

286

"Yes." Blood drained from my face. "Is Gobind okay? Is this a hospital?" Please God, not a morgue.

"Police, ma'am. Your son is fine. Perhaps you'd like to come down and pick him up?"

The next few hours were thick, muddled. Springing Arjan from a department meeting. Racing to the station. Finding Gobind on a wooden bench, frightened, forlorn, flabbergasted.

The speedy words of the desk sergeant: "Simple mistake . . . Security alert . . . Can't be too careful . . . Apprehended for questioning . . . Regrettable confusion."

"The turban." Gobind was shaking his head at his father and me. "They thought I was a Muslim terrorist because of the turban!"

"My son is, as I am," Arjan stood straighter, "a Sikh, sergeant . . ."

"Yes, Professor Singh, yes, we ascertained that after some questioning. And we also discovered he is an honor student, was born in this country, is, of course, a citizen."

"Citizen?" Arjan retorted. "He's a bloody Republican!"

Hard to tell whether Arjan was angrier with his son or the cop.

"We apologize for the inconvenience. No offense intended. But at this time in the history of our nation . . ."

"The inconvenience?" Arjan exploded.

Gobind reached for his father's arm, but Arjan pulled away and Gobind found himself with a fist of blue wool from the Christmas sweater my mom had knitted for her beloved son-in-law.

"You'll understand inconvenience." He removed Gobind's hand gently, then glared at the impassive sergeant. "When our lawyer gets in touch!"

Our lawyer? His squash partner, Michael, who worked for the ACLU, most likely. We'd never hired a lawyer in our lives. I hadn't seen Arjan this angry since that bureaucrat in Delhi told him we would have to wait another month for the marriage license.

Jay joined me on the overstuffed blue couch, resting her head on my shoulder. At fifteen she was rarely given to displays of family affection. The incident seemed to have traumatized her more than Gobind. Who knew? Who understood teenagers in normal circumstances, let alone during national-security alerts? Had they really thought that my hopelessly conventional, but loveable, CEO-in-training son was a terrorist?

"Mom, what were you like as a girl?"

"Why do you ask?" Mother-daughter bonding, I shouldn't have complained.

"Well, Grandma says you were 'intense,' so I know there was something interesting."

"Thanks a lot," I grinned.

"Come on." She stretched her long legs out on the hassock we'd bought in Lucknow last summer.

"Intense. Well, I became kind of a wild card in high school. But as a young girl, I was a worrier." Yes, that was my métier, worrying.

"What did you have to worry about?" She, who has

only known one of her American grandparents, the sober, open-minded knitter, was astonished.

"Oh, I had a *broad* palate. I worried about sin. About the state of my immortal soul. The future of democracy. The Communist invasion."

"The Communist invasion?" She grinned with perfect teeth.

"Those were different times. Well, in some ways. I worried about my parents' fights. About my buck teeth. About Mr. Sakov."

"Who?"

I drew a breath, for his name hadn't surfaced in years. "Our neighbor, the father of my best friend, Debbie Sakov."

"You've *never* mentioned her. So many of your school friends are still around."

"Not dead yet, you mean?"

"No, I mean get real. If she was your best friend," she softened her tone, "well, where is she now?"

"I don't know," I lied. "She moved away."

"Wow. Do you still think about her?"

"Sometimes. Sometimes quite a lot."

I leaned back into the couch. Each morning I sat in this very spot before the others awoke, sipping tea, summoning equanimity for my day. Equanimity seemed remote now as I pondered the unreliable partnership of conviction and fear. I recalled meeting Debbie Sakov in the side garden by the big rhododendron bush while my parents supervised the Mayflower movers.

❧

"Hi, I'm Debbie." A pretty black-haired girl. Something different about her accent.

I stare at her light blue eyes, then recover Mom's good manners. "I'm Alice. We're just moving in."

"I know. I was hoping there'd be a girl. What grade are you in?"

"I'm starting fifth."

"Me too. Do you like dolls?"

I nod, abashed by her enthusiastic embrace.

"And bikes? I got this blue Schwinn for my birthday."

"Mine's red. Still on the moving van."

"We'll go on adventures, then. I know a back route to Lake Washington," she laughs excitedly.

I giggle, amazed that making friends is so easy, wanting nothing more than to please this girl, to grow up together, having "adventures," meeting boys, double-dating, being each other's bridesmaids. It's not often that you recognize destiny, but that sunny July afternoon, I know Debbie Sakov is going to be pivotal in my life.

A month later—a month of cycling and swimming and playing dress-ups and dolls—life is perfect when we discover we're in the same class at Holy Cross Elementary School.

"How nice that Alice has found a friend," Mom says, settling into her place at the dining room table. "Someone in her own grade, right next door."

Dad is, as he often says, "dog tired" tonight. "Pass the spaghetti."

"Did you hear, Eddie? Alice has made friends with the girl from that nice Catholic family next door."

Baked spaghetti is a new item. Mom likes to *invent* in the kitchen. This dish contains last night's vermicelli, saturated with ketchup, topped with Velveeta, and baked in the oven for half an hour.

"Oh, yeah, good." He stretches, looking satisfied from the pork chops and the novelty starch. "This move was expensive enough. I'm glad somebody's benefiting from it."

"They're not from here, though." Patrick helps himself to the last slice of bread and slathers it thickly with margarine.

I hold my breath. Has he discovered they're Martians, this too-good-to-be-true family with the popular daughter who likes me?

"Well, honey," Mom frowns at what she calls Patrick's *critical nature*, which seems to me a scale model of Dad's explosive temper, *"we*'re new ourselves, you know, being as we've just moved out from Seattle."

"No, Mom, I mean, haven't you heard their East Coast accents?"

"Now that you mention it . . ." Mom is clearing the table. "Quite a change for them, picking up and coming all the way across the country."

I bring in the small bowls. Neapolitan ice cream

tonight. There's a way the chocolate slice tastes like a special treat here. You savor it more, in contrast to the vanilla and the strawberry.

"Why do you go fancy on us, Betty?" Dad complains. "I'd rather have a big bowl of real chocolate."

"It's good to try new things, to branch out."

I know she's thinking about her successful baked spaghetti.

"The neighbors," Patrick sounds bored with food talk, "they're from New York or New Jersey, one of those old 'new' states."

"A regular social butterfly," Dad teases. "That Debbie is cute, but a little young for you, Buck."

"Don't be ridiculous," Patrick rolls his eyes. "Mr. Sakov is my history teacher. He told us the family moved from back East three years ago. They visited Gettysburg on the way. We're doing a whole month on Lincoln. It's not too tedious, actually."

"Lincoln, yes. The Gettysburg Address, very moving." Mom always tries to move dinner conversation to a higher plane.

I like Mr. Sakov almost as much as I like Debbie. He's friendly and fun and asks us about classes. I enjoy sitting at their sleek kitchen counter talking about the places they've visited: different National Parks every summer. On weekends we play Scrabble in the living room, which is lined with bookcases and furnished with streamline chairs. Danish Modern, Debbie tells me.

What Debbie loves about our house is eating Mom's gingerbread and watching *My Little Margie, The Honeymooners,* and especially this new show, *American Bandstand.* At home she's only allowed to watch *Meet the Press, See It Now,* and the news. They read a lot. Novels. Books about wilderness.

Debbie tells me, "Dad has never even heard of the Ames Brothers, Al Martino, Patty Page, or Frankie Lane."

"Never heard of Frankie Lane?" Dad asks in one of his jovial moods. He rarely speaks to me or my friends. "What kind of *American* is he?"

"A patriot," Debbie answers quickly. "He was wounded in the South Pacific."

"Well, hats off to him," Dad says, offering us pretzels from the bag he's taking into the rec room. "I served in Europe, myself. Spotted General Eisenhower once."

"Oh, yes?" Debbie doesn't look as impressed as my father expects.

"The future President of the United States."

"If Stevenson doesn't win," Debbie answers quizzically.

"Stevenson, that Communist; he doesn't have a chance against the General."

Communism becomes a major preoccupation with me during the fall of 1952. In school we pray together to Mary to "turn Red Russia Blue." At home, Dad follows the crusade of Senator McCarthy from Wisconsin. He was a Marine, like Dad, only an officer. Watching the news with our neighbors, I learn that American soldiers are fighting to save the tiny nation of Korea from Communism. That year South Korea has four different Prime Ministers. Clearly they need our help.

"Stevenson," Dad says when Debbie leaves. "You think the neighbors are voting for Stevenson?"

Mom shrugs. "I doubt it seriously. Kathleen Sakov is a good Catholic. I see her and Debbie at mass every Sunday. Of course she's a little *different*. I mean, she went to some college in New York, and she drives. But she's a good soul. Not a working mother or anything."

Dad has lost interest, as he often does when Mom issues one of her neighborhood news bulletins.

We don't have time for much bicycling once school begins. Soon the rains come. But Debbie introduces me to the Brownies, where we do fun projects and practice good citizenship. Often I find myself at her house after classes, doing homework together. Mrs. Sakov makes the best hot chocolate. They say "chawklet."

My Seattle school had been a chore and a bore. Oh, I figured I'd do better than my parents, earn a high school diploma and find a job I liked. I fancied living on Queen Anne Hill in a little apartment, dating handsome boys for a few years before marrying and having children. Girl children. If surly Patrick was the alternative, I was sticking with girls.

But Debbie gets me involved in science projects and an essay contest. She says that if we stick with it, we can take college prep classes in high school and then . . .

"And then," Mr. Sakov joins in, "the sky's the limit." Since he's a teacher, he comes home earlier than my dad, about 4 o'clock each day. And he likes talking with us, says I have *an interesting mind*. "You could be a doctor, Alice, or a professor, or a Senator, or an artist."

Debbie grins, waiting to hear her own fortune.

I remain politely silent.

"Seriously, Alice."

He is reading my mind.

"You're *very good* at geography and history. You *should* be thinking about college. It's never too early."

My face flushes with pride and excitement and a prickly sensation of family betrayal. Because of this last, lingering feeling, I announce, "My dad says Adlai Stevenson is a Communist."

"Oh?" Mr. Sakov studies me.

Debbie walks into the kitchen, calling over her shoulder, "More lemonade anyone?"

"I like Ike," I say, then feel foolish.

"It's important to be interested in the election," he says in an edifying tone.

"Aren't you going to vote for General Eisenhower?"

"General Eisenhower is a brave, smart man. So is Governor Stevenson."

Governor. I've never heard him called *Governor* before. Is he making it up? I have a terrible feeling that I shouldn't persist but feel compelled.

"Are you voting for him?"

"Well, Alice, we have a system of secret balloting in

this democracy. But I believe in public discourse. Even dissent, among congenial neighbors."

I want to retract the question. Want to return to college prep and being an artist or a doctor.

"Hello, anybody home?" Pretty, blond Mrs. Sakov opens the door. I wish I was that blond—almost platinum. Mom says my hair is a nice "honey color," but Patrick calls it "dirty blond."

Mrs. Sakov is carrying groceries in both arms.

Mr. Sakov goes to her aid.

Her aid and mine. But I know what he would have said. Dissent. He's voting for Stevenson. Surely Mr. Sakov is confused.

On afternoons when the rains are mild, we walk home, over the hills, from school. I love the sharp scent of evergreens. So much more fun than sitting on that rattling bus being snubbed by the older kids and listening to the younger ones shriek.

Today I walk guardedly because I'm carrying the fifth grade rosary in the special sandalwood box blessed by our bishop. Tonight is "Pray Together, Stay Together" night at our house, part of the diocese campaign against divorce and Communism. Our primary intention—as in classroom prayers—is the conversion of Godless Russia. Sister Matthew suggests that tonight we also pray for victims of those terrible Mau Maus in Africa.

"So I think I have a crush," Debbie startles me.

"Who, who?" I spin on my feet, almost dropping the

sandalwood box. "Tim O'Rourke? Johnny Petrowski? Artie Romano?"

"You're one-sixth right, sort of," she grins.

"Come on." She could have all three of them. This is one of the first times I envy her beauty and confidence. Usually I just bask in these traits, proud that Debbie Sakov has chosen me as her best friend.

"Well, at recess today, Bobby flirted with me."

"Bobby? He didn't." I've never revealed my own crush on Artie Romano's older brother.

"Did too."

"How?"

"He said I should shake my 'beautiful hair out of those terrible pigtails.'" She giggles, whisking her long loose tresses over the shoulders of her Holy Cross uniform sweater.

We are standing on the last hill. Someday I want to live up here, in one of these homes with pretty gardens and a view of Lake Washington.

"Oh, come on," she's embarrassed now. "We're not going steady. Just talking to each other."

One thing leads to another, I've heard my mother say often enough, and somehow this makes me think of the rosary.

She's humming "Wheel of Fortune."

"You took the rosary home last week, right? Did you get your whole family to pray together? I mean, I'm afraid we won't be able to convince Patrick to join us tonight."

"Oh, sure, Mom and I knelt in the living room. You

know, we have that little wooden statue of the Blessed Virgin there. And we prayed the entire rosary aloud together."

"What about your dad?"

She looks surprised. "Daddy's Jewish. Didn't you know that?"

I draw a long breath. "A mixed marriage," I reply stupidly. Mixed marriages, like near occasions of sin, are to be avoided whenever possible.

"Mommy said it's good for one's education, being exposed to different traditions."

I wish it were storming and we were sitting on the bus, conversation impossible because of the screaming first-graders. I quicken my steps, but this last part of the route is endless.

At home, I'm relieved to find Mom alone in the kitchen, musing over the ingredients of a tuna noodle casserole.

"Can we talk?" I plop down onto a shiny yellow dinette chair and sip a glass of ice water.

"Are you worried about something again, dear?"

Already she's making it trivial. Maybe I should consult the priest. No, I need an answer now.

She turns down the oven, takes my hand across the Formica table. "Tell me what's on your mind."

At moments like this, I feel safe, for I know that it's possible to be sane and loving and good.

"Well, I'm worried about Mr. Sakov." I slump back in the narrow chair.

"Is he unwell?"

"About his soul," I whisper.

She regards me closely.

"I just heard from Debbie, on our walk, and it was such a surprise, and I don't know what to do."

"Slow down, dear." She speaks with exaggerated calm.

"Debbie tells me he's a, a, a *non-Catholic*." There, I've said it.

The refrigerator stops humming.

Mom takes a long sip of my water. "I guessed as much. Since I don't see him at church. Of course, your father doesn't come every Sunday. But Mr. Sakov is a different kind of man."

If only she knew how different.

I can't hold it in any longer. "Will he go to hell, Mom? Will he go straight to hell?"

"Oh, Alice dear." She's standing beside me now, tucking my apprehensive face toward her wide hip. "God loves many kinds of people. From what Patrick says about his lectures on Lincoln, their lively discussions, and from what you say about your nice conversations next door, I know Mr. Sakov is a *very* good person. I can't imagine God would send him to hell."

I take a deep breath. I'm not sure she's ready for this. "Debbie told me . . . Debbie said that . . ."

"Yes, dear?"

"Debbie says Mr. Sakov is *Jewish*."

"So?"

"Well, he's not even a *Christian*."

"Alice, love, there are many fine Jews in the world. Did you know, for instance, that Benjamin Disraeli, the British Prime Minister, was Jewish?"

I sometimes worry about my mother's wits. "But Britain is a Christian country."

"Britain is a democratic country."

I sigh, thinking about her pile of history and cooking magazines.

"Just like this one . . . at the moment."

"But Sister says we must pray to turn Red Russia blue. I've brought home the class rosary tonight. Isn't Mr. Sakov more important than some faraway stranger in Moscow?"

"Mr. Sakov is a smart, ethical man who lives with a devout wife and daughter. I don't think he needs to be our personal mission."

I don't tell her Debbie's mother says it's good for her education being exposed to different traditions.

The lawn signs start to sprout in mid-October. Mostly patriotic ones for General Eisenhower. Some cheerful *I Like Ike!* placards. Only two people in the neighborhood plant posters with dreary pictures of the horse-faced Stevenson. I hold my breath for a week, but the Sakovs's lawn remains clear. Dad says when we go trick-or-treating, at the end of the month, placards will help us know which houses to avoid. I bet Communists give out hard candy.

Now that the World Series is over—the stupid Yankees won again—my dad has a new favorite pastime: Bishop Fulton J. Sheehan's *Holy Hour.* And while Mom doesn't completely approve of priests appearing on television, she thinks it's good for my father to get his religion in any form. Bishop Sheehan doesn't come right out and condemn Stevenson, but he is very concerned about Communists. That Catholic Senator from Wisconsin is one of his biggest fans.

"Dad." I turn from the TV screen to my father stretched out in his recliner, wearing a T-shirt and boxer shorts. "Is Senator higher than Governor?"

"Doesn't work like that, hon. Senators are in Washington and Governors run states. Why do you ask? Planning on running for office?"

Unlike Mr. Sakov, he's joking.

"No, I was wondering about Senator McCarthy. If Governor Stevenson can run for President, couldn't Senator McCarthy?"

"You've got a good head on you. Wish your brother was that alert. Sure, Alice, he would make a fine choice someday. Why don't you write him a letter?"

This time, I can tell, he *is* serious.

"You just mail it to him in Washington, D.C."

That night I write the letter in my room and do all my homework there. I don't feel like going over to the Sakovs's after dinner.

Mom invites Debbie over for my birthday dinner. I can't have a real party because I don't know enough girls yet. But Mom has baked my favorite lemon cake. She says that after dinner Debbie and I can have a mini slumber party in my room and has let me move the Victrola upstairs.

Debbie's present is beautifully wrapped in silver foil with a blue satin ribbon. Too small to be a record. Too heavy for jewelry.

I've run out of guesses.

"A brick?" Patrick suggests.

Debbie giggles.

I pull a face.

Actually, Patrick has broken down and bought me a nice horn for my bike. Mom and Dad have come through with some cute clothes. So no matter what Debbie has brought, I'll be in a good mood.

She says she's saving the gift for later at our slumber party.

Patrick looks disappointed, in spite of himself.

"Oh, I hope you like it," she says breathlessly, watching me scrupulously unwrap the silver foil. Mom has taught me to save good paper.

"Dad gave me one last year and I absolutely *love* it."

The mention of Mr. Sakov, the Jewish Communist Stevenson-supporter, breaks my mood only momentarily. Her card is adorable, signed, *Love, Debbie, xxxx.*

Oh my, it's better than a record or a necklace. I could never have imagined something as splendid as this gorgeous red leather diary with a gold lock and special key. I stare at the present, feeling at once grown up and transgressive and, well, *artistic.*

"You don't like it?" she whispers anxiously. "I can

take it back to The Bon, get you something—"

"No, no, no. It's perfect. Thank you, Debbie." I kiss her reddened cheek. "Thank you!"

She covers her embarrassed pleasure by talking hectically. "It's good for writing down wishes and worries, you know, the sort of thing you can't really talk to another person about, at least not yet. And I have to admit, I've spent a number of pages on Bobby Romano."

Wishes and worries. Debbie never seems afraid of anything. I want to be more like Debbie.

We spend the perfect evening listening to Frankie Lane and drinking too much Pepsi and gossiping and eating popcorn, Fritos, and Oreos. Debbie has some interesting news about Bobby Romano, and I'm glad to tell her Larry Boudreau winked at me that morning.

Mom has made up the guest cot with an extra-fluffy comforter, not really necessary in October, but cozy.

Just as I'm sailing off to sleep, Debbie says, "Will you be my blood sister?"

I sit up in the darkened room. "You mean cut my hand and mix blood with you?" I hope she's teasing.

"No, something more mature than that. Promise to be each other's confidantes. You know, a sister you can tell absolutely everything without being judged or gossiped about. Like real, grown-up friends."

I am moved, glad she can't see my tears. Yet another level of loneliness excavated.

"Of course," I reply, then speed ahead. "Let's start now, by telling a secret."

"Tonight?"

"Short secrets, then."

"I can't think of anything just now." She yawns.

"Well, you could ask me something," I persist, wondering if I have anything to tell or ask.

"Okay, your brother Patrick. He seems kind of mean or something. What's he mad at?"

And without a second thought, I surrender the *big family secret* to my best friend: "Patrick got arrested in Seattle last year—unfairly, he says—when his stupid friends broke into a gas station." The main reason we've come to the suburbs is to help Patrick start over. The move has been for me what Mom would call "a blessing in disguise." Otherwise I wouldn't have met Debbie, who is the smartest, liveliest friend I've ever had.

"Oh, wow," Debbie gasps. "I had no idea. I just thought he had heartburn or something. Did he go to jail?"

"Of course not. He was let off because it was a first offense and he wasn't directly involved. Dad had to promise to 'rein him in.'"

"I see."

"But you won't tell, right? You promised that's the whole deal. Blood sisters, confidences, and—"

"Whoa, Nellie, don't worry so much. I'd never tell. People make mistakes. They repent. That's what confession is for. Mum's the word."

"So I get to ask you something."

"Yeah, I suppose." She sounds sleepy. "I had more in mind that we would come to each other with private concerns, things that bothered us or excited us. But we've started this way. Go on."

I can't help myself. "Your dad. Is he, a, well, a Communist?"

Debbie laughs. "No, I can't imagine . . ."

I heard the hesitation. "But . . ."

"But he did go to Moscow once."

I inhale sharply, silently, I hope.

"He taught English there for two years. A foreign-aid kind of thing. His grandparents came from there. It was his way of sharing. International solidarity, I think he said. But that was a long time ago. Before I was born."

"Oh," I nod.

After a few moments, Debbie suggests, "We should get some sleep. Happy birthday, blood sister."

"Thanks, Debbie. Sweet dreams."

Moscow. Solidarity. Jewish. Stevenson. It's all swirling through my brain.

I can hear her sleeping, the gentle, innocent inhale and exhale of the Communist's unsuspecting daughter.

This is how things begin, I read in Mom's *Catholic Digest*. They move into your neighborhood. Infiltrate your schools. Poor Patrick: first he's framed by his dopey friends and now he's learning Communism in high school. Poor Debbie and Mrs. Sakov. Surely they can't know. Kneeling in their living room praying for democracy while a Communist sits at their Danish Modern dinner table correcting history papers.

"Now I lay me down to sleep. I pray the Lord my soul

to keep. And if I should die before I wake, I pray the Lord my soul to take." Over and over, I quietly recite the Hail Mary, the Our Father, the Glory Be. "I pray the Lord my soul to keep." Nothing brings tranquility or sleepiness.

Hours later, endlessly wakeful hours, I slip out of bed with my diary and head for the kitchen. A small slice of cake and a large glass of milk should send me off to dreamland.

Seated at the dining room table, I feel better after one bite. *Count your blessings,* Mom always says, and I do. A decent family. A best friend. A blood sister. *It's good for writing down wishes and worries, you know, the sort of thing you can't really talk to another person about, at least not yet.*

Dad finds me in the morning, sound asleep at the table.

Vaguely, I remember him lifting me and carrying me back to bed.

Mom fixes us blueberry pancakes for breakfast and Debbie leaves for home about 10. When I return to my room to make the bed, I spot the diary key. Then I recall writing page after page about Mr. Sakov. Debbie is right, it helped relieve my worry, helped me fall asleep.

The Sakovs move out on Halloween. I won't be trick-or-treating tonight, not even to the *I Like Ike* households. Debbie hasn't talked to me forever. I only know part of the story, from eavesdropping on my parents' arguments, but I know enough.

After Dad reads my diary, he contacts the high school principal and our Congressman.

Debbie tells Bobby Romano her family is returning back East to care for her sick grandmother.

"And you never heard from them again?" Jay was astonished. Whether more amazed by her mother's callowness or the absurdity of the Communist boogie man, I don't know.

"Actually, years later," I sighed, suddenly craving a Scotch, but knowing I didn't want to follow my father down that path. "Well, when my first book came out, I got a note from Herb Sakov."

"You did?" Her green eyes widened. "What did he say, what happened to him?"

Behind her, I imagined the darkened lake, watched the lights blinking across the water from Seattle.

"In that first letter, he simply congratulated me on the book. Said he always knew I would become a doctor, or a professor, or a Senator, or an artist."

"I remember," she said eagerly.

I studied her animated face, amused how the story was hers as well now, touched by how good that made me feel. My daughter. My confidante.

"So I wrote, thanking him for the note. Apologizing, and asking his forgiveness. Inquiring about him and his family." I stared into space, following the long dark pigtails of a ten-year-old girl on a blue Schwinn bicycle.

"And?"

"Well, he wrote back, in a kind of summing-up way. I could tell he didn't want to revive an old friendship so much as close a chapter. He accepted my apology. Said one has to forgive *oneself* for being young. He started teaching again. The first few years back in New Jersey, Mrs. Sakov got an office job and found she liked it. Then he worked in a bookstore. Eventually, he started tutoring and returned to high school teaching a few years before retiring." I smiled thinly. "Debbie grew up, of course."

"Wow, so it all turned out okay. In the end."

"You think so?"

"Oh, Mom. He's right, you know, you were just an ignorant kid. You were anxious. By the way, that's still one of your probs."

"Hmmm." I looked past my wise and beautiful daughter, staring again at the glittering skyline.

"Those must have been scary times. We studied 'Reds under the beds' in school when we read *The Crucible*. A lot of people were frightened. I'm sure Debbie ultimately understood. So what happened to her, anyway?"

"She became a high school teacher," I said quietly. "History."

She took it in. Then a beat later, she grinned broadly. "That's really something about Patrick. Arrested. He's such a straight arrow, you know."

2011

THE ANODYNE DREAMS OF VARIOUS IMBECILES

by Daniel Alarcón

The Anodyne Dreams
of Various Imbeciles

In the second year of the war, the President of the United States was accidentally shot while hunting at his ranch. The hapless hunter at fault was an invited guest, a sheepish Senator from Arizona, for whom the President had recently named a Western lake. There was quite a commotion when the President fell. He was wearing a bright orange hunting cap. It was winter, and the trees and hillsides were bare. The bullet lodged in his upper thigh and shattered his femur. There was much blood and unpleasantness. The hunting holiday ended abruptly, as the Head of State was taken by train to Washington. There, the President refused to see a doctor. The wound neither worsened nor improved, his right leg still attached by a filigree of tissue and muscle. The President made a few speeches from behind his desk in the Oval Office, but otherwise stayed out of the public eye. People said he was depressed.

Meanwhile, the war was proceeding haltingly, almost

comically: a bomb here, felling a bridge in Montana. A bomb there, in downtown Los Angeles, destroying an abandoned building where a few addicts sometimes slept. No one would miss these constructions, certainly not the President. "We have so many bridges! So many crumbling buildings!" he was overheard saying to an aide. The President took pills and herbs

Figure 1: The President of the United States

for the pain and, in his less lucid moments, he prayed. His wife consulted tarot cards. In statements to the press, the President's spokesman ridiculed the crazies and their crude bombs, their patchwork ideology and their irrelevance. His injury was not mentioned.

A specialist was sent for, a young European doctor who had written extensively on these matters. It was said that he was an expert. The subversives made public a communiqué in which they asked the nation to pray for the President's speedy recovery. They lauded the decision to spend taxpayer dollars on a high-priced specialist. *For the greater good of the Fatherland,* read the document, *every sacrifice is worthwhile.* On his sickbed, the President was incensed. His wound was meant to be a state secret, but he had been betrayed. The rumors had swept across Washington and then throughout the country. He was being made fun of and everyone knew it. The specialist arrived from France and recommended the immediate amputation of the President's right leg at the hip joint. The wound was yellow and gangrenous, the leg atrophic.

"Have my reports been received?" the European asked.

They had not.

The specialist shook his head. "In any case," he said, "there is no time for that now."

The President was proud of his indifference to matters of life and death. He had fought in Vietnam. He had seen many people die.

How the amputated leg wound up in the possession of the subversives is not exactly clear. Perhaps someone had infiltrated the military hospital. Perhaps it wasn't the President's leg, but another, unfortunate man's leg. The masked subversives held an armed press conference in the remote Pacific Northwest, beneath the high green canopy of the millenarian forests. The subversives presented the appendage. The gathered media was invited to touch it and photograph it from all angles. The subversives took off the leg's shoe and sock, and played "This little piggy" with the formerly Presidential toes. *Godspeed, our one-legged leader,* they proclaimed. There were rumors. The amputation made the cover of the tabloids. The President ordered the offices of these papers shut down and firebombed. In response, the subversives organized massive protests, filling the streets of all the major cities. Thousands clamored in Times Square, along Lakeshore Drive. Traffic across the Bay Bridge ground to a halt. Cars were pelted with eggs. People carried placards bearing stylized portraits of the hobbled leader: the President on crutches, the President pulling his stump behind him. At Camp David, his devoted wife brought him each morning's newspapers. His convalescence was torture. Enraged, he ordered the French specialist detained, certain that the arrogant doctor had betrayed him.

His wife concurred. "I never liked his accent," she said.

A week later, still tormented, the President ordered the doctor executed. The specialist, he concluded, was a sympathizer, an educated and frivolous European of the kind who were entertained by the spectacle of America's decline. When the doctor was informed of the President's decision, he wept. His guards couldn't wait to be done with him. In fact, he was so inconsolable that after a routine and uninspired beating (during which the specialist's wailing grew almost unbearable), an impatient guard pulled out his weapon and shot the doctor dead, depriving the President the privilege of seeing the prisoner die. For this crime, the guard was also put to death.

Mr. President, as your medical handlers mentioned to me in their cable of last month, you are concerned about your wound. I assure you, I will come to your case without preconceived notions, my only intention, that of seeing you once again well and at the helm of your nation's forces as regards the ongoing war. Of course you are fearful, and certainly you must be concerned. I will attempt, as best I am able, to put your mind at ease. Some background on therapeutic amputation is in order, and here I can say that France has taken a pioneering role worthy of our national character. Indeed, the first instance of amputation for a gunshot wound of the upper part of the femur occurred in the French Army of the Rhine in 1793. The doctor in question was the illustrious Jacques Perault, then and thenceforth a zealous advocate of hip joint amputation. The patient, whose name is recorded only as S., bore the operation well, and for several hours afterwards his condition was most satisfactory. Unfortunately, it was necessary that S. should immediately follow the army in a precipitate march of more than twenty-four hours duration. It was winter. He died from exposure and fatigue. Undeterred, Perault again took to the knife in 1812, in this case to succor a French subaltern of dragoons named Goix, whose thigh was badly injured by a cannon ball at the Battle of Bordino. After surgery, the patient was removed to the Abbey of Kolloskoi, and thence to Witepsk, under the care of Surgeon Major Bachelet, until he was nearly well. Bachelet treated Goix with brandy and tincture of iron administered orally, while caring for the stump with daily injections of terebinth oil. Within three months, the patient had completely recovered. Perault celebrated, reportedly telling his aide-de-camp that a medical miracle had been achieved. In his memoirs, he cited this case as the first successful primary amputation, but as the patient never reached France, and his death is not accounted for, the adversaries of this operation will not admit it a success.

* * *

Years before he shot the President quite by accident, before the Second War of Rebellion, the Engineer, later Senator, from Arizona, said: "A fine spot for a lake, isn't it?" He was sunburned and loud, his booming voice echoing across the valley. It was the golden earth of the reservation, a slab of red rock slashed by a thin stream of water. His assistants smiled. Yes yes, they said with their eyes. The river cut a serpentine path through the base of the rock. It boiled silver in the bright sunlight. "A fine spot indeed," repeated the Engineer. He drew a sketch on a napkin and passed it to his assistants. "Well, get to it then," he said, and lit a cigar as he strolled back to the Jeep.

The first year of the dam was known as the year of drownings. They came from all over—from Maine and California, from Florida and Illinois—to step into the turquoise water and breathe it in, to fill their lungs with it and die. Native Americans mostly, and their sympathizers, earthy people who had protested the dam's construction at each step. They came and drowned in their indigenous costumes, plumed and painted as if for war. Their streaked, dead bodies floated to the surface, bloated and blue. The Park Service asked Congress for a pontoon boat to pull the corpses from the gentle waters. But there was no money. The war had begun in earnest. There were rumors that the President had been shot. It was the year of the Battle of Denver, the subversives' first military victory of any import, and the government was struggling to make ends meet. So the bodies stayed, bobbing helplessly on the surface of the lake, and that summer a few intrepid tourists braved the war zone to visit the picturesque lake, to watch the sun set over the water dotted with dozens of floating, colorful corpses. Seagulls too had found their way there, and flew over it in lazy, swooping circles. At dusk they could be seen pecking at the bodies, tearing at the water-logged flesh with their thin beaks.

The Engineer, for whom the lake had been named, found no humor in its macabre attraction. He looked upon the lake as one might a child suddenly grown into adulthood. He recalled that morning when he drew the first crude sketch of the place: the livid colors blooming from the rock, the bright sun, the altogether pleasing submissiveness of his assistants. It was a dream of his to see a lake there, and now the dam was in danger of becoming clogged with bodies. The whole Western power grid was in danger. He called the Speaker of the House. "I won't stand for it," he said. He called the Senate

Figure 2: The Engineer

Majority Leader and spoke with the same harsh tone: gruff, pained, gravelly. He very nearly called the President, though they had not spoken since he'd shot him. In interviews with the press, he didn't hesitate to call the body of water *"my* lake." After all, hadn't he conceived of flooding the desert? And hadn't the President named it after him?

* * *

Of course, there are dangers, Mr. President. It is true that the combined mortality rate for amputations by the British in the Crimean War and the French in the Franco-Prussian War was a startling 76%. These were indeed the dark early days of battlefield medicine. But you are right to judge that 10,000 dead out of 13,173 is not acceptable. And yes, you may have heard that amputations at the hip joint are particularly dangerous, with 100% mortality rate during those two military engagements. Yet I am optimistic for two reasons. First of all, the progress in these fields of medicine cannot be ignored. The survival rates have improved with each successive campaign, so that by the time of the First War of Rebellion in your country, only 83.3% of hip joint amputees perished within a month! Secondly, I believe Americans are quite simply stronger and have within their grand and heroic souls a greater will to live. On this second point, I turn to Mrs. Phoebe Y. Pember, who wrote of her experiences as a matron at the Chimborazoo Hospital in Richmond, Virginia during the First War of Rebellion:

> Poor food and great exposure had thinned the blood and broken down the systems so entirely that amputations performed in the hospital almost invariably resulted in death after the second year of the war. The only cases under my observation that survived were two Irishmen, and it was really so difficult to kill an

Irishman that there was little cause for boasting on the part of the officiating surgeon.

I have been told, Mr. President, that you are of Irish stock. Is this true? Take heart, Mr. President: The Irish are lions!

The President's doctor's name was Céphas. Before he was killed, he dreamed of Paris. He was in Washington, of course, in the dim bowels of the White House, but he dreamed of the city where he was born: the graceful indolence of the Seine, the gentle winds, the bustling plazas and crowded, smoky cafés. His parents were Senegalese. His older brother sold phone cards at a subway stop in the 17th arrondissement. His younger sister was a housekeeper for a wealthy couple in Montmartre. He'd never been to Senegal, and left the French capital on only a few occasions. He studied, excelled, and reached heights that he could scarcely explain to his mother and father. They wanted him to marry, to stop fooling with so much education. "A man in your position could have two wives or even three," they told him.

He laughed when they told him things like this. "Ah, my simple parents," he said in Wolof, and kissed his mother on the forehead. He was young, not yet forty, when he was called to serve the American President. This they understood, and were proud. Céphas studied the President's condition in preparation for his trip. His family saw him off at the port. Crowded in a waiting room, his brother embraced him, pressed a stack of phone cards into his pocket, and said to call "every day, if you can." The voyage by sea would take only two weeks, so improved were the newer fleets. There were tears in his mother's eyes. *Inshallah*, his father said somberly, God willing, we'll see you again soon. The news from America was grim. They were afraid to send their son to a war zone, but it was an honor to serve a great nation and ally like the United States.

Now Céphas dreamed of a Paris empty of people. Even in his ghastly cell, it was a startling image. No dramatic Parisian beauties dressed in black, smoke coiling from their ruby lips; no jaded young men with scarves wrapped tight around their necks; no Algerian cab drivers pretending to know their way, boasting as they drove in circles around the sullen, industrial neighborhoods at the southern edges of the city. Nothing human, not a soul: only the buildings, but even they were somehow changed. In his reverie, he squinted: What was it? Windowless, he could see it now, a city of tomblike structures, shuttered constructions. Everything bricked-over, monuments too encased in concrete, as if each building were the site of a tiny nuclear explosion, as if the city had, for its protection, buried itself block by block, neighborhood by neighborhood. Denuded trees stood like skeletons along the Seine. A city of miniature Chernobyls. My parents, Céphas dreamed, have fled, back to Dakar with my brother and sister, but the rest of the city has perished, perhaps even the rest of France.

The images played out before him in high-definition: first the dead city of his birth, then his family, at the pier in Dakar, scanning the horizon for a boat from America that would bring their youngest son home again. He wept at the thought of it. The ocean is turbulent, and ships do not carry Africans east across the Atlantic.

Will you be disfigured, Mr. President?
You will.
But allow me to interpret: Aren't we all mere vessels, carrying on our persons the sundry wounds and scars of living? Is not the very character of a man molded in his darkest moments? And yet, you can count yourself fortunate: Times have changed since Private Thomas A. Perrine of the Michigan Regiment (Union) penned these melancholy verses:

> I offered her my other hand
> Uninjured in the fight;
> 'Twas all I had left.
> "Without two hands," she made reply,
> "You cannot handsome be."
> War has left me with empty sleeve,
> but she, alas, with empty heart.

A great variety of cripples are now allowed in polite company, and marriages these days are constructed of firmer stuff, are they not? The treachery of a woman such as is described in the poem is not oftentimes seen in our day. And in your case, dear sir, stories of your wife's devotion have reached Paris, I assure you.

But let us look upon your potential disfigurement another way: Think of the level of solidarity you will have achieved with the soldier who is now waging war in your name against the insurgency. These are facts of history: Two years after the First War of Rebellion, your government authorized the purchase of 4,095 prosthetic legs, 2,391 arms, 61 hands, and 14 feet—all for the exclusive use of Union veterans.

I'll be clear: Add them up, Mr. President. More than 6,500 voters, dear sir, and their grateful families. With the advances of modern war, we can only assume that these figures will rise. The infirm, irrevocably disfigured veteran will see in you a picture of himself. And in the pensive quiet of the voting booth, their steadfast women will marvel at how much you resemble their courageous husbands.

And what of the Rebels? History is clear: They were stripped of their suffrage. They hobbled about for years, without succor from their government, in what was surely just punishment for their transgressions. If you allow me to operate, Mr. President, you will carry your wound with you throughout this great land, a testament to your sacrifice. You will be the nation.

The President asked that his leg be brought to him. "One way or another," he said. The order shivered its way through the great brain of government. The next day, Secret Service agents were kicking in doors in Brooklyn, rousing migrant farm-workers from their sheds in the fertile valleys of California, tearing through rustic mountain cabins in Appalachia. They looked in schools and factories, patted down office workers cubicle by cubicle. The newspaper offices were bombed. While the great cities of the nation fell into protest and chaos, the army marched through the forests of Oregon with chainsaws. They cannot hide, Mr. President.

But the subversives had vanished. The leg as well. There was a network of sympathizers, people said, all over the West. Denver was theirs. They were preparing to bring the war East. Forget your leg, the President's advisers told him, it could be anywhere in the vast hinterland. In a cave, they said. Anywhere.

The President despaired.

"You'll feel better once you execute the African," his advisers said.

"I thought he was French," the President said.

That evening, the Eastern power grid failed. There was looting in New York, riots in Boston. In a White House lit by candles, the President lay with his wife. Who was he kidding? The country was quite obviously falling apart. The government army was in disarray, camped outside Denver awaiting orders. In the West, parents had begun keeping their children out of school. The subversives were forcibly conscripting boys as young as ten, snatching them from Little League practice, from shopping mall parking lots where they congregated to smoke cigarettes. The disasters were multiple and hideous. He felt a pang in his right leg and his heart leapt, but he looked down on the stump and felt the terror of recognition.

The White House was stifling, even with the windows thrown open.

The President's wife massaged his stump. She wrapped it in warm towels. He fought back tears. The room shone orange in the candlelight. "I am a failure," he said.

Oh, dutiful First Lady! "Mr. President," she purred. "Mr. Commander-in-Chief! You're the next Lincoln!" she cried.

It was 1860, Mr. President, when Dr. J.J. Chisholm, in a manual of military surgery for the use of Southern medical officers during the First War of Rebellion, observed the following:

Amputation at the hip joint is born of an unfortunate ambition—one might even use a stronger term for it— a criminal desire on the part of overzealous medical technicians. These hooligans traffic in cruelty when it is more humane to abandon the languishing patient to inevitable death than to subject him to a mutilation that is so rarely successful.

He further remarked that hip-joint amputation "should be expunged altogether from the military practice. It is savage and not fit even for Indians or Negroes."

I take issue with this final remark, of course, but choose to see hope in the final outcome of that first war: Dr. Chisholm's retrograde philosophies were roundly defeated. The Union was preserved so that it might serve as a beacon in the world. Not only has human society advanced, Mr. President; medicine has as well. In the nearly hundred and fifty years hence, medical progress has made amputation fit for men and women of all races and creeds, dear sir. Fit for a king. Fit even for you, Mr. President.

Céphas was received in the Lincoln bedroom. Guards stood at the door. The First Lady lay on the bed reading. "It was good advice," Céphas said, when confronted. "Sound medical advice and I stand by it."

In his wheelchair, the President registered pure hatred.

Céphas felt his face flush. "No, no," he apologized, "a clumsy choice of words, Mr. President, I beg you. My English is not so good."

"Your reports have arrived," said the President. "Your English is fine." He threw a stack of papers at the African. They spilled like confetti over the carpeted floor.

In his cell, Céphas dreamed of Paris, and his jailer dreamed of Salisbury steak. The jailer's name was Jackson and he liked to tell everyone that his wife Mae "could really hook up dinner." Um-um. Céphas wandered along the empty streets of Paris, city of tombs. Hate vegetables though, Jackson thought to himself. His mouth watered.

Jackson got hungrier as the night wore on and so to pass the time, he and another guard pulled Céphas from his cell and beat him. Jackson liked to beat prisoners and imagine himself being videotaped, starring in a television special on rogue cops, and maybe have the videotape set to music, something dark and bass-heavy. At the oddest times—in the shower, during sex, on his morning commute—he liked to roll his r's as if he were emptying a clip from a machine gun.

Figure 3: Jackson

Céphas wailed as they kicked him. Jackson tried out soundtracks in his head: the taut snap of a snare drum, the metallic splash of a cymbal! Bongos, congos, juju music! Jackson shouted at his prisoner and felt he was flying. He rolled his r's in a cascade of bullets. Céphas's pain was also a song: syncopated, atonal, the music of the murdered. Jackson wasn't hungry anymore: the music was in his head, in his heart; he was an animal. His soul was stirred beyond all reason and he could walk on hot coals or handle poisonous snakes—surely he could!

He pulled his gun instead and shot the African doctor. The loud clap of the weapon echoed in the cell and silenced the music.

Céphas was dying. Up two stories was the White House and its administrators, the bureaucrats and figureheads who made the country great. Ahead of him was a vast and turbid sea, and beyond that, waves cresting and crashing on a distant shore. Paris went black.

The room was thick with catastrophe. Jackson's partner was already on the walkie-talkie, calling someone to do something about what had just happened. "Well, what's happened?" the voice on the other end asked. Jackson could barely hear his partner. "I don't know," he was saying. "Hurry up and get down here."

Now that the Second War of Rebellion has begun, Mr. President, it may be instructive to review a case history from the first such war. Again, you will take solace in the outcome. Case #3354, 1863: Private Henry Robinson of Louisiana (Rebel) Regiment, aged thirty-five years, was wounded at the confluence of the Tallahatchie and Yalobusha Rivers on March 13 by a fragment of a twenty-four-pound shell fired from United States gunboats. Surgeon William M. Compton was standing near the wounded man when he fell. Hastily exposing the wound, Dr. Compton found that the immense projectile had buried itself in the upper part of the left thigh, smashing the trochanters and neck of the femur and wounding the femoral artery. The necessary preparations were made on the spot. The patient was desirous that an operation be practiced. He was of a hopeful, buoyant nature and was sanguine of a favorable outcome. Chloroform was administered. Dr. Compton made an irregular incision just above the lacerated margin of the wound and dissected upwards, retracting the skin and trimming away the muscles. Strangely, Private Robinson evinced scarcely a symptom of shock. Soldiers in those days—even Rebels— were hardened men, unafraid of death. When the anesthesia had passed away, the patient was cheerful, even jocular. Febrile reaction was slight. The patient was placed in a shelter tent and given a dose of opium. On the fifth day, Robinson was sent by steamer to Yazoo City, where the stump was covered with yeast poultices. Beef essence, stimulants, and anodynes were also administered. However, within two days there was yellowness at the surface and pus of a very offensive nature, though the lips of the wound were united in nearly their entire extent. Need I say the patient did not rally? Smile, Mr. President: another Rebel dead, a victory for human progress: first came delirium, then coma, and then death!

There is an argument on the floor of the Congress. Listen: "If the good gentleman from Arizona has no further answers for the Committee, will he kindly yield the floor?"

"I will not," said the Engineer. He was red-faced and angry. The President and First Lady were in attendance, seated in the upper gallery of the Capitol. "I will not," he said again, and bared his teeth. There it is, he thought, I've done it: I have growled at the Speaker of the House on national television. It's about fucking time, he thought. A flurry of cameras flashed and clicked. They were asking him questions about things he knew nothing of: Who were these supposed suicides? Did he know anything about the death squads that had been dumping bodies in the lake? Had he ordered the killings himself?

The dam had been bombed. The lake had grunted and spilled. Who cares of the death squads? Isn't there a war going on?

How did the President's leg wind up in your lake, Senator?

"It's not *my* lake," he said.

The leg had been found that morning in the drying sludge of the lake bed. It had been rushed to the lab, badly decomposed, for DNA testing.

The Engineer wondered where it had all gone sour. By today, of course, it was far too late to salvage anything from the sick nation. But yesterday? Last week? A year ago? A decade? Or was the moment of our fatal turn buried somewhere farther in the distant past? When the nation was only an infant, learning to crawl? Who were these people questioning him, and by what right? He could feel the President's eyes on him. His inquisitors did not smile. Did they want contrition? Did they expect groveling? They'll have their spectacle if they want it! His teeth were still bared.

"Senator, please!" they shouted, but he couldn't stop: He felt a blood vessel might explode. His teeth poked like fangs from his open mouth; he dreamed them sharp and ferocious. He sprouted hair werewolf-like and prowled around the Capitol, yellow-eyed, a feral beast, something savage. "In a moment the power will go out," he shouted, "and I'll bite the first man who lays a hand on me!"

The guards swarmed from all sides. The President,

with help from the First Lady, rose to the edge of the balcony to watch the commotion. "That man nearly killed me," he whispered to his wife. The Engineer was an animal, after all, bounding from table to table on all fours, his hands bent into claws. He attacked the Committee, tore the legs and arms from the Speaker of the House. The Engineer's suit seemed to come apart at the seams, his chest swelling. Beneath the gilded dome of the Capitol, he roared like a lion.

Figure 4: Dr. Céphas Diem

What did these men dream of, Mr. President, when death eclipsed them? When they marched a full winter's day with a rotting wooden crutch? When they joked, legless, with their doctors in an opium daze? When they swallowed in suicidal mouthfuls the blue waters of Arizona's artificial lake? Did they dream of love and women, of family and friendship? I submit that if they were soldiers, true warriors, they did not waste their dying moments with such maudlin concerns. If they were warriors—indeed, if they were men—they dreamed only of vengeance. This is the lesson you must take with you, the lesson you must weave into your heart. It will lead you forthrightly into battle. Now ask yourself: Do I trust this doctor? You must and you will. Everything will proceed like this: The first incision must be precise, or else all is lost. I cannot hesi-

tate even for an instant without risking hemorrhage. I will take the scalpel and press its blade firmly against your skin, and slice as if I were cutting into an apple or a steak. Like a warrior, I must be merciless. Infection and disease are the enemies at the gate. Yes, there will be blood, but am I not a surgeon? Presidential blood is the same as any other, dear sir, the same shade of red, the same sticky consistency between the fingers. It can be spilled, as surely the earth can soak it up. Only joking. I will take the scalpel and I will cut you. Really, it isn't so dramatic. Don't worry over the blood, and never mind the bone. It will be sawed through, disarticulated. Your femur is destroyed, there are no options. See how easily the skin pulls back? Surgery is a species of murder. You must be calm. I will finish and go home, and leave you to lose your war. Godspeed. Inshallah. I will finish and marry three wives. You will feel no pain, not until later, but then, aren't you a man? You have suffered for months with this wound and I will relieve you of it. You will be sedated, asleep and dreaming in Technicolor, eyes darting about beneath the lids, beatific as I cut you. And, of course, no one will know anything, Mr. President. These are state secrets.

[Note: Some material adapted from Amputations at the Hip Joint: A Study, *published by the War Department, Washington D.C., 1867, and* Civil War Medicine: Challenges and Triumphs, *by Alfred J. Bollet. Tucson: Galen Press, 2002.]*

A SHORT HISTORY OF THE
CONTRIBUTORS TO THIS VOLUME

Olivia Armenta

DANIEL ALARCÓN is associate editor of *Etiqueta Negra*, an award-winning monthly magazine based in his native Lima, Peru. His first book, *War by Candlelight: Stories*, was published by HarperCollins in 2005.

Sigrid Estrada

AMY BLOOM is the author of two short story collections, a novel, and a book of essays. She lives in Connecticut and teaches at Yale.

KATE BORNSTEIN'S groundbreaking *My Gender Workbook* and *Gender Outlaw* are the principal books used in college gender studies courses. Her latest book is *Hello, Cruel World: 101 Alternatives to Suicide for Teens, Freaks, and Other Outlaws* (Seven Stories, 2006). Bornstein lives in New York City with her partner, two cats, two turtles, and two pugs.

Michael A. Johnson

ALEXANDER CHEE was born in Rhode Island and grew up in South Korea, Guam, and Maine. He is the author of the novel *Edinburgh*, and his second novel, *The Queen of the Night*, is forthcoming from Houghton Mifflin. He is a recipient of a Whiting Writers Award and a NEA fellowship in prose, and has taught writing at the New School and Wesleyan University.

Diane Baldwin

T COOPER is the author of the novels *Lipshitz Six, or Two Angry Blondes* (Dutton, 2006) and *Some of the Parts* (Akashic, 2002). T lives in New York City.

VINAY GANAPATHY (Illustrator) grew up in Connecticut and attended Syracuse University. After graduating, he moved to New York City, where he continues to live and make art.

KEITH KNIGHT is an award-winning San Francisco cartoonist and rapper. His comic strips can be found in over thirty-five alternative, ethnic, political, and college newspapers across the country. He has authored five comic-strip collections, and his latest book is *The Beginner's Guide to Community-Based Art*. Knight's hip-hop band, the Marginal Prophets, won a 2004 California Music Award for their latest disc, *Bohemian Rap CD*. For more information, visit www.kchronicles.com.

RON KOVIC is the author of the American antiwar classic *Born on the Fourth of July*. He served two tours of duty during the Vietnam War and was paralyzed from his chest down in combat in 1968. Along with Oliver Stone, Kovic was the co-screenwriter of the 1989 Academy Award–winning film *Born on the Fourth of July*, based on the book (Tom Cruise stars in the role of Kovic in the film).

PAUL LA FARGE is the author of two novels, *The Artist of the Missing* and *Haussmann, or the Distinction*. His stories have appeared in *McSweeney's, Fence, STORY,* and elsewhere. He was the 2005 recipient of the Bard Fiction Prize. He is also the translator of *The Facts of Winter* by Paul Poissel, recently published by McSweeney's Books.

FELICIA LUNA LEMUS is the author of the novels *Trace Elements of Random Tea Parties* (FSG, 2003) and the forthcoming *Like Son* (Akashic, 2007). She lives in New York City.

Matthew L. Kaplan

ADAM MANSBACH is the author of the novels *Angry Black White Boy* (Crown), *Shackling Water* (Doubleday), and the forthcoming *The End of the Jews* (Spiegel & Grau/Doubleday). He lives in Berkeley, California.

Tom Foley

VALERIE MINER is the award-winning author of twelve books, including *Abundant Light, A Walking Fire, The Low Road,* and *Blood Sisters.* Her work has appeared on BBC Radio and in the *Georgia Review, Ploughshares, Salmagundi, Ms.,* and many other journals. She teaches at Stanford University and her website is www.valerieminer.com.

Viet Le

THOMAS O'MALLEY was raised in Ireland and England. Author of the novel *In the Province of Saints* (Little, Brown, 2005), he is the recipient of the Grace Paley Endowed Fellowship at the Fine Arts Work Center in Provincetown, Massachusetts. O'Malley has published fiction in various magazines, including *Ploughshares, Glimmer Train, Shenandoah, Natural Bridge, Blue Mesa Review, Crab Orchard Review, New Millennium Writings, Vanguard, FRiGG,* and *Mississippi Review.*

Niles Fuller

NEAL POLLACK is the author of three books of satire, including the cult classic *The Neal Pollack Anthology of American Literature,* and editor of *Chicago Noir* (Akashic, 2005). His short fiction has appeared in several anthologies and magazines, and he's a regular contributor to *Vanity Fair* and *Nerve.*

DAVID REES is the author of the comic strip "Get Your War On," which appears in *Rolling Stone,* and "My New Filing Technique Is Unstoppable," which appears in the *Guardian* (UK).

SARAH SCHULMAN is the author of eight novels, most recently *Shimmer* (Avon, 1998) and *The Child* (Carroll and Graff, 2006), and two nonfiction books including *Stagestruck: Theater, AIDS, and the Marketing of Gay America.* Her plays include *Carson McCullers* and *Manic Flight Reaction.*

DARIN STRAUSS is the best-selling author of *Chang and Eng* and *The Real McCoy.* He is also a screenwriter who has collaborated with Julie Taymor, Disney films, and—for the upcoming movie version of *Chang and Eng*—Gary Oldman. His fiction has been widely anthologized, translated into thirteen languages, and published in seventeen countries. He teaches writing at New York University.

BENJAMIN WEISSMAN is pictured here with Ted, his snow-romping pal. Weissman is the author of two books of fiction, most recently *Headless* (Akashic, 2004). He teaches writing at Art Center College of Design.

Also from **AKASHIC BOOKS**

SOME OF THE PARTS BY T COOPER
*A BARNES & NOBLE DISCOVER PROGRAM SELECTION
264 PAGES, A TRADE PAPERBACK ORIGINAL, $14.95

A novel that's changing the way we define "family." The Osbournes, Sopranos, and Eminem are only "some of the parts" that make up the whole story of the new American family.

"A wholly original novel that's both discomforting and compelling to read."
—*San Francisco Chronicle*

"Cooper's scenes have a quirky appeal . . . [D]eftly capturing the seamier motives of her unconventional characters."
—*Publishers Weekly*

HEADLESS STORIES BY BENJAMIN WEISSMAN
*A SELECTION OF DENNIS COOPER'S LITTLE HOUSE ON THE BOWERY SERIES
157 PAGES, A TRADE PAPERBACK ORIGINAL, $12.95

"*Headless* is fearless, fun, and sometimes filthy. Weissman invites you into an alphabet soup of delight in language. Eat up."
—ALICE SEBOLD, author of *The Lovely Bones*

"Weissman is an impishly audacious writer, and that's reason enough to love *Headless*."
—*San Francisco Chronicle*

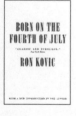

BORN ON THE FOURTH OF JULY BY RON KOVIC
*WITH A NEW INTRODUCTION FROM THE AUTHOR
225 PAGES, A TRADE PAPERBACK ORIGINAL, $14.95

"As relevant as ever, this book is an education. Ron is a true American, and his great heart and hard-won wisdom shine through these pages. "
—OLIVER STONE, filmmaker

"Classic and timeless."
—*New York Times*